SECOND ACTS OF

WEARY

WARRIOR

WOMEN

ELIZABETH F. SHEARLY

ISBN (ebook) 9781068934605

ISBN (paperback) 9781068934612

For more information, visit www.elizabethshearly.ca

Editor: Maggie Morris, The Indie Editor

This is a work of fiction. The story and characters are strictly products of the author's imagination, and any resemblance to real people, living or dead, is unintentional and entirely coincidental.

CONTENTS

CONTENT NOTES

This book contains stories with sexually explicit scenes and stories with violence. Each story has general content notes at the beginning, and you can find detailed content notes at www.elizabethshearly.ca.

SHE'LL GIVE UP HER POWER—
JUST TO KEEP IT FROM HIM

THE
KING'S
PIXIE
SEER

ELIZABETH F. SHEARLY

CONTENT NOTES

Imprisonment of pixie, threat of execution, sexually explicit scenes, D/s relationship.

Please see the book's web page at www.elizabethshearly.ca for detailed content notes.

1

Sarafine drew a card from her custom-painted oracle deck and glanced from the silk-draped table to her patron. As usual, the bejewelled lady watched her, wide eyed, hanging on her every mystical word.

"Hmm," said Sarafine. "I see a journey in your future."

"Let me pick one!" said Jixa, fluttering near her ear.

A shaft of sunlight drifted across the card table through the velvet-draped window and highlighted the curl of smoke rising from the stick of camphor Sarafine had set burning before her patron arrived. This patron's time was almost up. Might as well end with a flourish. "The pixie shall choose the final card." Sarafine fanned the cards out on the table, and Jixa landed beside them.

Jixa pushed one of the cards toward the patron, her tiny feet digging into the silk-covered felt.

"I see her footprints!" the patron gasped.

Sarafine smiled indulgently. Jixa's dramatic flair had got them started in the fortune-telling business, and Sarafine had got the knack once the gold started rolling in. She drew the card Jixa had chosen as the pixie fluttered back to her shoulder, and Sarafine finished out the reading with the appearance of a stranger into the patron's life.

"Thank you so much, Ms. Laurius! Really, I don't know what I used to do without you." The patron struggled to pull her coin purse out of her pocket and scooped a handful of glinting gold onto the table, scattering coins over her cards.

"I merely report the cards' unknowable wisdom," said Sarafine.

The pixie on Sarafine's shoulder giggled and clapped her hands. "And help relieve her of her coin."

Sarafine ignored her.

"You're an absolute angel," said her patron. "And thank you too, little pixie!" Her patron's winning smile was aimed at entirely the wrong shoulder. She bustled to the door and waved at Sarafine. "Ta-ta, darling! I'll be back next week. Same time? Of course the same time!" She laughed gaily, and her mincing steps retreated down the carpeted hallway. The front door opened and shut with a click.

Sarafine laid out a wispy purple kerchief and gathered the coins into it. Jixa fluttered from her shoulder and pussyfooted around the cards. She tilted a coin onto its side and rolled it into the pile.

She licked the coin. "Mmm."

"That's gross, Jixa. You've no idea where that's been."

Jixa cocked her head and squinted at her. "I know a bit. Why don't you ask your fortune-telling cards?"

"Don't be silly. The cards are just cards. You're the one who tells me the future."

"What will we buy with this pile of gold?" Jixa hovered over the coins. Her tiny feet knocked one, and Sarafine straightened it.

She tied the corners of the kerchief together and slid it into her pocket. Jixa fluttered back to her shoulder as Sarafine stood, and Jixa gripped onto the epaulette that acted as her throne.

"This thing needs new padding," said Jixa. "I can feel your bony shoulder right through."

Sarafine shrugged gently. "We have the money. I'll look into it."

"Good, I want to be comfortable for our trip."

Sarafine nodded to her butler, who still waited by the door, and turned to the stairs. "What trip is that?" They weren't planning to go anywhere. Sarafine padded up the carpeted steps.

"To that fortress in the mountains. It's coming up soon." Jixa kicked her heels against Sarafine's collarbone.

Sarafine reached the top of the stairs and turned down the wide hallway. "You'll have to tell me more about the trip. This is the first you've said about it." Her chatelaine jingled as she unlocked her office door, then her lockbox, and tucked the gold inside with the other knotted kerchiefs.

"There's a fortress and a lord on a horse, and he's telling them to open the door, but they won't."

A siege? Their little corner of the world had been at peace since she'd chosen Corniston to disappear to, the second-largest city in the kingdom. Bracetree was larger, but she couldn't have hidden *there* for years on end.

"A lord on a horse" could be anyone, and "a fortress" could be any of a dozen scattered along the border. No matter which one it was, it didn't concern them, not anymore.

"Do you want to draw a picture?" said Sarafine, already pulling the paper and watercolours from her desk drawer. The sooner Jixa dropped this trip idea, the better.

Once the pixie was settled, grabbing handfuls of paint and rubbing them over the paper, Sarafine drew her stack of correspondence close. She flipped through the letters, most from patrons . . . but not this one. The royal lion rampant graced this one's seal, and below that, a stylized *D*. Her throat closed. He'd already used her and Jixa to become king. What else could he want from her, sending letter after letter?

She flicked the parchment unopened into the fireplace where the edges charred black and curled, and the wax seal lit and melted away.

The next letter on the stack came from her parents, and she almost tossed it after Darion's. Sarafine sighed and cracked the seal. Once again, they had found "a most promising suitor" for her and begged her to impart her whereabouts so that they could descend on her and drag her back into their grasp. Not that they said that last part.

Her intermediary, who handled her mail, could be depended upon not to give her location away, not even to the king. Especially not to the king.

"Oh yeah!" Jixa was green to one knee, pink to the hem of her skirt, and a smudge of yellow stretched across her entire face. "The lord is Darion! He has a bunch of horses with him."

Sarafine froze, her throat working again. No crying over him, and no vomiting over her desk. King Darion was laying siege to a fortress or would do so "soon." Still not her problem.

"I hope Amelia isn't in trouble." Jixa smeared orange paint across the top of her paper as she shattered Sarafine's calm.

She had to swallow twice before she answered. "Why would Amelia be in trouble?"

"The fortress. Can we go? I miss the birds there. Remember that robin that used to talk to me?"

Langswold. Home. Sarafine and Darion's home, where they'd lived with Jixa, Amelia, Marcel, and their high ideals. Where Amelia and Marcel probably still lived. Where Darion was approaching with "a bunch of horses."

No trace remained of Darion's letter in the fireplace. Maybe she shouldn't have been so quick to burn it. Force of habit.

She could stay here and leave them to it. Just because Darion was king didn't mean he knew where she was. And if he did, nothing had stopped him showing up here over the past eight years. Sarafine cracked the wax seal on the next letter and unfolded it, but the cultured handwriting blurred as she looked through it, through her desk. If Amelia and Darion were at odds, someone was going to die. Marcel could keep Amelia in check, but no one would rein Darion in, and he was the king.

If she could do anything, she would have to try.

"Want to come up to the attic with me, Jixa? We'll need all your warmest clothes if we're going home to Langswold."

2

Sarafine's horse, Mandrake, picked her way across the field toward Langswold Fortress. The grey stone wall dwarfed the sentries that stood atop it facing east where the king's camp lay, just out of bowshot. Not that she could see the camp over the rise that lay between them; Darion's soldiers patrolled the road, not the goat tracks by the stream like the one she and Jixa travelled.

Last time she'd been here, she had picked her way through bodies on foot while Jixa helped her locate anyone still living, and while Darion betrayed her at the parley with the elders. The lush grass was the only remnant of that battle, besides the black scorch mark that marred the wall of the fortress.

"The men who catch us are so mean," said Jixa.

Sarafine tried not to let her shoulders tense. No need to scare Jixa. "Catch us?"

"Here, by the brook."

"Where do they come from?"

Jixa fluttered toward the brook and gestured into the trees on the other side.

Sarafine clucked their horse into a trot, and Jixa squeaked and zoomed back to her shoulder. "We'll make it to the postern," Sarafine muttered.

Mandrake's hooves beat the earth, and her tack jingled in time.

Someone shouted from the trees, but Sarafine didn't look around. The postern gate yawned ahead, a dark tunnel at the base of the thick stone wall.

Jixa clutched her perch on Sarafine's shoulder. "Do we have to go so fast?"

"Yes, we do." If Darion's men caught them now, he would use Jixa for his own gain, just as he'd done during their rebellion.

The hollow thump of hooves on dirt filled the quiet morning, and the jangle of harnesses drifted to Sarafine over the water. Still, she didn't turn; it would only slow her down.

Sarafine stood in her stirrups and urged her horse into a canter until the postern gaped in front of her. She reined up hard, sliding onto her belly and down from the saddle, urging her horse to jog with her into the low tunnel. Whinnies echoed into the tunnel over the clacking of Mandrakes hooves as two arrows drove into the ground outside in quick succession.

The rebels' archers hadn't shot at her. She slowed to a walk and craned back over her shoulder. The riders were out of sight, clearly, no friends of the rebels inside the fortress.

At the far end of the postern, the portcullis blocked Sarafine and Mandrake from entering. A helmed guard peered through into the darkness, trying to make them out. Sarafine waved.

"Ho, I come as an ally. A friend to Amelia and Marcel of old."

"This gate's not going anywhere until they vouch for you. I already sent a runner." The guard didn't look familiar, but why would she? Sarafine had been gone for eight years, and besides, half of the folks she had known had surely chosen Darion when he became king.

"I would expect nothing less from Amelia's people." Sarafine led her horse into the pool of light cross-hatched on the flagstones, and

Jixa leaped off her shoulder and darted through the grating, right past the guard's ear.

The guard furrowed her brow and eyed Sarafine's shoulder perch. "Don't go back out there. The king's soldiers won't be kind to a seer."

The rebels wouldn't allow Darion's soldiers to come within bow-shot of the walls, let alone into the tunnel behind her. True, Amelia might be holding a grudge about the way Sarafine had left without a word, but she'd never throw her on Darion's mercy. They would let her in, and she wouldn't have to see him alone—and risk a resurgence of old feelings.

Jixa fluttered back into view and perched on the portcullis. "They got rid of my spot in the kitchen. Make them put it back!"

"I will have them put it back as soon as I can," said Sarafine, mindful that the guard could neither see nor hear her conversation partner.

"There's a person right there! Tell them to put it back. I'm hungry!"

"Jixa!" Sarafine gestured to the metal grid penning her in.

"It's not my fault you can't fit through. Humans are too big."

Sarafine ignored her and unbuckled her saddlebag to pull out a kerchief of raisins. She untied it and dropped a couple into the thimble on Jixa's perch.

"Yes!" Jixa leaped to her seat and snatched a raisin. She nibbled it and settled herself on Sarafine's shoulder.

The guard peered through the grating as, from her perspective, the raisin floated through the air, hovered, and then disappeared, bite by tiny bite.

"What is it, Carmela?" The voice came from around the wall, out of sight, but it was Marcel; there could be no mistaking him.

"Marcel!" said Jixa, tossing her half-eaten raisin back into the thimble and zooming through the grating again. "It's Marcel!"

"I can hear him, Jixa," said Sarafine.

"Sarafine?" Marcel stepped around the corner. His blue eyes shone from a light-brown face only a bit more lined than the last time they'd spoken. His straight hair still shone black, with only a few streaks of grey around the temples.

Jixa landed on his shoulder and nuzzled her face into Marcel's cheek. He startled at the invisible touch, but his eyes met Sarafine's, and he smiled at Jixa before gesturing to the guards on the wall above her head to raise the gate.

They didn't try to speak over the cacophony of the chains raising the portcullis, and as soon as the way was clear, Sarafine led Mandrake carefully over the uneven threshold into Langswold.

"I heard Darion was here, and I thought I could be of some help to you and Amelia." The fortress seemed calm despite the pending siege. Shouldn't Amelia be wandering the ranks, nitpicking everyone else's work?

"I'm sure you will be. You must be hungry after the ordeal getting to our walls."

"Yes! We're famished!" said Jixa.

"Food would be lovely," said Sarafine. "Maybe somewhere you can detail the situation?"

Jixa settled on Marcel's shoulder as he led them deeper into the fortress. The pixie intermittently stroked his neck, saying things like "good human" and "steady now" that he couldn't hear. Sarafine didn't bother relaying them.

The outside of the wall hadn't changed, but in eight years, most of the buildings inside had been repainted, some entirely rebuilt. That house had been white, and a stranger watched from the doorway.

The ringing from the forge, at least, hadn't changed, though the blacksmith of her time had liked to leave the door standing open. They wound up to the keep, and Marcel called into the stables.

A voice barked back. "What could you possibly need me for? Not like we have tons of visitors—" The speaker poked his head out of the stable, and his mouth fell open. "Sarafine!"

"Gregory?"

"By the gods' whiskers, never thought to see you again, girl! How have you been keeping yourself?" He clasped her hand in both of his and leaned in to air-kiss her cheek, his beard brushing her face as she returned it.

"Jixa and I have been keeping well enough in Corniston."

He turned and spat. "The city! Surprised you still have a horse to carry you here. I'm sure you've been sitting on cushions and taking baths all day." He chuckled. "And who's this now?" He clucked to her horse and rummaged in his pocket until he produced an apple.

"Mandrake. Don't you go spoiling her. She's a city horse, but she's a hard worker."

"Yeah, yeah." Gregory was already leading her horse away. "Sure, you can have this if you let me take that tack off, Mandrake, my girl."

Marcel had his arms crossed over his chest, and Sarafine averted her gaze from his steady stare. He didn't have to say anything: he disapproved of her having left with nary a word to her rebel family. She'd run from more than just King Darion when she rabbited all those years ago.

"Can we get to the food now?"

Sarafine gave Jixa a sharp look, but the pixie just pouted back at her. "Jixa's hungry," said Sarafine, suppressing a smile.

"We can't have that," said Marcel. He brought his hand gingerly to his shoulder where Jixa sat, and she hugged his fingers, wrapping both her arms and legs around them and squeezing. Marcel laughed. "I think we might even have a few cherries."

"Cherries!" Jixa let Marcel's hand go and zoomed around his head twice.

"Calm down before you hurt yourself," said Sarafine, but Marcel smiled.

He led them down a familiar path up the main staircase, where Darion used to keep his favourite painting, a grey rendition of a ship tossed in a roaring sea, the wall now standing empty.

She paused in the doorway to Darion's office, tracing the ornamental scrollwork with a numb finger. But Darion's voice didn't call out from behind his desk for her to come in, and Marcel beckoned her inside.

"When Darion . . . left, I took it over. We can sit somewhere else if—"

"Here is fine."

She edged across the carpet, the same one that had cushioned her knees from the bite of the stone floor while he laced his fingers through her hair—

The shelves behind the desk that used to be lined with books now held knick-knacks and trinkets from all over the continent, and the desk that Darion had bent her over so many times, scattering forgotten correspondence heedlessly while he gripped her hips and— The desk was immaculate: one pile of paper, perfectly squared, lay on the right-hand side, and no ink dotted its top. Shouldn't there be scratches in the surface from her nails where she'd clawed the wood?

"Feel free to make yourself comfortable." Marcel gestured to an unfamiliar table and two chairs by the mullioned window that overlooked the inner courtyard.

Sarafine sank into the chair in front of a platter. A bowl of cherries sat in the middle of the table, and the other place stood empty. The branches below were clustered with small green fruit, some apples, some pears. Jixa stepped gracefully from Marcel's shoulder and attacked the cherries, knocking one flying from the bowl and off the table.

Marcel laughed. "Still likes her cherries." He swiped the fallen cherry off the rug, perched across from Sarafine, and crossed his legs.

Sarafine picked at her platter. A small bun, no butter, but freshly sliced strawberries, whole blueberries, and melon somehow cut into perfect balls.

"The king's men showed up two days ago. Darion didn't join them until yesterday. Amelia wanted to ride out right away and meet him. I was on patrol in the forest, otherwise I would have gone with her. I would never have let the two of them meet alone."

The little green apples bobbed as the wind picked up.

Jixa pelted Sarafine with a cherry pit that rattled off her platter. "He's waiting for you to tell him it's fine, that it's not his fault."

Since when was she so perceptive?

"There's nothing anyone could have done. You know Amelia when she gets an idea stuck in her head."

"I can usually divert her. If you rode all the way from Corniston, someone must have told you Darion was coming . . ."

Had Darion tried to tell her in that letter she'd tossed in the fire? Had he been asking her advice all this time and she'd been too stubborn to help? Even if she'd given her advice, he would have been too stubborn himself to take it. "Jixa told me."

Marcel nodded and smiled at the cherry bowl, now but sparsely populated, and Jixa perched on the edge. It wobbled, the little pixie narrowly avoiding overturning it on herself.

Sarafine sighed. Marcel was being his typical patient self with her, but he deserved better. She caught his gaze. "I'm sorry I left you. All of you. When I realized Darion had used me to take over the monarchy,

I couldn't bring myself to stay and find out what he was going to use me for as king."

Marcel took her hand and squeezed her fingers gently. "Amelia and I understood." He shrugged. "Most everyone did. The way he betrayed us . . . He betrayed you tenfold."

Jixa hopped onto the windowsill and strutted along. "I used to have a nice bed here."

"We'll find you a bed, pixie. Do you want any of my food?"

"Maybe a crumb or two." She fluttered onto Sarafine's platter, burrowed into her soft bun, and pulled out an armful of the fluffy middle.

"Would you like to set up in the kitchen?" Marcel directed his question to the bun. "Francine would be glad to have you."

Jixa paused, her handful of bread forgotten, and fluttered a few inches off the table. "Francine? She sings to me!"

"I'll take the hovering bread as an affirmative."

"I'm sure all of Langswold knows we're back by now." So many people Sarafine had once considered family. A family Darion had ripped apart.

"It wouldn't surprise me if Francine has already dusted off your spot on the kitchen windowsill."

"Make sure she knows you're there," Sarafine called after her re-treating pixie.

"Oh, she'll know!" Jixa called back as she wriggled under the door into the hallway.

Sarafine shook her head slowly. "She's going to get swatted one day."

"Francine will take good care of her. She's been missed around here. Both of you have." He held up a hand. "I know. You already apologized. I'm not trying to guilt you. I just mean that you're welcome. Welcome to stay, I mean. After."

"After what, exactly? How did you and Amelia manage to bring the king himself to your doorstep?"

"Made friends with the wrong lord." Marcel scrubbed a hand over his face.

"You said Amelia met with Darion already. What did they talk about?"

"I don't know." Marcel looked about ready to vomit.

"She didn't tell you?"

"She hasn't come back."

"They're still in negotiations?"

"Who knows? We haven't heard anything at all from him."

Darion had kept Amelia in his camp overnight with no demands? The two of them certainly hadn't come to a compromise about . . . whoever the lord was.

"Who exactly is this lord that Darion hates so much?"

"You'd know him as the crown prince, Quinton, old King Iron Fist's firstborn. He's been badgering Darion for the duration."

No doubt royally disgruntled that he'd been denied his birthright.

"And you want him to become monarch?" Had Amelia and Marcel changed so much?

"Not on your life. He's promised Amelia reforms once he's in power, and she takes him at his word. Darion finally reached his limit on traitors in our midst and told Amelia to turn him out."

"Those must be some reforms. I'll bet she told the king to go to hell. Quinton is here?"

Marcel shook his head. "Rode out two days ago on some secret business—"

A rap on the door cut him off. "Marcel? The king has sent demands."

Marcel rubbed a hand over his face. "Come in here, and let's hear them."

The messenger poked his head around the door and glanced at Sarafine. "He wants the seer. Otherwise, Amelia will be executed."

Marcel flinched. "How long do we have?"

"Until sunset."

Marcel waved the messenger out and cradled his head in his hands.

Sarafine pressed her palm onto the table, barely breathing. "He's taken her hostage?" Her nostrils flared, and she made an effort to unclench her jaw. "Underhanded rat bastard."

"His Majesty, the underhanded rat bastard." Marcel raised his eyebrows.

"With at least two hundred men at his beck and call." Sarafine slumped back into her chair.

"Knowing Amelia, she stormed in there and told him where to shove his army, or else. I don't think even she knows what the *or else* would be. But of course, His Majesty can't have anyone speaking to him in such a disrespectful fashion."

Sarafine had delighted in speaking to him in a disrespectful fashion, right here in this office. But Darion and Amelia didn't resolve their problems that way; they were more inclined to have a screaming match and storm off, leaving Sarafine and Marcel to talk them each down. Inevitably, Amelia and Darion were best friends again in the morning. Had been.

"Darion won't back down. He's going to execute her as an example to the rest of us."

Marcel nodded. "When Darion gets something into his head . . ." Marcel gazed out the window, off into the distance.

"And no one can get under his skin quite like Amelia." Sarafine had often said they'd kill each other with no one there to play buffer between them, but she'd meant it figuratively.

Darion didn't know she was here. His soldiers had spotted the perch on her shoulder and reported a seer entering the rebel fortress. She could keep it that way, send Marcel off to bargain with the stubborn jerk without her. But he would carry through on his threat to murder Amelia, friendship be damned. They couldn't count on his ruthless streak faltering at the last moment. They needed to be sure of a way to get Amelia safe now.

They'd all been stubborn enough to stand against King Iron Fist, but Darion was the only one ruthless enough to take the monarchy despite their agreement to abolish it entirely. And with that, he'd burned all their dream of distributing power to the ground.

In the intervening years, had King Darion shown any sign of using his power to bring the monarchy down? Of course not. Now that he had his power he wielded it. Maybe not quite as ruthlessly as King Iron Fist, that was true. No one was selling their children to the clergy to pay back taxes as Marcel's family had tried to do to him and his sister. No orphanages were being stripped of the king's patronage and shuttered as Amelia's had been under Iron Fist. No stories had reached Sarafine of merchants' prized goods being seized to pay for the king's latest indulgence when they tried to take them to market, as Darion's best horses had been.

Still, taxes were demanded with no regard to the family's situation, orphanages stood at the mercy of rich patrons, and tariffs on merchants' goods still went to buying the king's jewels. Darion wanted the seer and he wouldn't back down.

"I'll do it. Me for Amelia. But you do the bargaining." If she could delay her encounter with Darion, all the better.

"We'll meet and agree to the terms. Get Amelia back. After that . . ." He ran a hand over his face again. He'd wear his nose right off if they didn't get Amelia back soon.

"Let's just deal with the impending death of our friend before you worry about the future of the kingdom. Meet with him, agree on the exchange, and then we'll get Amelia back." She couldn't sit still any longer and paced to Marcel's shelves of knick-knacks.

"Are you sure? You escaped him once . . ."

Had she ever wanted to escape him? No. But the news that he was to be crowned king had sent her fleeing. She hadn't given him a chance to trap her and Jixa; she'd just disappeared. Marcel was right. If she went back to him now, she wouldn't be able to leave again; he wouldn't give her a chance. She and Jixa were too valuable to relinquish.

"Let's just get Amelia safe and get them both calmed down. We'll go from there." She'd think about the implications of having Darion in her life again later. If he asked her to tell him Jixa's prophecies, she'd simply refuse. They could find a way to keep that power from him once Amelia was safe.

3

On the ramparts, Sarafine gathered her cloak more closely about her shoulders. The thick wool mostly kept the icy wind at bay, but it didn't touch the chill in her bones watching Marcel, Carmela, and another guard ride out to the meeting point midway between the walls and the king's camp. Marcel had set two of his most steadfast archers to cover them; they stood poised along the wall, neither one close enough to hear her muttering to herself. Her feet had carried her up here of their own accord. Had Darion changed as king? Had he really turned into a power-crazed maniac?

Four riders filed through a gap in the palisade. One of them had windswept black hair and an arrogant tilt to his bare head. He held the reins loosely and guided his horse with his knees alone, as comfortable in the saddle as on his own feet. Darion.

Sarafine fought down the tightness in her belly, the fluttering in her chest as he drew closer and his gaze seemed to take her in, though he wouldn't be able to identify her at this distance with her hood raised against the chill. Sarafine had left Jixa in the kitchens. It wouldn't do to have her zooming off to nuzzle the king's cheek as she had with Marcel; Jixa adored Darion, totally oblivious to what he'd tried to do to them.

The wind carried snatches of Marcel's voice up to the ramparts, but Darion scanned the battlements, his gaze catching on her again.

Darion's gravelly timbre, even from so far away, made something try to crawl up Sarafine's throat. Possibly her lunch, possibly her heart. She swallowed it down.

Marcel spoke again, and Darion nodded, glanced toward the archers on the wall, spared one last covetous glance toward his goal, the seer, and wheeled toward his encampment.

Sarafine slumped against the embrasure. Fucking Darion. How could he still affect her this way, after all this time? If she was so affected by hearing a snatch of his voice, how could she possibly hope to resist when he demanded Jixa's prophecies? One of those commanding looks of his, a simple caress of his deft fingers, and she'd spill every last prediction Jixa offered. And he would use them.

The king and his soldiers disappeared behind their palisade, and Marcel and his guards turned their horses back toward the fortress. Darion would use her predictions to crush rebellions like this one, like theirs, back when Darion had rebelled with them. He'd use her for her pixie, and he wouldn't even have to hide it anymore.

Sarafine trudged down to the keep, where Marcel met her, dismounting.

"If there's anything you want to do before we throw you to the wolves, you have an hour." He gave her a sympathetic look, and she turned away.

"Thanks." The worst part was how sure she had been that they were all working together, using Jixa's prophecies to propel their rebellion, all of them dedicated to the cause, not trying to seize power for themselves. But Darion had fooled her, along with the rest of them. She'd been a particularly useful tool to him, that was all.

She and Marcel parted ways in the bailey, he going to check their defences in Amelia's absence, and her to the kitchen to collect Jixa. She took her pixie up to Marcel's office; they didn't need their own quarters because they wouldn't be staying overnight. She sat her pixie on the windowsill and then pulled her chair in close.

"Jixa, we're going to see Darion."

Jixa squeaked and darted around the room like a hummingbird.

"But you're not to touch him, and you're not to tell me any prophecies while we're with him." If Sarafine didn't know them, she wouldn't be able to pass them on to Darion.

Jixa giggled. "Nope! I loooove Darion! I'm going to snuggle him! Does he still have that fuzzy beard?"

"He doesn't. His face looks prickly now." Come to think of it, his face had been thinner. "What about the prophecies? Can you at least keep those to yourself while we're with him?"

"But he likes them." Jixa landed on her shoulder and rested her head on Sarafine's earlobe. "He always says they are so helpful. Besides, you know I can't keep prophecies from you, silly." She snuggled into Sarafine's neck.

Jixa wouldn't be any help with this. As long as he had them, Darion would use their prophecies for his political manoeuvring. She would be back under his spell again; already she couldn't get his dark eyes out of her head. She could almost see him across the room, sitting at his desk, working on some missive.

He'd look up and catch her staring, *Come here*. He'd watch her cross to him and sink to her knees, then he'd pat his thigh, and she'd settle on her cushion with her head resting in his lap while he finished up. He'd run a hand through her hair. *What would please you, my lord?* A smile would curl his lips; he hadn't been finishing his work, he'd been planning every detail of their evening, beginning with leaning back in his chair and spreading his legs—

Sarafine shook her head and squirmed in her chair, trying to ease the ache between her thighs. Jixa strutted along one of Marcel's knick-knack shelves, ringing a tiny bell over and over again. Darion wasn't even here, and Sarafine could barely keep it together. She wouldn't be able to keep Darion from taking advantage of Jixa, and Jixa couldn't help her; she'd already said as much. Only one option remained: leave Jixa behind.

Sarafine couldn't pass on prophecies that she couldn't hear, and Jixa loved it in Langswold kitchen. Francine, Marcel, and Amelia would take good care of her. But none of them could see her or hear her. What if something happened and they didn't realize? What if someone really did step on Jixa or crush her somehow? She'd lie, invisible, hurt, and alone until she lost her strength entirely, with no hope of being rescued. No, she couldn't leave Jixa here.

Not only that, but Jixa was right: pixies needed to share their predictions. If no one could hear her, Jixa would drive herself to exhaustion trying to make someone listen. The only others who could see and hear her were her relatives, the pixies who lived in their village deep in the wood, up the mountain, where Sarafine had found her little friend. She and Darion had fetched her there, a tiny pixie raring for adventure and hungry for a human to see and hear her.

Yes, that would be the only way. Return Jixa to her home, and then Darion would have no use for Sarafine. If he tried to make her reforge her pixie bond, she would refuse. He'd realize that Jixa hadn't been part of their bargain, and he'd let her go. Later, perhaps she would think about where she would live, what she would do without Jixa by her side, but not now. She had an hour to trek to the pixie village and back. They had to leave right away.

Sarafine beckoned to Jixa, who flew to her perch and hung on as Sarafine hurried into the bailey.

"Where are we going?" asked Jixa. "You know I love a good adventure."

"I thought it might be nice to visit your family."

"My family? I never thought of that. I can show you how to ride a squirrel." She fixed Sarafine with an assessing stare. "You might be too big for it, though."

"Probably."

Mandrake wouldn't make it up the narrow path to the pixie village, so she hustled toward the postern gate on foot.

"Where are you going?" Carmela stood guard in front of the portcullis.

"I'm sure Marcel told you that I have free rein to come and go as I please."

"Trying to escape now that you've made your bargain with the king?"

"Of course not. I care for Amelia as much as you do."

Carmela planted her feet firmly. "So, where exactly are you going?"

"I'm taking Jixa to visit her family in the wood. It might be our last chance now that . . ."

Carmela narrowed her eyes, but she stood aside and waved for the gate to be lifted, and the portcullis ground up. The dark tunnel seemed shorter in this direction, and in a moment, Sarafine was stepping into the late afternoon sun. It would be twilight when she returned, but she knew the terrain. She hopped across the stream and began to climb, sticking to a goat track. No clear path led to the pixie village; they had only found it that first time after months of searching, but with Jixa's guidance, she would find it easily.

Jixa chattered about her village, correcting Sarafine's path a few times. Sarafine paused to look over her shoulder. Surely someone, Marcel or even Darion, must be about to jump out and stop her. But no one appeared.

They emerged into a glade gilded in the lowering sun. Her pixie leaped from Sarafine's shoulder and zoomed over the wee toadstool houses, calling out to the pixies as she flew. She landed in the middle of the faery ring. A door in the side of a toadstool opened, seemingly on its own, and then shut again. Jixa tracked someone Sarafine couldn't see, grinning and nodding.

"She wanted to bring me for a visit!" She threw her arms around nothing—the other pixie. "It is nice to be home."

Do it now, before you lose your nerve. Jixa will be fine.

"I disavow my bond with Jixa." Sarafine kept her voice low.

Jixa was still chattering to the other pixie and hadn't heard her yet. Was she a little less solid than she had been?

"The link is severed, the compact broken."

Jixa screeched and fluttered toward Sarafine, definitely translucent now. "What are you doing, Sara? Why are you . . ." Her voice trailed away to nothing as her being disappeared completely. Sarafine closed her eyes, and something pelted her face, tiny fists pounding at her skin.

"You can't come with me, Jixa." Sarafine dashed away a tear and sniffed. "I know you wanted to see Darion again, but you won't be safe. You have to stay here with your family."

The pixie's tiny body still pressed against her face, shuddering with sobs. There was still time to undo it. Sarafine could reforge the bond as long as she was here. She had Jixa's name; she knew the words.

No, this was the only way to keep Darion from entrapping them both, using them for his own ends, using their power to invade their neighbours or whatever underhanded schemes he was weaving these days.

Sarafine gently wrapped her fingers around Jixa and pulled the pixie away from her cheek. She crouched and placed the shaking pixie in the centre of the faery ring. Jixa didn't cling to her again. As soon as Sarafine let her go, it was as though she had never been.

4

The trek back through the forest seemed to take an eternity and to pass in an instant. Sarafine kept on downhill until she reached the stream, which she could follow back to the fortress.

Jingling harness and creaking leather snapped Sarafine out of her stupor too late, and she emerged onto the forest road mere steps in front of two riders. Their conversation stopped short as they reined in their mounts. Were they Darion's soldiers or rebels?

"There you are." Marcel's relief was mixed with irritation as he looked down on her from horseback. "We should be at the parley."

"I just wanted to clear my head. I'm on my way there now."

"I was told you went out. I guess it's too late to reprimand you for not telling me first." He reached a hand down. "Want a lift?"

Sarafine took his hand, and he swung her up behind his saddle.

The sun touched the horizon as they trotted across the plain toward a small tent, a few figures waiting outside. She'd been almost out of time. The tent's canvas snapped in the evening breeze, outlined by the sunset.

"You took your time with your outing." Marcel's voice was level, but he fidgeted and glanced at the king's encampment.

Darion's black charger emerged from between the palisades, a rope trailing behind leading Amelia, hands bound in front of her, head held high despite her hair being a nest and dirt coating her knees. She didn't stumble as they crossed the plain, and Darion kept his horse at an easy walk, his soldiers leaving ample space behind Amelia.

The procession stopped outside the little tent.

When they drew close enough to see Sarafine's face, Amelia and Darion both did a double take.

Darion's eyes darkened, but he didn't say a word to her through his clamped jaw; he just swung down from his horse and picked at Amelia's bindings.

Amelia glared at Sarafine. "I thought you were gone for good."

"I thought I was too," said Sarafine.

When Amelia was free, Darion laid a firm hand on her shoulder and steered her toward the tent, pushing her inside. Marcel dismounted and Sarafine followed, the rest of the soldiers making no move to join them.

Darion and Amelia glared at one another across the tent, and they both turned to Marcel and Sarafine. The four of them were alone.

"What the fuck are you doing, Your Majesty?" said Amelia.

Marcel ran a hand over his face.

"I think I've been clear with you, Amelia. I can't allow local lords to flout my directives, let alone stir up sentiment against me."

"Is he fucking kidding me with this?" Amelia snapped to Marcel. "Godsdamn hypocrite."

"I am not kidding you, Amelia." Darion's voice was steely.

"You would have executed me in cold blood to put my people in their place." She spat at his feet.

"You are very lucky that no one else is here to see that," Darion ground out.

Someone needed to step in before this got out of hand—more out of hand.

"Darion has different priorities now that he's the monarch," said Sarafine.

Amelia glared at her. "And why the fuck have you crawled back out of the woodwork? Decided your precious *lord* needs your services again?"

Sarafine glared right back. Using her and Darion's relationship dynamic—former relationship dynamic—against her was a low blow. "At least I'm not getting myself killed for no reason."

"Scurry back to your mouse hole—"

"Godsdamn it, Amelia. Shut your mouth for five seconds," said Marcel.

Darion shook his head. "And you didn't bother to mention that the seer we were bargaining for was *her*?"

Marcel ran a hand over his face again. "Sarafine came to warn us that Darion was on his way, and when she learned that Amelia was in danger, no thanks to you, Your Majesty, she agreed to trade places. So maybe try to be nice to the person who just saved your asses?"

Amelia looked back and forth between Marcel and Sarafine. She let out a deep breath. "I'm sorry, Sarafine. This hasn't been my best day. When I saw you here again . . ."

Sarafine glared up at Darion, and he returned it with a hard stare.

"Not your lord anymore, I guess," Amelia amended with a smirk. "At least he won't kill you. I think we can all be sure of that."

Darion broke the stare. "You've caused me a lot of trouble, Amelia."

"Good." She flounced from the tent.

Darion deflated a fraction. "I'll deal with Quinton and the elders, Marcel, but you're going to have to give me something. I never wished for noble blood until I became a royal."

Marcel and Darion were halfway through a conversation that Sarafine wasn't a part of, so she shut her mouth and listened.

"We just need an excuse to change tacks on Quinton, and we'll hand him over. Amelia won't break her word, but if you goad him into betraying us . . ."

Darion nodded.

Marcel nodded back and followed Amelia out.

Leaving Darion and Sarafine alone.

"That went better than expected," Darion muttered, staring at the tent flap where two of his former best friends had disappeared. Had he intended for Sarafine to hear that?

He turned to her and set his jaw. "Come."

"Oh no you fucking don't, Your Majesty. You threaten to kill my friend to drag me out and then expect me to follow like a dog?"

Darion paused, his back to her. "This isn't the time. And you could show some gratitude after I saved your ass as well." Without waiting for her retort, he strode out of the tent to his horse. He swung up into the saddle and reached down for her.

"Afraid I'll make a run for it?"

"You wouldn't get ten yards."

She suppressed a tingly shiver and wrapped her fingers around his wrist, his leather-clad hand doing the same to hers, and swung her up in front of him. They trotted back to the encampment, past the palisade, and reined up in front of a large tent.

Darion swung down and made to help Sarafine, but she ignored him and swung a leg over, narrowly missing his face. His charger topped Mandrake by a good three hands, and she clung to his pommel to avoid getting a foot caught in the stirrup. Darion seemed to restrain himself from steadying her as she landed on the ground, his hands hovering near her shoulders.

"Your tent, my lord?" Shit. Why had she called him that? "Your Majesty," she amended.

"A private tent is prepared for you. But please, join me for a . . . talk first." Dark circles shadowed his eyes, and a line creased between his brows. He gestured her to precede him into the large tent, and she straightened her spine and strode in.

A wave of warmth hit her; the thick canvas blocked the wind, and a brazier in the middle kept the chill at bay.

An actual desk sat on one side, a proper bed on the other. Darion followed her in, stripped off his shirt, and grabbed a cloth from the washbasin in the corner. Sarafine stood frozen, watching Darion's back muscles rippling as he swiftly washed the riding dust from his neck and shoulders. Eight years ago, he'd been more lithe, strong, but wiry. Who would have thought being monarch would have him putting on muscle?

Darion tossed the cloth into the basin and turned, his chest damp and glistening in the brazier's glow. A dusting of fine hair covered his chest where it had been smooth before. Would it feel different pressed against her bare back as he crushed her to him and—

She tore her gaze from the trail of dark hair disappearing into his breeches.

Darion's desk was unruly as ever, papers scattered across the surface.

"What do you think you'll find?" said Darion, close behind her, not quite touching.

"What?"

"When I asked you to come, I never thought you'd take their side."

Asked her to come? He'd never asked her to come to Langswold . . . . The letter she'd tossed in the fire. "You are a fool if you thought I'd take yours."

"True enough. After you betrayed me and disappeared like a shadow the second the battle was won."

"Betrayed *you*?" She whirled, heedless of how close their bodies were, how close his bare skin was. "We promised, *swore* that we would not accept the monarchy, even if it was offered to us. All of us did! How did you imagine we would react when you snapped it up at the first opportunity?"

His eyes darkened, and he took a step back. "Why are you here, Sarafine? Spying on me? So desperate to get into my tent. More fool I, I thought you might be— But that doesn't matter. Clearly, I was mistaken."

"To save my *friend* whose execution, if you will recall, you already would have carried out."

Darion shook his head. "How else was I supposed to get you here?"

"Maybe try asking next time, Your Majesty."

Darion flinched. He opened his mouth but perhaps decided he had no right to tell her not to address him by his title, the title that he'd betrayed her to take on. Rehashing the past wouldn't get them anywhere.

"You told Marcel you would take care of Quinton. What does that mean?" Quinton had been a smarmy, opportunistic prince with a selfish streak a mile wide. Served Darion right, working with people like Quinton all day now that he was king.

"He never got over my being chosen as king instead of him. He's like a buzzing fly I haven't been able to swat. No thanks to your friends."

Her friends. Not *their* friends. They'd been like a family and now they weren't even counted as friends. "Now you can?"

"Now I have you and Jixa. He can't keep pestering the elders to dethrone me now that I have a seer at my side."

"A seer?" Not Sarafine. He just needed a seer.

"Quinton won't stop yammering on about the peace agreement stipulating the loyalty of a seer to support the monarch. Lucky for me, no one has a better claim than I do, and once we confront the elders tomorrow, his only argument will disintegrate."

Tomorrow. The elders. Confronting the elder, play-acting as the seer she no longer was. "So you could have roped in anyone with a link to a pixie—"

"Or Quinton could have, yes. Believe me, he's been searching for the faery ring."

The faery ring that she'd just jaunted off to without bothering to cover her tracks. "But you know where it is . . ." He'd searched it out with her, been there when Jixa had agreed to link herself with Sarafine. He could have taken anyone there to bond with a new pixie and solved his problem himself.

"I've been there a few times. No response from the pixies." He sat at his desk and pulled his boots off.

Sarafine idly traced the papers on Darion's desk with her fingertip: missives from neighbouring monarchs and from local lords, reports of all kinds, and a letter that Darion had been in the middle of writing to the elders. "I guess pixies like Jixa are rarer than we thought."

Darion watched her unflinchingly. "You are the rare one, princess." His mouth snapped shut. He'd made the same blunder she had fallen into earlier that day when she called him *my lord*. His gaze softened into something more familiar, almost pleading, before he shut it down.

His puppy eyes couldn't make up for his betrayal and were not enough to make her come crawling back, but after the day she'd had—after losing Jixa—she needed someone to be there for her, even if it was only nostalgia, even if it was only temporary comfort that would fade away the moment they left this tent. Besides, once Darion found out that Jixa was long gone, he'd turn her out, and she'd probably never see him again.

She swallowed and looked up at him as she sank to her knees on the wool rug at his feet. "My lord."

Darion stepped toward her, reaching out, but he snatched his hand back and glanced around the room. "Is Jixa here?"

Sarafine jolted. He couldn't know that she'd returned Jixa to the forest. Did he even know it was possible? Sarafine still had Jixa's perch on her shoulder, so Darion had no reason to suspect that she was gone forever. When she and Darion had been together, they'd always been careful to dismiss Jixa before engaging in any of their intimate activities. It wouldn't have been appropriate for Jixa to see them . . .

Sarafine's pussy clenched. "No, my lord."

"You don't have to do this, princess. I don't . . . require your service." His fingers brushed her jawline, trying to coax her to her feet. "That wasn't intended to be— Our arrangement is complete. Amelia is safe. You don't have to . . ." Darion brushed a lock of hair from her forehead.

There were no words for what she wanted from him. She couldn't ask for his love when she wasn't prepared to give it in return. She didn't trust him, not in general. But with her body? Her pleasure? She would always trust him completely.

Sarafine unbuckled the straps of Jixa's perch and propped it on Darion's desk on his sea of papers. She tilted her head up to him and licked her lips.

He growled and laced a hand in her hair, but he shook his head, looking away from her. "Sarafine, whether you like it or not, I'm your king. You are my prisoner. I can't just . . ."

He was going to deny her after she'd practically prostrated herself before him? Would he banish her to sleep alone in a cold, silent tent? She wouldn't even have Jixa's chatter for company.

She caught his hand before he could let go of her hair. "Please, my lord."

His fingers tightened under hers, and she leaned into his touch. He shook his head again, but this time, he smiled down at her. "I can't call you princess, not now that I'm king."

Sarafine grimaced. *Princess* had been a half-joking, half-reverent term back in the day. Now that he was the monarch, it had a gross edge to it. "Call me seer." That was the only reason he wanted her, anyway.

He cocked his head and gave her a quizzical look, but he didn't argue. "My little seer."

Sarafine shivered. That wasn't what she'd said, definitely not what she'd meant. And yet, the way he watched her as the words rolled off his tongue, the emphasis on *my*, made it impossible to forget who this was: Darion, her lord. And she was his seer.

Darion's fingertips massaged her scalp. "What do you need from me tonight?"

The familiar words refused to filter into her mind. What did she need from him? She reached toward his bare stomach, and it contracted as he gasped, but he nodded, and she trailed her fingers down the planes of his abdomen, brushing the hair leading downward. "This is new."

He grunted. "I can barely wait to explore your body, remap every inch of you. Do you still make that noise when I stroke your ribs just right?"

Sarafine's lower belly tightened; it had been so long since he'd feathered his fingertips over her. She went for the laces of his breeches, but he caught her wrist with a chuckle.

"Still in such a rush. Bed."

Sarafine stiffened. This was like old times. Too much like old times. They had had fun. The banter, the games. But this was not old times. The years between them might not mean anything—they'd fallen back into their comfortable rhythm—but the rift between them couldn't be so easily breached. Their past betrayals were still there, waiting to overtake them the moment they were most vulnerable.

Darion pulled back, hand still laced in her hair. "I said bed, my little seer."

Sarafine stared at his feet. Why couldn't she just let him bring her pleasure and give him pleasure in return? Would it really be so hard to bury these strange feelings and carry on, at least for tonight? Once he found out that Jixa wasn't with her, he would throw her out. Couldn't she just let herself enjoy it for one night?

"Sarafine." His eyebrows were drawn together, his gaze fixed on her. Not *seer*, Sarafine.

"What?"

"Tell me your safe word."

"You don't remember it?"

"I remember. I want to make sure you remember."

"You think that I would be using it right now, but I've just forgotten it? It's *monarchy*. Satisfied?" He used to say that *monarchy* was a good safe word because it made his balls want to crawl up inside his body. Had he been playing her from the beginning, with all his talk of abolishing the monarchy itself?

"I don't know if you'd be using it right now, but you're dissociating so hard, I bet you can't even feel your legs."

He was right, the bastard. Everything below her collarbone might as well have disappeared for all she could feel it. "Don't you fucking dare go into another power imbalance spiral. I know. We don't have to do anything I don't want to do."

Darion crossed his arms over his chest. "Then answer my question. What do you need from me? Clearly there's something or you would let this go and stalk off to your own tent, which is waiting for you, by the way, whenever you want it."

I want to go back in time. I want to know why you betrayed me. Were you always planning to use us to make you king? Or did you just jump at the chance that presented itself? Were you always using me and Jixa for our power, or did you ever care for me? She kept all of those questions inside: *never ask a question if you can't handle the answer.* Couldn't they just pretend everything was normal between them, that she hadn't just banished her best friend in the world? Pretend that she'd never found out that Darion didn't love her at all. "Fuck me like you love me, Darion."

He closed his eyes and took three deep breaths before his lashes fluttered open and his eyes darkened. "Look at you, kneeling at my feet, ready to worship my cock. I bet if I said so, you'd spread your legs for me right now, wouldn't you?"

Sarafine reached to open his breeches again, and this time, he didn't stop her. She lost herself in a world where her only goal was to draw out those little grunts, growls, and words of praise from Darion's lips, let his hand in her hair guide her, feel him hot and pulsing on her tongue.

He tugged her gently off him and tilted her face up, leaned forward, and kissed her. His tongue nudged at her lips, and she opened for it to dart inside.

He pulled back, and one hand snaked up under her skirt, brushing her slick thighs. He half lifted her into his chair and seemed to soak in her every expression as he brushed her clit in a steady rhythm. Her head fell back, and her entire body condensed into his fingers on her tender bud.

"Did you like my letters, my little seer? Did you send Jixa away so that you could read them alone? Did you take them to bed with you and pretend I was there?"

His letters? The letters that she had tossed in the fireplace unread . . . had been love letters? Not orders from the king, not official missives demanding her presence, but secret correspondence from Darion? How could she tell him that she'd never even opened one? That she'd watched them curl to ash in her fire without so much as breaking their seals?

Her belly tightened, and her pussy tingled, saving her from devising an answer. "Don't stop," she breathed.

"That doesn't sound like the appropriate way to address your lord." But Darion had a smile in his voice, and he kept a steady pace.

"Please, my lord, don't stop!"

Darion wrapped an arm around her thigh as her back bowed and her pussy spasmed; her mouth hung open, no sound coming out. "Beautiful. My exquisite little seer." He kissed the inside of her knee and extricated his hand from her skirts.

He didn't seem to need an immediate answer about the letters.

"What has you so troubled?" Darion stood, pulling her with him.

"I just want you to take your pleasure, my lord." Not a lie, not exactly.

Darion circled her and unhooked her skirt and bodice, loosened the laces on her stays, and soon she stood naked before him. She shivered.

"Bed, get under the covers."

This time, she obeyed. He banked the brazier and stripped off the rest of his clothes in the shadows. Next time, she'd insist on seeing him in all his glory. If there was a next time. Once he discovered that she no longer had her pixie . . .

He slipped under the covers. "Have you imagined me inside you? I'll admit I had to take more than one break from writing your letters to imagine you, hot and wet around me." He settled between her thighs, and she tried to imagine a world where she'd read his love letters instead of letting them burn. He thought she'd known how much he cared for her and missed her, and he'd been trying, all this time, to reach out to her the only way they'd been able to connect, and yet she'd still stayed away. And he'd kept on writing.

She reached between them, finding his hard length, but he chuckled and replaced her hand.

"Spread your legs."

She shivered and complied. This man thought she'd betrayed him.

"Beg for my cock."

"Please, my lord." Sarafine squirmed. He was nudging her entrance. Perhaps if she wriggled just right—

He hummed and sheathed his cock deep inside her. "My dreams can't compare to you, Sarafine." His lips tickled her ear. "Even my memories were faded. The way you beg, the way you give so beautifully." He rolled his hips, coaxing her closer to the edge. His words so soft that they were almost lost. "Don't leave me again, my little seer." He ran a hand down her ribs, over her hip, and circled her clit.

Sarafine's hips jerked, and she fluttered around Darion's pulsing length, as if she never wanted to let him go. Even she could almost believe that she'd never leave him again.

5

Sarafine surfaced from sleep as a powerful arm pulled her bare back against a hard body. She snuggled in, still dozing.

Darion.

His habit of cuddling in his sleep. Instead of melting into him as she always used to do, she waited until his arm went limp, and slipped away. The cool air kissed her bare skin as she hunted for her clothes in the dim tent, the brazier having faded to embers under its shield. She donned her chemise and pulled her stays over her head to lace firmly in the front, where she could tie it off herself. She tied on her pocket, heavy with her card deck, and tossed her skirt over her head to settle on her hips. Her skirt she could hook herself, but her bodice hooked in the back. She couldn't leave the king's tent half-dressed like a common slattern. *They* wore clothes they could get into—and out of—themselves.

Staying would mean being forced to talk about Jixa, about the letters, about meeting with the elders today and what the hell she was going to do. She hefted Jixa's perch onto her shoulder and buckled it roughly. That would keep her bodice in place somewhat. Maybe a camp follower would be stealing out of a soldier's tent and she could beg their aid. She couldn't stay here either way.

Sarafine ducked out of the king's tent and shivered. Boisterous conversation and wood smoke from crackling fires floated on the morning breeze. Dawn hadn't yet warmed the day, though the sky was light enough for Sarafine to pick her way toward the sounds of life. The cooks and servants were always the first to rise, and only one or two soldiers milled around the camp, none taking much notice of her. The one who did caught sight of Jixa's perch and backed off.

A bonfire crackled toward the back of the camp, outside the noisy tent, a robust woman bending over a cauldron that sat in the fire. She looked up when Sarafine approached.

"Nellie?"

She scowled and brushed her hands on her apron, but her face cleared as she caught sight of Sarafine. "Sarafine?"

"How are you? How have you been?"

"Same old, serving His Majesty. Last time I saw you, you were"—she looked Sarafine up and down—"properly dressed."

Sarafine's face heated. "I found myself without any assistance this morning."

"Turn around. I'll get you sorted." Nellie tugged Sarafine's bodice into place and fastened her hooks. "I'm glad His Majesty was right about you, Sarafine. Some of the others thought—" Nellie's tap on her back gave her leave to turn around. "Never mind what they thought. I'm glad you're back with us. Just a few more minutes until breakfast. Porridge again. As you can imagine, being in camp like this, we only brought the essentials. Now that you're here, we'll be able to pack up."

That Nellie had joined Darion was no surprise; she believed in him, and she always had. "Pack up and go where?"

"Back home. Bracetree."

"Home." Bracetree was Darion's home and had been for years. Of course it would be; he was the king, and Bracetree was the monarch's seat. Bracetree, their eternal enemy under King Iron Fist, was Darion's home now.

"You'll get used to it. Damned sight different from when we lived here, that's for sure." Nellie jerked her chin at the fortress behind Sarafine. "Where have you been all this time? Hanging around Amelia in Langswold?"

"No, I actually live in Corniston."

"As far from His Majesty as you could get, eh? The important thing is you're back now. No more worries." She nodded sharply, as if everything were decided.

They filled the silence with small talk, but it was different than it had been when Nellie was the mother figure to the rebels and Sarafine and Darion were idealistic young folks with their heads in the clouds. Now, Nellie's bits of wisdom seemed trite and simple, too simple for the real world that Sarafine lived in. Nellie thought if everyone was just honest with each other and the monarch was compassionate and cared for their people, everything would run perfectly smoothly. The right man was on the throne now, so nothing could be wrong.

The soldiers soon roused and descended on Nellie's porridge, leaving Sarafine to melt into the background. Everyone here could identify her by Jixa's perch, and her skin crawled at even the thought of donning her fortune-teller manner if she was asked to do a reading.

All too soon, a breathless runner drew her out of her seclusion, on orders to bring her to the king. Every moment in Darion's presence was a chance for him to realize that Jixa was not there with her, but delaying would only arouse his suspicions more, so she followed without complaint.

Darion stood outside his tent with his horse and . . .

"Mandrake?"

He turned and ran a hand through his hair, still rumpled from their bed. "Marcel sent her along. I presumed you would want to ride her, so she's ready when you and Jixa are."

Mandrake tossed her head and stretched her nose toward Sarafine. The soldier holding her reins passed them over, and Mandrake snuggled her face into her human's shoulder. Sarafine muttered soothing words to her horse and stroked her blaze; she seemed unsettled but calm enough to ride, at least.

Darion mounted his black charger. "We'll go on ahead, and the camp will be struck. There's no need for anyone to stay here now that matters are settled with Langswold."

He hadn't asked her a question, so Sarafine held her tongue. She was his subject, and monarchs didn't discuss matters with their subjects, at least not in front of a camp full of soldiers.

Darion moved closer. "Sarafine?" He was looking down at her, concern written in the line between his brows.

"Yes, Your Majesty. I— We're ready." She adjusted the perch on her shoulder, more through habit and muscle memory than as a pretense, but it would serve as such, regardless. She would have to remember to talk to Jixa sometimes, though pretending to feed her would present problems. Had Darion forgotten that Jixa used to make footprints? Hold objects and make food seem to disappear? Eventually, he would remember. She had to finish this before he did.

Sarafine mounted Mandrake, and they were off. Kings didn't ride with their advisers, didn't fraternize with the help. Monarchs were far too good for those around them and stood alone. Still, Darion rode abreast of her and Mandrake, opposite where Jixa would have been sitting. The soldiers remained around them, some riding ahead and some on foot behind, all close enough to overhear their conversation.

"Jixa seems quiet."

"She's had a busy few days."

"Is she sleeping?"

Sarafine just grunted. People appreciated either keeping close to the truth or being as vague as possible when it was necessary to lie. During readings, being more vague always elicited awe and profuse thanks. Patrons filled in the details for themselves, supplying precisely what they wanted to hear more effectively than she ever could. Certainly, Jixa had added a touch of drama, a little finesse, but Sarafine could more than cope without her. Of course she could. It would be no problem.

A scout dropped back to report in midmorning. She leaned in to speak to Darion, who nodded, and she rode off.

"It seems Quinton has set up just outside the next village. We'll take him in and carry on to Bracetree this afternoon."

"Yes, Your Majesty." She kept her eye on the road, but Darion glared. Her behaviour was perfectly proper in the king's presence. If he expected her to treat him as her friend, then he should have considered that before accepting the monarchy.

By the time they reached Quinton's camp, Sarafine had "had a conversation" with Jixa and "fed her a few snacks" from her still-stocked saddlebags. The time to mourn Jixa's loss would come, but for now, Sarafine clamped down on her own feelings to maintain the facade that Jixa was still with her. Quinton would be searching for any excuse to claim that her presence didn't fulfill the peace agreement, and Jixa being gone was a damned good reason.

Quinton's camp was little more than a single temporary shelter; soldiers huddled around the bonfire wrapped in blankets.

When Darion's people asked about Quinton, they were directed to a cozy cottage in the nearby village, where smoke curled from the chimney.

"Did he turn the family out to have the place to himself?" Sarafine muttered, but Darion caught it.

"That wouldn't surprise me in the least. Quinton isn't known for his self-sacrificing nature."

A soldier dismounted ahead of them and rapped on the door. A guard opened it and ducked aside when he caught sight of the king.

Sarafine followed Darion inside, and as her eyes adjusted to the dim interior, someone scrambled and the door shut on the second of the two rooms in the cottage. Quinton reclined on a couch by the fireplace, surrounded by what looked like every candle in the village. He didn't make to get up when the king entered.

"Ah, Your Majesty, you've made it. And with your seer in tow." He said *Your Majesty* in the tone of voice that Sarafine used when she and Darion were alone.

"Quinton. Finally outside your high walls. If you think I'll forget your treason now that I have my seer with me, you're very much mistaken."

Quinton shook his head and gestured Darion and Sarafine to two chairs across from him. "I wanted to have my fortune read by the infamous fortune teller of Corniston."

Darion didn't cross to the chairs, and Sarafine remained blocked by his shoulder. "You will come with me back to Bracetree where you will face—"

Quinton waved him away. "Yes, yes, of course. Dire punishment, I understand. The reading first, perhaps?"

Darion shifted to block Sarafine more thoroughly. "I don't think that's—"

She stepped around him. "I'd be happy to, my lord." Faking a reading for Quinton would be simple enough, and it might help to convince him that Darion's claim to the monarchy was legit. As King

Iron Fist's heir, he no doubt had sway among the elders. "Allow me to fetch my supplies."

Darion didn't follow her out to Mandrake, who tossed her head to have a stranger holding her reins. "This won't take long, my friend." She'd never been much for talking to her horse in the past, but without Jixa, she had to talk to someone. She drew three kerchiefs, a stick of camphor, and a tin of incense from the saddlebag, gave Mandrake a pat on the neck, and ducked back into the cottage.

Darion stood by the small window. Had he been watching her? A tea table had appeared in front of the chair across from Quinton, but he didn't appear to have moved from the couch. For a prisoner accused of treason against the crown, he was awfully cavalier.

Sarafine moved a half-knitted sock, still on the needles, from the seat and took the hard chair. She smoothed the first silk kerchief over the tea table. A quick reading, nothing too specific. She draped the second overtop and set up her incense. If Quinton asked to have Jixa choose a card, she'd just claim that Jixa was feeling ornery. That wouldn't be surprising to Darion, who was plenty familiar with the temperamental pixie. She used the last kerchief to waft the incense smoke toward Quinton and brought her cards forth with a flourish.

Sarafine shuffled the cards and began her reading. They were random, as always, and she made up some guff about a journey, an alliance, and shifting power that made Quinton sneer at Darion.

Finally, she turned up the last card: a crowned woman in a crimson robe seated on a throne. The Monarch.

"Ah, a good omen, my lord. This card portends a—"

A crash, as of a basket falling from a shelf, echoed from the other room, and someone berated the perpetrator. No second voice responded during the following pause, but the first started up again. Almost as though someone was speaking to a pixie. But that wasn't possible. Darion had said that no pixie besides Jixa had wanted to come into the human world.

Quinton scowled at the closed door. Darion, behind her, hadn't made a sound.

Sarafine cleared her throat and continued the reading. "A path of great wisdom and great opportunity lies before you."

"Very enlightening. But I wonder if your pixie could choose a card for me?"

"Jixa, would you be so kind?" Sarafine addressed her own empty shoulder. She grimaced. "I'm very sorry, my lord. She cannot be convinced. She is out of sorts today after travelling so far. You understand."

Quinton's sly smile made Sarafine's heart pound and her stomach clench. "I certainly do." He turned to Darion. "I think it's only fair that I warn you of your precarious situation before you confront the elders. After all, lying to them would be punishable by death. And you know that I am not without mercy, however much I might rejoice at your beheading, of course."

"Get to it, Quinton. I'm eager to resume our journey and get home to Bracetree."

Quinton nodded, as though acquiescing, but his wolf's smile didn't falter. "Carmela!"

The door to the chambers opened, and Carmela appeared holding a battered birdcage—empty. "Now behave." She shook the cage and tried to smooth her hair, many strands having been tugged from her bun and poking out at odd angles. Tiny scratches marred her neck, perhaps from the small creature that had escaped from the cage?

She turned, revealing her opposite shoulder, upon which a perch rested. A chill crept up Sarafine's spine. A perch, twin to the one strapped to her own shoulder. The birdcage shook again, but Carmela wasn't the one shaking it. It was as if a small invisible bird were trapped inside—

Sarafine tried to speak, but all she could do was croak. They'd trapped a pixie. In a *birdcage*. They were keeping a pixie imprisoned like an animal.

"She's not your master anymore, you little vermin." *Not your master*? What did that mean? Unless it wasn't just any pixie in the cage—after all, Darion had said no other pixie wanted to come with the humans he had offered. *No.* Sarafine held herself still to keep from snatching the cage and smashing her pixie free on the dirt floor. Jixa was imprisoned in that birdcage, bound to Carmela, the only one who could hear the pixie.

"Your seer is a wily one, Darion. Twice now she's slipped through my fingers, first in Corniston and then Langswold, but as you can see," said Quinton, gesturing to the cage, "I no longer have need of her. We have her pixie right here."

Sarafine growled and lunged for the cage, but Darion's arm wrapped around her middle like iron before she could go two steps.

His jaw was set, and his arm didn't slacken. "I see nothing, Quinton, as you well know. Your person, here, may be skilled at pantomime, but this proves nothing."

Sarafine gripped his forearm. He'd implied that Quinton was the one lying even though it must be obvious to Darion by now that Sarafine had tricked him.

"Attacking the heir apparent wouldn't be wise," Darion muttered into her ear.

He . . . was protecting her? Even after she left him on the day he became monarch, left him in a very precarious position, no less. She didn't respond to his letters for eight years; she came to Langswold to oppose him, and now, despite the compelling evidence right in front of him that she had betrayed him again, *still* he backed her?

Part of her wanted to fall to her knees before him, tell him the truth, and beg his forgiveness. But not in front of Quinton and Carmela, who poked a stick of kindling through the bars of the cage. A cage that could very well contain Jixa.

"We've seen enough of your inane attempts to prevent me from securing my place as monarch, Quinton." He nudged Sarafine to precede him from the cottage. His dark gaze promised that they would have a private conversation, just the two of them, soon enough.

But did she want to? Continuing this facade might allow Darion to remain king, but did she want that? When she had left Corniston, she'd only been looking to keep Darion and Amelia from ripping one another's throats out. And that, she had done. If she sided with Quinton now, Darion wouldn't stand a chance of remaining king; after all, Quinton's loyal follower was the one with the bond to a pixie, and that was the elders' stipulation for the monarchy. Quinton would become king, Darion would be executed, Jixa would be a prisoner for the rest of her life, and Quinton would take everything from the people and give nothing back, just as his father had done. Darion had had eight years to abolish the monarchy, and yet it was still firmly in place, but Quinton assuredly never would, and would string up anyone who so much as whispered such an inclination.

She scrambled to stack her cards and wrap them in silks, gave Jixa's cage one last look.

Quinton clearly couldn't contain one last taunt. "I think you'll find your claims against me will no longer be well received in Bracetree, *Your Majesty*. But don't worry. My seer and I will make our own way there. No shackles required." His smarmy face was so punchable that

Sarafine clasped her cards in a white-knuckle grip as she stalked past him.

They rode in silence the last leg of their journey to Bracetree. Darion's mount walked ahead of hers, and Sarafine almost dropped the pretense of Jixa's presence, except that Darion fell back to ask about her pixie and gave her a meaningful look. And so she "fed" her a few times during the ride and kept up a one-sided conversation with her own shoulder, feeling more and more inane as the afternoon wore on.

Finally, they entered Bracetree, winding up through the village, up the scarp, over the flying bridge to the bailey on top of the hill. An elder tried to hail Darion as he rode into the bailey, but the king waved her off, pleading fatigue from the journey. Sarafine trailed him, dragging her feet to put a little distance between them so that she could slip away, but Darion was having none of it and grabbed her hand in his gloved one, tugging her up to a gilded chamber, the guard shutting the door behind them with a resounding thud.

His canopy bed was similar to the one at the camp, the carpet on the wood floor soft beneath Sarafine's boots. Darion dropped her hand and peeled his gloves off. He flung them on a chair and turned to her: the harsh planes of his face weren't angry exactly, but he knew what Sarafine had done.

It was the chance she'd been waiting for to admit to her dissembling. "It's true, Your Majesty. My bond with Jixa is broken. I'm no longer a seer." She stood across from him, staring him down, daring him to toss her out now that he knew the truth.

"And you were going to let me lie in the faces of the elders and tell them I had secured a seer? Do you hate me so much?" He still didn't sound angry. His voice was level, almost cold.

How was she even supposed to answer a question like that? *I thought I'd be able to hide it.* Why hide it in the first place? She'd been so focused on making sure Amelia was safe, so focused on keeping Jixa out of Darion's hands, that she hadn't thought of herself. Would he not reveal her lie now and have her executed for treason? And if he didn't, Quinton would have no such compunction. Where had she been going with this ruse? Had she been planning to keep it up for the rest of her life? Lying to the *king*! What had she been thinking?

Betrayal, revenge. Darion had already used her once to climb to power, and he had been planning to use her again. "I couldn't let you get Jixa. I didn't want you to use her."

"And now Quinton will use her."

Sarafine recoiled. It had never crossed her mind that someone else could claim Jixa, or that she would accept some unknown human barging into their village trying to claim her. But all the evidence suggested that Carmela had followed her to the faery ring, claimed Jixa, and returned with her to Quinton.

"I never thought Jixa would go with someone else."

"We don't always know those closest to us as well as we might like, *fortune teller*."

So he'd caught that, had he? She wouldn't apologize for the life she'd built after he'd betrayed her. "Very true. The people closest to us can betray us on a whim, *Your Majesty*."

"I thought everything was clear from my letters. I thought perhaps we were past that."

"We said we would never accept the monarchy, Darion, never! I returned to the fortress after spending hours picking over a corpse-strewn *battlefield* only to learn that you were to be the new king! I trusted you to parley with the elders. I left it to you because I thought you would do right by me, by all of us! But you didn't." She turned to the window. "You took power for yourself and left the rest of us to rot."

"And you? You're blameless in this scenario you've devised? I came out of that parley utterly defeated, forced to take on a kingship I've always despised, and where is my—" He caught his breath and then pressed on. "Where were you? Disappeared. No one knew where. Gone. Without so much as a goodbye."

"Oh, yes. The seer you needed to cement your place as monarch. That must have been quite a shock."

His fingers dug into her shoulder and wheeled her around. "No. Sarafine, I don't give a fuck about you being a seer. I don't give a shit about your pixie." He shook his head. "I care about Jixa, whether she's yours or not. I fucking loved you, Sarafine. And you disappeared on me at the first opportunity. I thought you loved me too, but I suppose you loved the rebellion, the vision for the future that I represented. And when I wasn't perfect? You were out."

Wasn't perfect? Betraying everything they'd ever fought for, everything they valued *wasn't perfect*? Her face twitched into a sneer. "I did. I loved that vision for the future. I won't deny it. I still love it, Darion." She sniffed and swallowed down the last words: *I still love you*.

Darion's fingers coasted over her jaw and tipped her face up. "And me? You were willing to part from Jixa to bring me down. What was your next move, my little seer?"

"It wasn't about you. It was about Amelia's life."

He didn't drop his hand. She could have batted him away, but she let him keep their gazes locked. "Are you under the impression that I'll let you go now that I have you?" His voice had deepened.

"Without Jixa, what am I to you?"

His hand slid lower to circle her throat. "Still mine, little seer."

She swallowed under his hand. He still wanted her. Without Jixa, without the power to finally crown him king, without any visions of the future, he still wanted her.

He had even loved her, once. He'd written her love letters, dozens, over the eight years they had been apart. Love letters that she had thrown in the fireplace without a care for his feelings on the matter. He had imagined her reading his letters, enjoying them, thinking of him, if not fondly, at least lustfully. He hadn't imagined that every time she'd received a missive from the king, she'd been stabbed through the heart again at his betrayal, driven to destroy his letters and leave no trace of them. He hadn't imagined that *she* was the one who felt betrayed by *him*.

She'd trusted him to parley with the elders. She'd trusted him to take the path they had agreed upon. She had trusted him not to make decisions about her future without her, the way her parents had. And yet.

He spoke the truth: she was his. Not an equal partner, entitled to deliberate with and come to an agreement, but a pawn to use however he saw fit. Clearly, that hadn't changed in the intervening years.

"Yours to do with as you please."

His grip flexed around her throat, never impeding her breath. "Exactly as I please."

"Yours to drag to Bracetree to be your personal assurance that you will remain king." Her hands twisted in her skirts.

Darion's fingers loosened their hold and fell away. "I thought my letters explained all, Sarafine. If you'd stayed in Corniston, Quinton would have found you within a fortnight, and there would have been no escaping him."

Quinton had been looking for her? Of course. *Twice now she's slipped through my fingers.* He had needed a seer to take the monarchy, and she was the only one available. Had been. And Darion had tried to warn her that Quinton was hunting her, tried to have her come to him, even threatened Amelia's life to keep Sarafine out of his grasp. So that she could remain under Darion's protection.

A protection she would never have needed without that stipulation in the peace agreement about the monarchy being tied to whoever possessed a seer. "If you cared to protect me from Quinton, why sign a peace agreement that effectively bound the monarchy to me?"

Mud caked the toes of Darion's boots. Birds sang outside the window. Sarafine twisted her fingers together.

"You never read my letters." Darion's weary voice was not accusatory.

She shook her head.

Darion dropped to one knee before her, looking up so she had to meet his sharp gaze again. "Why?"

"I told you already." Sarafine's hands clenched into fists, her nails digging into her palms. "You betrayed me—us. We all agreed not to take the monarchy, even if it was offered up to us."

"As it was offered up to me, free for the taking." Darion's mouth twisted in a mirthless smile. "You believe that it didn't pain me to take the mantle of king? You don't think I would have taken any other viable choice that was offered to me?"

"I . . ." It *had* been his free choice . . . hadn't it?

"Certainly, I was free to refuse. Free to turn my back on the elders, leave that tent, come back to you and the rest. Free to bind you to Quinton for the rest of your days."

Bind her to Quinton? What was he talking about? Her hands tightened into fists. "Make yourself plain, Your Majesty."

"The elders' offer was as follows: whoever had the loyalty of the seer would also control the monarchy. As the representative for our faction, I was the natural candidate. And if I declined the offer, then and there, it would pass from our grasp. Quinton would have been all too happy to claim his status as your betrothed. You must know that your father would have given you to him and been overjoyed at the prospect of his daughter marrying the prince-turned-king."

Indeed, she had run away from home and joined the rebels to avoid her parents' attempts to marry her off to the most powerful suitor they could manage. Darion spoke truly: they would have been ecstatic to bind her to the king, with or without her consent.

And she had run away from Darion before he could give any explanation for his actions at the parley. The parley that she had sent him to alone, too busy hunting the battlefield with Jixa for any survivors to go herself. Would her presence at the parley have made a difference? Perhaps. Perhaps not. The elders would have been happy to talk over her and give her in marriage without listening to a word that she said, fixated as they were on her status as seer.

Darion still shouldn't have made the decision without asking her . . . but he had made the best of a very perilous situation. Had Quinton been allowed to continue his father's legacy with her and Jixa at his side, the rebels would have been crushed, Darion, Amelia, Marcel, and everyone she cared about included. A fate that awaited them still if Quinton kept Jixa bound to him through Carmela.

Darion brushed his fingers over her jaw. "Speak to me, my little seer."

"I'm not a seer anymore."

"True enough. I see the wheels turning in that head of yours. Quinton has all he needs to take the monarchy from us."

"With a king already on the throne? If you don't step aside—"

"Now that Quinton has a better claim, it would be treason to stand against him." But Darion would.

Traitors were executed, and Quinton would take great pleasure in decapitating Darion.

This might be Darion's last day on Earth, and she'd had a part, however unwitting, in his demise.

She bowed her head to her lord. "How would you have me atone, my lord?"

The line between his eyebrows smoothed. "First, rid yourself of your clothing, my little seer, and then we shall see what can be done with you."

Despite his words, he helped her undress until she knelt naked on the rug, the woven wool scratching at her knees.

Darion stripped off his tunic and boots and rolled up his shirt-sleeves, the curls of his chest hair peeking through the V of his open collar. He paced back and forth before her, and Sarafine dropped her gaze and smiled down into the carpet. He must be devising some penance for her, something to clear the air between them. She wriggled at the possibilities that flashed through her mind. Instead of giving her an order, he crossed to his bookshelf, slid a book out, and took it to the bed, where he lounged back into the pillows and opened it.

He intended to read at a time like this? Sarafine kneeling naked before him, the elders practically beating down the door for an audience with him, Quinton following close behind them, ready to brand Darion a traitor?

He turned a page. He *was* reading. He had not told her to be silent and yet had not given her permission to speak. Did he expect her to simply kneel there, bored, knees itching while he . . .

Yes, he did. She'd expected penance, and penance was what he was doling out. Unable to touch him, to take comfort in him, to distract herself from their plight. More cruel than any intimate game he could play with her.

Quinton and Carmela were on their way there with Jixa, who seemed miserable being bound to Carmela. When they arrived, they would demand an audience with the elders immediately, show that Jixa was with them, loyal to Quinton, and convert the elders to their side, inclined as they already were toward supporting the former king's son.

They would be too late to intercept Quinton's party on the way to Bracetree, and blocking them from entering the keep would require a very good reason, something that would only make Darion seem more suspicious in their eyes. The elders were more than willing to give Quinton an audience, judging by the way they had accosted Darion upon his arrival, and Quinton would grasp his chance immediately. Jixa, last Sarafine had seen, had been caged and trapped, bound to Carmela physically. But she hadn't been cooperative and indeed still seemed to view Sarafine as her *master*, a word that had never passed between Sarafine and her pixie.

The elders could no more see Jixa than Quinton or Darion could. Would they believe that Sarafine and Jixa were still bonded? No one but Carmela and Sarafine could tell for sure. Could she convince them that Carmela had caged Sarafine's pixie, that they were still bound and Sarafine was still the rightful seer, as she had always been?

"What are you cooking up in that brain of yours?" Darion snapped his book shut.

Sarafine allowed a slow smile. "I think we might have a chance, my lord."

He dropped his feet over the side of the bed, set the book aside, and patted the coverlet next to him. Sarafine's smile widened, and she crawled the few feet to him and climbed up to sit, arms and legs touching, beside him. But for a moment: he dropped to his knees before her.

"Now you have paid your penance, little seer, but I have yet to pay mine." He hooked one of her legs over his shoulder and wrapped his arms under her, pulling her to him and dipping his head down to lick through her folds, the shocking, warm sliding making Sarafine cry out.

"You consider this penance?" she gasped.

Darion chuckled into her flesh. "Do you?" He lapped at her clit.

She arched her back, bracing her hands behind her on the bed. "I don't care, just keep going."

Later, they would discuss her plan. For now, they would indulge themselves. If the plan failed, it would be their last chance.

6

Darion went along with Sarafine's plan. The elders had no conception of how the pixie bond worked—even less than Quinton did, if that was possible, so they would believe whatever Sarafine told them.

Hooves clattered from the courtyard below Darion's bedroom window, and there they were, Quinton and Carmela, birdcage strapped to her saddle. Mercifully, Sarafine couldn't see how miserable Jixa must be, huddled in a corner of the barren cage, not even a cushion or a scrap of cloth to ease its jolting.

Darion's hands landed heavily on her shoulders. "Your plan will work."

"I know it will." But it wouldn't get Jixa back. She couldn't do that. What would happen once Darion secured the kingship? They might win Jixa's freedom from her cage, but she would still need Carmela close by to pass on her predictions, and keeping Carmela around would be inordinately suspicious . . . but keeping Darion's head attached to his shoulders was the priority for the time being. Quinton would execute Darion as soon as possible, so even if they were only buying time, convincing the elders of Sarafine's bond to Jixa was their only choice.

Sarafine turned from the window as Quinton and Carmela dismounted and Carmela released the cage from her horse's saddle. An elder met them and led them out of sight beneath the window. Straightening Jixa's perch on her shoulder, Sarafine turned to Darion.

The king. His crown glittered; his regal red velvet cloak rippled as he moved, and even his boots sparkled with gold thread in a lion rampant pattern as he stepped toward her.

Darion offered her his satin-clad arm. "Come."

"Yes, Your Majesty." Sarafine looked at the floor and allowed the king to lead her from his chambers.

When they reached the throne room, Sarafine forced her gaze from the inlaid marble. The elders sat on embroidered couches ranged around the room, servants in royal livery standing by to serve them refreshments. Quinton and Carmela stood together at the bottom of the steps that led to the monarch's gilded seat. Carmela quietly admonished the empty cage she still held, but gouges marred the bars in several places, as though a rodent had gnawed at them. Sarafine's heart broke for Jixa.

Keep to the plan.

Darion squeezed her shoulder and swept up the aisle, lightly mounting the steps to his throne. Even Quinton bowed to him as he passed. Once the king was settled on the cushioned seat, Sarafine flicked her train straight and made her entrance.

Stained glass windows behind the throne depicted Quinton's forebears in a carefully crafted portrayal of the formation of the kingdom.

Sarafine lowered her gaze back to the inlaid marble floor and curtsied low to the king. "Your Majesty, they've taken my pixie. I demand her immediate return."

"She is no longer yours, and you are just as aware of that as I am." Carmela swung around to face her, and the bars of the cage shook as though Jixa had been thrown against them.

"You believe our bond can be broken simply by locking my pixie in a cage?" Sarafine had no need to pretend. She allowed the truth to tumble from her lips. "Jixa will always be my pixie, just as I will always be her human." *I may have given her up, but some bonds can't be broken so easily.* She kept that last thought inside; it wouldn't do to reveal that she had broken their link.

"Your pixie begs to differ. She says that she no longer wants anything to do with you, since you abandoned her."

It might not have been a lie, either. Jixa would be angry with her, probably beyond all reason. Sarafine *had* abandoned her in the forest; that was unquestionable between them. But there was no chance whatsoever that Jixa preferred her current predicament to being doted on by Sarafine.

Carmela flinched and removed one hand from the cage, holding it only by the ring on top. Tiny scratches marked her palm where it had been pressed to the cage. No, Jixa was certainly not pleased with Carmela's treatment. Perhaps enraged enough to take Sarafine's side in this.

She turned to the elders. "I demand that my pixie be released at once. I will prove to you that she has been taken from me despite our bond." She slid her deck of cards from her pocket. "She will do a reading for you."

Quinton groaned. "This again? Honestly, I'm weary of your *seer's* pretenses, Darion."

"You will address the king as *Your Majesty*, Lord Quinton. He remains the king for the time being." The foremost elder spoke mildly. "As this dispute concerns his title, I would ask him to allow the elders to deliberate on the matter. We will be the judge of the rightful claim to this pixie."

Darion steepled his fingers and inclined his head. "Of course, Elder Rowan. I have no doubt you will devise a suitable test."

Test? That wasn't part of the plan, and yet, she couldn't decline a chance to prove her claim to Jixa beyond all doubt. How could they test Jixa's bond? The pixie could speak to no one except her own human, and she had never learned her letters. All Jixa could share with other humans involved objects. If the elders were not immediately convinced by the scratches on Carmela's neck and hand and the gnaw marks on the horrid cage they had shut her in, what would convince them?

Jixa had impressed patrons with her antics, making footprints in powdered sugar, picking cards from her oracle deck, and sometimes even touching their fingers. But that would only convince the elders of her existence, not her bond.

The elders deliberated quietly and, finally, Elder Rowan addressed the king and the pretender. "The pixie will predict what colour of kerchief I have concealed and tell its master, who will tell me. Whoever has the correct answer has the true bond."

Sarafine almost laughed. Jixa couldn't be forced to predict a specific fact in that way, at least not in all the years they had been bound. Carmela had just as much chance of guessing the correct answer as Sarafine did. But Carmela didn't look at all worried; triumph gleamed in her eyes and curled her lips.

"Sarafine, as the challenger, we will begin with you."

What should she guess? It would be worse to deliberate too long. Instead, she addressed the cage. "Jixa, please tell me what colour kerchief the elder will pull from her pocket in a moment." She paused, pretending to listen to Jixa's answer, trying to ignore Carmela's unsettling smile in the corner of her eye. "Jixa has imparted a prediction." The elder was dressed fashionably in their customary purple from head to toe. "Purple, of course."

Elder Rowan cocked her head but only gestured for Carmela to take a turn.

"Jixa has imparted to me that your purple kerchief was ruined by your laundress two days past and that you carry a white one made by your mother."

The elder held Sarafine's gaze as she drew the white kerchief from her pocket. Sarafine's chest tightened, her heart pounding against it. She'd lost. She'd lost Jixa; she'd lost Darion . . .

Quinton's sharp smile taunted her from over Carmela's shoulder. No, she hadn't just lost Darion but condemned him to death. Had Jixa imparted such knowledge to Carmela? Or had the elders set up this entire meeting to defeat her and Darion? Quinton's favoured status was no secret among the elders; they would be greatly relieved if the hereditary line of monarchs were to remain unbroken, their divine claim to the throne unquestioned.

Quinton stepped forward. "Only one thing remains." He turned to his seer. "Carmela, do you swear that I have your loyalty?"

"Yes, of course, my lord."

They had lost. The peace agreement stipulated that the rightful king must have the loyalty of a seer. Nothing Sarafine did mattered now.

She snatched Jixa's cage from Carmela's fumbling hands and thumbed a card from her deck, jamming it between the cage door and frame and popping the latch free. The door was kicked open by invisible pixie legs and swung free, a light brush of wings on her cheek the only sign of Jixa. The cage dangled unheeded from Sarafine's hand as she hunted around the room in vain for any sign of her pixie. *There!*

An elder squeaked as his tea cake exploded into crumbs. Sarafine threw the cage to the ground and stomped it into kindling.

She whirled on Carmela. "Never cage her again, or I swear to you, I will kill you while you sleep, seer or no."

Carmela recoiled a step. Jixa was lost to her; Darion faced death; Quinton would turn on Amelia and Marcel and the other rebels and crush them under his royal heel.

And then she felt it. A familiar weight on her shoulder. Tiny hands stroking her neck, a familiar little face burrowing into her hair. "Jixa?" Her pixie had come back to her, even after Sarafine had abandoned her in the woods. When it would have been best for her to escape home, fly away, and leave humans behind forever, Jixa had come back to her.

Sarafine raised a trembling hand to her invisible friend, mindful of her own massive strength in the face of the tiny pixie, and Jixa wrapped her arms around two of Sarafine's fingers. Tears blurred her vision, and Sarafine closed her eyes. Seeing didn't matter, only the warmth of Jixa's little arms, her breath . . .

"Interesting." Darion's murmur made her open her eyes again. "We can all see the pixie's loyalty, can we not?"

"What are you implying?" growled Quinton.

"It appears that, when given a choice, the pixie has chosen my seer, not yours."

"Be that as it may—" Elder Rowan began.

"It's a trick," Quinton snarled. "There is no way to prove that the pixie is really there. Elders, she tried the same trick with me earlier today. Before she was aware that her pixie had a new master. Tried to convince me that the pixie still conversed with her through pantomime and deception. Surely you do not believe—"

"Lord Quinton, that's enough." Elder Rowan glared at Quinton, clearly unused to being interrupted. "Your seer gave the correct answer to my test. However, it is possible, however unlikely, that you deduced the information some other way." She turned to Carmela. "Tell me, can the pixie communicate directly? Can she tell us in no uncertain terms who holds her bond?"

"I— I don't know, elder, I—"

"She can paint," said Sarafine.

"Paint?"

"Yes, Elder. I often gave her watercolours to paint with, using her feet and hands. She loved to . . ." Tears choked her again, and Sarafine shook her head, Jixa gripping her fingers all the tighter, as though she would never let her hand go.

Watercolours were called for and an easel. Jixa had always worked on a flat desk before, but hopefully her wings would allow her to paint on the tall surface.

Sarafine brought her shoulder close to the easel and eased her hand out of Jixa's grip. "Paint something good, Jixa. Show them where your loyalties lie."

The daubs of paint seemed to float through the air, an unsettling display, to say the least. How had Darion and the other rebels accustomed themselves to this strange invisible presence that made small objects float and food disappear? Had Quinton and Carmela fed Jixa at all since they had kidnapped her? While the others watched Jixa paint with four colours at once, one on each extremity, Sarafine pulled a servant aside and requested that berries be brought for Jixa.

Jixa had always painted like this: daubs and swirls that might resolve themselves into something concrete, but not always. What would they do if she decorated the paper and no coherent image emerged? Sarafine needn't have worried. A sparkling crown took shape, dotted with gemstones; flowing black hair; and a red robe, twin to the one Darion wore.

"She's painting a portrait of Darion," Quinton snapped. He turned on Sarafine. "You knew she would paint whatever was in front of her. This test is meaningless."

The elders murmured, but Sarafine cut in.

"She is not painting King Darion. Mark the background, the trees, the stream at their feet. Mark the curve of the figure's breast." And the border around the whole thing. She wasn't painting Darion, and she wasn't just painting a picture of a monarch. She was reproducing a card.

Sarafine fumbled in her deck and held up the matching card: the Monarch.

The elders broke into a babble.

"Does that mean she's loyal to whomever the monarch happens to be?"

"I told you this would yield nothing—"

"The former seer has been trying to trick us—"

"Another," said Elder Rowan. "Tear that off. Pixie, paint us another. You are speaking of the monarch. Yes, so are we. Tell us, to whom are you loyal as monarch?"

The pristine paper being attached to the easel rippled, Jixa flew by it so fast. The paint on her limbs let Sarafine track her as she zoomed up toward the throne and threw her tiny body at Darion, nuzzling into his neck and smearing paint in his beard.

Quinton's face matched Darion's robe. "Esteemed elders, this means nothing. The pixie is not the one who decides our politics. The peace agreement clearly states that the monarch will be chosen by a seer's loyalty, and it is clear that I have the loyalty of the seer." He shook Carmela by the shoulder, and she bowed her head.

"Evidence points to your being correct, Lord Quinton." Elder Rowan gave Sarafine an apologetic look. "I'm afraid you did fail the test. And without a seer's support . . ." Darion would be disposed of to make space for the next monarch.

King Quinton, descended from old King Iron Fist, the king she and the rebels had only taken down with Jixa's help. Descended from the ruthless family who had seized power over the people of this kingdom and then blatantly mythologized themselves for all to see in the very glass of the throne room windows, the inlaid marble floor, the ornate throne carvings, the very fabric of the monarch's raiment. As though all this was their right, a right that would be impossible to wrest from their hands after all. These last moments of King Darion's precarious reign should be savoured.

Jixa and Darion looked so natural together, as they always had. He had never been able to see Jixa, and thus her invisibility was no impediment to them now. Jixa communicated yes and no through nuzzles and pinches, Darion speaking and laughing with her quietly, old friends reunited. They could practically get on without Sarafine as intermediary, even after all this time apart. *Without her as intermediary.*

Sarafine grasped the last fibre of hope and stepped forward. "As your wisdom here has proven, elders, my bond to the pixie Jixa had been broken. I am no longer a seer."

The whole room stilled. Darion and Jixa's conversation ceased, and Quinton smirked at her while Carmela's eyes narrowed.

"But nor is Carmela. I'm sure you'll agree that Jixa is, in her own right, the seer. She is the one who imparts prophecies of the future, makes predictions. The human is but the vessel. I was honoured to be that vessel for many years, but as you can see, his majesty and the pixie communicate quite effectively with no human intermediary at all."

"And the pixie is obviously loyal to King Darion." Elder Rowan spoke wryly; the tiny paint-splattered hugs and nuzzles imprinted on

Darion's face and neck contrasted with the scratches on Carmela's. "Though you may only be trying to cement your own choice of monarch, your logic has merit. It seems the pixie can trade master whenever she wishes. It would be wise indeed to choose the monarch the pixie herself prefers."

Of course, Quinton piped up. "And you, former seer, lied to the elders. Since you yourself have admitted that you are not needed to be the intermediary between King Darion and his pixie seer, there is no reason to be lenient with you." His chances of becoming monarch were slipping away, and it seemed he insisted on taking his revenge out on her.

But Darion and Jixa would be safe. With his protection, no one would cage her again, and with Jixa by his side, no one could question his claim to the kingship again. If securing their safety meant that she had admitted her own treason, so be it.

The elders all tried to speak at once, but Elder Rowan raised her voice. "Lord Quinton, let us deal with your initial claim first, since some kind of order must be maintained in this chamber. Your claim to the throne on the basis of a seer's loyalty, a loyalty that you claimed King Darion did not possess, is denied. If it was once true, he has since proved beyond doubt that he has the seer's favour, as stipulated in the peace agreement. Shall this be agreed?"

"Agreed," echoed the rest of the elders, a wizened matron striking her cane on the floor.

"As to your second claim, I will admit I find it troubling." Her gaze flicked to the smashed cage on the floor, to the bowl of cherries that had been brought to sit on the arm of Darion's throne, from which a fruit flew to roll down the steps as they all watched. A smile touched her lips. "I believe that the king should decide the fate of the traitorous former seer, as is customary in such cases."

"But he conspired with her to—"

"Lord Quinton! I suggest you consider leaving here with your own head intact as a blessing and depart forthwith."

Quinton's glare was livid, but he grabbed Carmela's arm and dragged her from the chamber.

Elder Rowan's voice pitched lower. "What say you, Your Majesty? What should the fate of the former seer be?"

Darion watched her, leaving Jixa to burrow into her food—someone had brought her a dish of buttered breadcrumbs, which stuck all over her body when she dived into it, and a thimble of watered wine that decorated her face, almost enough that Sarafine could make out the features she longed to see again.

Perhaps she should be focused on the man who held her life in his hands. He descended the steps from the throne, each footfall ringing through the silent throne room. Sarafine's low belly surged under his fixed gaze. She lowered her eyes, and when he stepped onto the level floor beside her, she dropped to her knees before him.

His callused fingers stroked her jawline. "My little seer," he murmured for her ears only. "Elders, I cannot pardon the former seer."

Sarafine squeezed her eyes shut and pressed her hands together. Would he have her killed after all? She was no longer useful to him, and perhaps he couldn't allow her to join Amelia and Marcel and make his life more difficult.

But Darion wasn't done. "When Sarafine spoke of her bond with the pixie Jixa, I believe she spoke of the bond you have all seen here today. The ineffable bond that caused her to call for food. The bond through which she knew that the pixie loves to paint. Elders, I do not grant Sarafine's pardon. I declare that no treason took place at all."

And then his emerald eyes gleamed, level with hers, but he hadn't pulled her to her feet. The king knelt before her.

"I would humbly beg Lady Sarafine to stay by my side. Whether seer or no, her presence, her wisdom, is invaluable to the kingdom and to me." Perhaps if Jixa's paint hadn't still decorated his face and neck, it would have been a more solemn moment. Darion cocked an eyebrow. "You want to abolish the monarchy?"

Was he really asking *now*? Just like that? "Of course I do."

Darion drew her to her feet at his side. "Now that my seer is present"—he gestured to Jixa, still spraying breadcrumbs wildly—"the position of monarch is abolished, and the elders will now have autonomous rule over the nation, subject to an advisory council that will be put in place at a later date." He gestured to a liveried man by the door. "You will find the proper agreements already drawn up, lacking only the seer's signature to make them binding."

He had already written up the documents that they had planned together all those years ago? He'd already signed them, only to be told that his signature didn't have the power to make them law without the seer's backing?

"I tried to tell you, in my letters." Darion shrugged.

Letters she had never deigned to read about a precarious agreement of which she'd had no inkling.

Sarafine stepped into his embrace. "You never hunted me down?"

"And force you into a union with me, just as a means to an end?" He shook his head. "You were free from the chains of the monarchy that had ensnared me, and I would never have bound you to them unwillingly."

"Even to free yourself?"

The liveried man brough forth a document and affixed it to the easel, where Jixa smeared a series of multicoloured squiggles below Darion's illegible signature.

Darion chuckled. "Says the woman who was willing to die a traitor to keep Quinton from taking the throne."

Darion smiled down at Sarafine and bent his head toward her lips—but an invisible set of tiny hands pressed at her mouth. They had always sent Jixa away before they so much as kissed. Clearly, she was going to accept nothing less.

"Let's get you set up somewhere comfortable," said Sarafine to the invisible pixie. "Darion and I have things to discuss."

7

Jixa's weight swayed on Sarafine's shoulder as they hiked through the woods, Darion trailing them. The three of them had left the rest of the guard and Amelia and Marcel at Langswold Fortress. It would still be safer if no one else knew where the faery ring was.

And there, in the trees, stood the ring of toadstools, tiny doors shut against the wind. Sarafine held her hand out, palm up, and minuscule feet dimpled her skin as the pixie's feather-light weight settled in her palm.

Sarafine fixed her empty palm with a hard stare. "You're sure you want to do this?"

Jixa stomped one tiny foot.

"We can always dissolve the bond again once you've properly told me off for tricking you, if that's what you want."

A stinging pinch to the delicate skin of Sarafine's wrist was Jixa's answer, and a laugh emerged from deep in Sarafine's belly.

She bowed her head toward the ring and began. "I humbly beg a bond with Jixa."

Darion's hand rested on Sarafine's shoulder, opposite the perch.

"The link is forged, the compact sealed."

". . . so I *told* that horrible human the white handkerchief was going to cause *lots* of trouble, but she didn't even *listen* to me . .

." Her gossamer wings sparkled; her tiny face faded into view, its pinched expression a promise of many stolen knick-knacks, stops for snacks, and non-stop half-intelligible chatter to come. Jixa flew from Sarafine's hand to land in the ring and natter to some other pixies, forever invisible to humans they had no interest in. Her little hands waved in the air as she described being caged and shaken around, hovering two inches above the ground as she became more animated.

Darion wrapped an arm around Sarafine's waist. "You see her again?"

"And hear her."

"You won't abandon her anymore, will you?" Darion was watching the scuffs in the dust that marked the passage of pixies.

Sarafine leaned into his body. "I love her. I won't abandon anyone I love."

He did look at her then, and when their lips came together, nothing stood between them to hold them apart.

END THE NIGHTMARES.
LOSE YOUR BEST FRIEND.

To Break a
Dragon
Bond

ELIZABETH F. SHEARLY

CONTENT NOTES

Choosing to die, exile, intrusive thoughts.

Please see the book's web page at www.elizabethshearly.ca for detailed content notes.

1

Their eyes stared sightlessly at the ceiling. No breath nudged their chests up and down. They were all frozen, unmoving. In her dream, Raisa recoiled, but a heavy hand seemed to shove her close to one of the corpses. The child's eyes were closed, as if asleep, but the little girl was just as still and silent as the rest.

Raisa gasped and startled awake, the staring eyes still dancing before her in the darkness. She slammed her mental defences into place, as she did every morning. That thrice-damned dragon *knew* she couldn't defend herself while she slept.

Raisa dragged her heavy limbs out from under her wool blanket into the too-silent cottage. She settled her thick shawl about her shoulders and crept across the room out of habit: Jarom was no longer here to disturb.

He'd given her a perfunctory hug as he settled his pack on his back.

"I'll come back soon, Mum," he'd said and grinned.

She'd smiled back at him. How could she be dejected when he looked so happy? He wouldn't be back very soon; his apprentice duties wouldn't leave him any time to visit her. These days, the only way to get up here into the mountains was by horse and cart.

"Write me every week, let me know what you're learning in the capital," said Raisa.

"Of course, Mum," said Jarom.

She gave him one last hug, and he scampered out the door. Or maybe *strode* would be more accurate now. He wasn't a little kid anymore. Raisa watched him from the doorway as he bounded down past the bend in the road and disappeared behind the trees. She went in and shut the door.

Her shoulders hunched as she surveyed the cold hearth, the empty chair beside it, the wood Jarom had stacked carefully in the corner for her. Only a week had passed since he'd left, far too early to start wondering when he was going to come back. She stirred the fire in the hearth to life.

"I should go into town, check for a letter from him," she said to the empty house. It *had* been a week, and she *had* asked him to write. If they'd still been able to channel the magic, she would have gotten his replies instantly. Having a rider carry a piece of paper was painfully slow. Even if he'd written her immediately, the letter might not arrive until next week.

She hauled the heavy cast-iron kettle to the water pump in the corner and filled it. Raisa paused to brush her unruly hair out of her eyes, the scales at her hairline bumpier than skin. She hung the kettle over the fireplace and sat back to braid her hair.

Too bad her dragon bond was able to survive without the magic. How convenient it would have been if that too had withered with the retreat of their channelling. Her routine had become reflexive: block the bond in the daytime and suffer through the nightmares while she slept. Breaking the bond for good was out of the question, what with her parental responsibilities . . .

Raisa swallowed hard. Jarom would be fine without her from now on if something did happen. Her heart pounded and her mouth went dry. Breaking the bond had seemed impossible for so many years, and she had spent the better part of two decades reminding herself it was too risky, dismissing it out of hand. But now?

Raisa tied off her braid, added oats to the kettle, and stirred them.

Every dragonrider knew the only way to break a dragon bond was by the monarch's hand, but it hadn't been done in generations. Raisa shivered. Legend had it that the rider and dragon had begged the queen to dissolve their bond, though the reason for it was lost to time. The queen had granted them a favour and dissolved the bond as requested. Neither the rider nor the dragon had survived.

Raisa stirred the oats again and gathered her shawl about her shoulders.

Older records of the procedure being successfully performed did exist, but without the specifics, death had to be an accepted risk, and Raisa hadn't been willing to accept that risk.

But what kind of life was this? Alone up in the mountains where Kalanthi couldn't follow, far from the capital and her son. Hiding from her past. If she broke the bond, she'd be able to move to the capital permanently and be near Jarom while he studied. Maybe she could even reach out to her old friends, the friends she'd had to leave behind when Kalanthi started terrorizing her with the constant barrage of heartbreak and death.

Raisa scooped some oats into her bowl.

No, she couldn't keep on like this. Breaking the bond was her only option, risks be damned.

2

The palace towered high overhead, all shining marble and gilt rooftops. The iron bars out front were cool in her hands. Truth be told, Jarom had seemed a little disappointed to see her, eager as he was to strike out on his own. Her plan had worried him, though she didn't tell him how high the chance of her death was.

Petitions from the populace were accepted today, so Raisa had every right to be here. After the last time she had seen the king, would she really be welcomed back?

Twenty years earlier . . .

Kraisa peered down at the palace far below, the afternoon sun glinting off the roof and sparkling over the white facade. An image popped into her head, seamlessly imparted by her mental link with Kalanthi.

The wide courtyard, easily large enough for a dragon to land.

"We'll head that way," said Kraisa and pictured the two of them circling and landing in the spot Kalanthi had imparted.

She squeezed the dragon's neck with her knees as they dove, skimmed over the wrought-iron fence, glided over the palace walls, and touched down in the middle of the courtyard. Kalanthi's claws scraped on the stone, but no damage was done; the place had been made for dragons. Kraisa alighted, patted Kalanthi's neck, and strode into the palace. An aid jogged after her.

"This way, dragonrider," said the aid, gesturing her down a long hallway.

"Kraisa," she said. Her new dragonrider name came naturally to her already.

"Dragonrider Kraisa," said the aid and inclined their head toward a large set of doors, standing open.

Kraisa paused on the threshold. Was that the king? The actual real king standing over a table in the middle of the hall? Yes, it was. And she was a dragonrider. An actual real dragonrider. She squared her shoulders and marched into the throne room. She ducked her head in a quick bow, and the king looked up from his maps.

"Dragonrider," he said, taking in the green luminescent scales scattered at her hairline.

"Yes, Your Majesty," said Kraisa.

"As you have no doubt gathered, I have requested a dragonrider's assistance contacting some of my subjects in Rams Village. The bridge to Rams Island has been destroyed, likely by raiders from the Northern Kingdom, and they are not responding through the usual communication methods. Please ensure their safety, as rebuilding the bridge will take several weeks."

A milk run. Her first assignment was to count heads in some tiny village?

"Not what you had in mind, dragonrider?" said the king, and Kraisa startled.

"Of course it is, Your Majesty. Any task you set is my honour to perform," she said.

The king chuckled, the lines on his face deepening. "Good to hear. Do some simple work, and I'm sure the Roost will see fit to assign you something more exciting." He went back to his map. Kraisa had been dismissed.

As Kraisa strode through the vaulted corridor back to Kalanthi, she pictured the location of Rams Village and imparted their assignment to ensure that the villagers were safe and reassure them that their bridge would be rebuilt as soon as possible.

Rain slashed down, and waves crashed against the base of sheer cliffs.

A bit of a storm wouldn't keep them from their task. They'd flown in all kinds of weather as part of their training. She pictured the sun at its height in the sky (the only way to impart time to a dragon) and flying to the village.

Kalanthi didn't respond.

Kraisa pictured the mountain pool at the Roost, Kalanthi diving into it and rolling under the water. Kalanthi soaring through the clouds, mist gathering on her scales.

The route to the village and Kraisa talking unintelligibly to the villagers.

The images flickered through her head so fast she could barely make them out.

Kraisa laughed as she reached the courtyard and patted Kalanthi's snout. "The sooner we get this errand over with, the sooner we can go have fun."

Kalanthi rumbled in response. She didn't understand the words, but she could often get the gist of anything Kraisa said through their bond. Kraisa leaped to her back and crowed aloud as they took off in a cloud of dust stirred by Kalanthi's huge wings.

Present day . . .

"Dragonrider," said the guard at the palace gate and stepped aside.

How had he recognized her? Her confusion must have shown on her face, because he brushed a hand over his hairline. Her ever-present scales. Of course. She ducked her head and hurried through the wide courtyard to the huge double doors, which stood open in the mild air. Another two guards nodded as she passed through. She joined a lineup in front of the throne room; many more supplicants awaited an audience with the king than the last time she'd found herself here.

Raisa's head throbbed with the effort of keeping Kalanthi out. After twenty years of practice, shielding herself at this proximity to the Roost, where Kalanthi most likely was, still took most of her energy.

The afternoon was mostly gone by the time Raisa crossed into the throne room and trudged to the dais to address the king. Twenty years ago, his calm face had projected an air of confidence, comfort. Now his cold eyes surveyed her lethargically from beneath the heavy crown adorning his brow.

"Dragonrider," he grated.

"Your Majesty," said Raisa and bowed.

"You've been gone a long time," said the king. Did he really remember her, after all these years?

"Yes, sire," said Raisa.

Glassy eyes stared up at the ceiling, frozen forever . . .

Raisa shook her head and fought to keep the images out. Was it getting *more* difficult?

"I would ask that you break my dragon bond," she said. A drip of sweat rolled down the side of her face.

"Are you quite well, dragonrider?" said the king.

"No, sire," said Raisa. "The dragon—"

A roar shook the windows and the ground trembled. It couldn't be . . . Why would Kalanthi be here? Raisa took a deep breath, closed her eyes, and opened her mind.

The palace, guards gathering, retreating with confusion . . .

The doors to the throne room burst open, and a guard sprinted inside.

"A dragon!" he shouted. "A dragon without a rider!"

"No rider?" said the king. He pierced Raisa with a glare, and she nodded. He turned back to the wild-eyed guard. "Please let the beast be. It is under this dragonrider's control."

Under her control might be a bit of an overstatement. Still, she didn't want Kalanthi to be hurt.

Raisa pictured the sun moving forward in the sky and then herself coming out to the courtyard. Another roar rattled the windows, but Kalanthi imparted an image of curling up to wait for her.

"Now," said the king wearily. "What did you say you wanted from me?"

"I want to break my dragon bond," said Raisa. "You're the only one with the power to do so."

The king's gaze narrowed, and he steepled his fingers. "You must be aware of the magic shortage. Most people are unable to channel at all."

"But that doesn't affect your magic?" said Raisa. "Right?"

"Unfortunately, I am unable to perform the level of magic necessary to do as you've asked, even were I inclined to, which I must be frank, I am not." He shook his head. "Breaking a dragon bond is both complex and dangerous. Surely you and your dragon can find another way?"

"No, sire," said Raisa, more sharply than she'd intended. If the king wouldn't help her, she would have to keep living this way. "Please, she won't— She's not—" Raisa fought down the panic in her chest. "She keeps imparting the Massacre," she finally whispered.

The king lifted his chin. "I see only one way forward, if you insist on this path. We have been unable to effect any diplomatic relations with the Empire since your . . . since the Massacre. The Roost refuses to mediate, and we do not have the magic to travel to Ferrin Isle, their chosen neutral ground. I'm sure you're aware that ships cannot make landfall there. I expect the Empire is aware of these limitations, hence their choice of meeting place. If you can negotiate peace between our nations, break this stalemate, and get the magic flowing into our kingdom again, I will have the power I need to break your bond."

He'd said himself he didn't want to break the bond. What if she got him his magic back and he still refused to help her? "May I have your word that if I successfully restore the kingdom's channelling ability, you will perform the procedure to break our bond?"

The king sat back in his throne. "I swear to you, dragonrider. If you restore peace between the Empire and my kingdom, you will have earned anything within my power to grant you. If you still wish to attempt the procedure, I will perform it."

Raisa nodded and bowed. Time to go out and deal with her rogue dragon. The rogue dragon would have to ride again, for the first time in twenty years, if she was going to Ferrin Isle to restore magic to their kingdom. She trudged through the corridors to the courtyard where Kalanthi stood, neck arched and talons scraping the flagstones.

Raisa stood in the archway to the courtyard, hands on her hips. Kalanthi raised her head and blinked slowly at her rider. She snaked her head down on its long neck, and her wide nostrils flared.

Kraisa, as she was when she'd last seen Kalanthi. Tears running down her face, sobs shaking her chest. Kraisa, snapping something unintelligible, turning her back on Kalanthi, and walking away.

Raisa swallowed and laid her hand gently between Kalanthi's huge eyes. Kal might not have understood what she'd said that day, but Raisa remembered it all too well.

"I'm sorry," she whispered, the words tumbling from her lips before she could hold them back. Not that the dragon could understand her. The sharp stab of guilt in her chest would be far more legible to

Kalanthi than a thousand words. Kal's snout nuzzled into her body, and she wrapped an arm as far around it as she could. For once, Kalanthi wasn't filling her head with gruesome images. Raisa leaned against the warm muzzle and relaxed, perhaps for the first time in two decades.

3

F ar below Raisa's feet, the ocean peaked with whitecaps, but the
sun shone from a painfully blue sky. They would make good
time to Ferrin Isle. The king's aides had insisted on outfitting her with
fancy robes and supplies for her journey, considering she was going
as an official representative of the king, not a Roost dragonrider, let
alone a poor backwoods spinster. The Empire had agreed to a two-day
meeting, at the end of which Raisa would bring the magic back to her
king and get her dragon bond taken care of.

Kalanthi imparted an image of their route, and Raisa tensed. It
would lead them right over Rams Village.

The last time they had flown this way, storm clouds had blackened
the sky, and the tall waves had dwarfed even Kalanthi.

Twenty years earlier . . .

Kraisa smiled as Kalanthi imparted an image of curling up warm
and snug in their den. She swiped the rain from her eyes for the
millionth time and bent her head against the howling wind. Frolicking
in the lake would wait for another day.

Kraisa squinted down at the frothing ocean below. Shouldn't there
be land somewhere around here? She asked Kalanthi, who sent back a
wavering image of the island they were supposed to be headed toward.

Lightning flickered and thunder roared. Kraisa cried out and clung to Kalanthi.

The Roost, their warm den. The sun moving through the sky . . . night . . . day . . . Kalanthi and Kraisa going to the island.

"No, we have to go today," said Kraisa. "We're almost there. We must be." Botching her first assignment would drop her so far down the duty roster that she'd be scrubbing pots in the scullery the rest of her life. Sure, it was a milk run, but the king had said that if she did well, he'd give her more to do. Assignments straight from the king would cement her place at the Roost.

Finally, Kraisa sighted land way off to their left. Not where land was supposed to be. What the heck was that island? Craggy, barren cliffs jutted straight from the crashing waves below. It was likely un-inhabited since the jagged shoreline certainly wouldn't allow ships to approach.

Kalanthi circled; with any luck, there would be a place to land to wait out the storm. A rock shelf sheltered by a cliff face appeared through the driving rain, and Raisa imparted it to Kalanthi. The huge dragon staggered upon landing in its shelter, too used to being buffeted by the wind. The cliff face gave them a bit of protection, and they huddled together, Kalanthi's wing wrapped over Kraisa. Kalanthi crooned to her as her teeth chattered.

"We'll just wait out the lightning, then get this damned errand over with," she said. The gusts had driven them way off course, despite Kalanthi's inherent navigational acumen. "Where do we need to go from here?"

Keep our backs to the setting sun until we reach the coast, then follow it south again.

Kraisa craned her neck up at the cliff face. An archway etched into the stone arced overhead. A huge door? "What is this place?" she breathed.

Kalanthi rumbled.

A man wearing rich clothes, a channeller making the entire island shake as they drew rocks from the ocean floor, a bright portal.

Kraisa shook her head. The confusing images from her dragon, in this case, were far inferior to just looking it up or asking someone. Sometimes, Kalanthi's images left out crucial context required to understand her meaning.

Lightning flashed, and Kraisa counted to ten in her head before the answering rumble of thunder.

"What do you think, Kal?" she said and patted her dragon's side.

Soaring through the breaking clouds and sweeping in to land over a dense forest and rolling fields.

"Let's go, then," said Kraisa and climbed to Kal's back with numb fingers.

Present day . . .

They had to be getting close to Ferrin Isle now.

Kalanthi rumbled.

A cliff in the rain.

"*That's* where we're going?" said Raisa.

There it was again: *a man wearing rich clothes, a channeler making the entire island shake as they drew rocks from the ocean floor, a bright portal.*

That must be the ancient Empire channeller creating this place. An island they could control with no outside interference.

The cheerful sunlight stripped Ferrin Isle of some of its forbidding nature, but still, the waves roared over the craggy shore. Flying was the only way to access it. That or use the portal Kal had imparted, if it was still active. Hopefully, one of the Empire's emissaries could fill her in on the history of this place. Kalanthi's images would be much more useful once she had some context.

4

Their lovely room overlooked the ocean, and even had a large balcony that Kalanthi could use to come and go. She and Kal had probably unknowingly sheltered on one of these balconies during the storm twenty years before. The room would be big enough for Kal to come into for the night, though the doorway to the corridor was human-sized so she would be able to go no deeper into the halls. An image flashed unbidden into her mind, though it was her own: sleeping peacefully curled up in Kalanthi's warm body. The dragon crooned to her. She hadn't shielded her thoughts.

Tiny, fragile human cradled carefully in a huge dragon body.

"I'll let you know when I'm going to bed, then," said Raisa. "I just have to meet the diplomat from the Empire." She imparted an image of an old person in a long robe and lots of human talking.

Kalanthi rumbled and launched herself out over the ocean, rose into the air, circled once, and then disappeared over the isle. If only Raisa could go with her. But playing the diplomat was the only way she'd be able to break her dragon bond, if she still wanted to after this. *If?* One day of peace from her dragon, and she was ready to consider keeping the bond intact?

Raisa straightened her robes and stepped into the rough-hewn hallway. Moisture beaded the walls and hung in the air. Raisa's steps echoed through the still corridor. The rooms intended for her retinue remained sealed since Raisa was the only one from her kingdom who could reach Ferrin Isle. Not so the Empire representatives with their access to magic.

An old man in a robe, strikingly similar to the image she'd imparted to Kalanthi, met her just outside the negotiation hall and gestured her toward the doors. She bowed her head.

"It's a pleasure to be here. Thank you for giving me the chance to work things out between our nations."

"Save it for the emissary, dragonrider," he replied gruffly and hauled the solid door open.

Every seat on the Empire's side of the hall was filled, once the man at the door shut it firmly behind Raisa and stalked to his place. The representatives were uniformly old and dour. All except one.

The sole young man was poised in the centre of their party, in the place of honour. His long fingers gripped the arms of the carved chair; his legs were crossed, and his mouth twisted at the sight of her.

Eleven kingdom seats faced those of the Empire, all empty. There was nothing for it. Raisa lowered her gaze and trudged to her side of the long table. She settled herself in the centre seat, across from the young man. Outnumbered eleven to one by real dignitaries. That didn't bode well for Raisa's chances, but if she failed here, there would be no magic for her kingdom, no bond-breaking procedure for her, and no freedom from the nightmares.

"Shall we begin?" said Raisa.

"As the one who called the conclave, I believe protocol dictates that you begin," said the young man. "What do you want?"

"As I'm sure you are aware, channelling has been rendered impossible within our kingdom. We are willing to pay for the magic if the Empire will only supply it," said Raisa.

"Who are you, and why should we allow you to buy us off so easily?" said the young man.

Buy them off? Wasn't her proposal an obvious win-win situation? "I am Raisa, emissary from the king. Who are you?" she said. If he meant to rattle her, he would be disappointed. She'd raised a child through the toddler years and into teenagehood.

His eyes narrowed. "I'm Thane. I have full authority to negotiate for the Empire. So convince me."

Convince him? This was supposed to be a negotiation. Convincing him would only be an option if she understood his objections. They were going to have to talk about the Massacre. It was bound to come up, but did it have to be quite so soon?

"The Massacre occurred twenty years ago," said Raisa.

Thane's mouth tightened.

"We have been deprived of magic for all of that time. It has been years since our channellers have been able to work. To be blunt, we need the magic. All the gold in the world can't feed a family or heat their home."

The woman to Thane's left began, "We are open to a mutually beneficial—"

Thane cut her off. "Your kingdom began this conflict. You accused the Empire of committing a massacre on your people, which ever so coincidentally caused the diplomatic agreement with our mutual neighbour to the north to fall through. We have been at war with them ever since, our coffers emptied, while your kingdom across the sea wants for nothing. And now you tell us that your people are suffering, and we should find it in our hearts to provide you with the magic to make your lives soft and comfortable?"

"Eating food is hardly what I would call soft and comfortable," said Raisa. "And the diplomatic agreement between the Empire and the

Northern Kingdom had nothing whatsoever to do with us." The king may have overestimated her negotiation skills.

Thane shook his head. "Even twenty years later, you deny it. I will say, I didn't expect the kingdom to come begging on their knees, but no contrition at all?"

"Contrition would imply that there was some wrongdoing, which there was not. Might I remind you that it was *our* people who were massacred!" said Raisa.

Ocean lapping at a tall cliff face. A dangling bridge.

No, not right now, Kalanthi. She slammed her mind shut.

"Not only your people," hissed Thane. "My sister never came back. She was trying to help, and instead, she disappeared. You believe us to be capable of murdering innocents, but you can't possibly think our people would sacrifice one of their own. No. It was not the Empire who massacred those people. We have lived under the shadow of your kingdom's accusation for too long." He shot to his feet.

"Perhaps a walk in the gardens? A less formal discussion forum may do you good," said the woman beside Thane. He glared at her, but contradicting her in front of Raisa would be rude, and he must have known that as well. He nodded and glared at Raisa, which was perhaps intended to be an invitation to follow him out?

Once they were outside, Thane's shoulders dropped. Not all the way, but it was something. Raisa kept pace with him as the wind whipped her curly hair across her face and her robe around her legs. They followed a path around the isle and passed between two outcroppings into a secluded walled garden, protected from the wind. A pear tree grew flat against one wall, and a stone bench sat across from it. Thane stood beside the bench, and Raisa sat down and stared at the intricate pear tree.

"Magic won't solve all your problems," said Thane.

"Money won't solve all of yours," said Raisa.

"You only think that because you have it," said Thane.

"Same to you," said Raisa. "Gold and magic together can solve damn near anything, in my experience."

"Neither can bring my sister back. What are you looking to solve?" said Thane.

Raisa sighed. Her troubles were her own business, and they had nothing to do with the current negotiations. "You might have noticed that without magic, my people can't even travel to this isle," she said and gestured to the ocean around them. "What chance do they have at diplomatic relations when the only emissary they are capable of sending is a disgraced dragonrider who's been hiding from politics for the last twenty years?"

"Disgraced?" said Thane, his face clouded.

"I'm the one who reported the Massacre," said Raisa. "I thought you knew that."

"You?" Thane's eyes burned into her, and Raisa recoiled. His fists clenched at his sides, and he took a step back from her.

Cave opening and bodies lying everywhere, staring, limp, sightless . .
.

"Kalanthi, not now," Raisa hissed.

"*Kalanthi*," said Thane. "It really is you, Kraisa. I thought it was a coincidence." His fists opened and closed. "Does your king know he sent you here to die, murderer?"

Raisa shook her head, too much of her energy was focused on shutting Kalanthi out.

"This afternoon, you will hear our terms. Quite simply, you give us our vengeance, and we give your king his magic," said Thane. He turned on his heel and strode away.

Their vengeance. They, quite literally, wanted to kill the messenger.

Twenty years earlier . . .

Kalanthi stumbled in for a landing on Rams Island, near the village, and Kraisa slid from her dragon's neck onto her knees on the hard stone. Waiting for the storm to blow itself out would have been a better idea. But they were here now. Might as well check it out.

The bridge was broken, dangling against the opposite cliff face, so these folks were cut off from the mainland, but that didn't explain why they hadn't been able to contact anyone by channelling a message out.

The storm clouds billowed overhead in the fading light and spat rain onto Kraisa and Kalanthi as they crossed to the main entrance to the cave network that housed the village. Everyone must have been inside sheltering from the storm. Kraisa poked her head into the dim cave. What little sunlight there was barely filtered in through the high windows. Kraisa imparted Kalanthi lighting a brazier or a torch for her. Kal could see in the dark much better than Kraisa, and she'd be able to find something flammable faster.

The two of them leaving and flying away.

"We will," said Kraisa. "We have to check on everyone." She imparted talking to a group of humans.

Kalanthi growled. *Kraisa crying.*

"What do you mean, Kal? I'm not crying. Just light something so we can find our way into this cave," said Kraisa. Something tightened in the pit of Kraisa's stomach. Why wasn't anyone coming out to meet them? A huge green dragon landing on this little island would be hard to miss.

Kalanthi puffed a tiny flame onto a brazier, and it took slowly, shedding light in an ever-widening circle.

Wide blank eyes danced with demonic flame. A little boy clutching his stuffed animal tight to his chest, even in death. Kraisa's breath hissed and caught, and she backed out of the cave mouth. No one was answering because everyone was dead.

Present day . . .

Kraisa gripped the edge of the stone bench. The king must have known what he was sending her into. He had known the Northern Kingdom, at least, had been pillaging the coast. Kraisa and Kalanthi had been the only ones to witness that scene. In the tumult that followed her report, the dragonriders refused to be involved, the Empire withdrew their magic before anyone could try magical means to access the village, and they were left there, no doubt to rot away in the dank cave.

5

Raisa smoothed her robe. Again. Dinner with the Empire emissaries would be rough, but it was a chance to make them see her humanity, the humanity of everyone in her kingdom. A chance to persuade them that they didn't need to kill her.

Thankfully, dinner would be served in a less formal hall, so Raisa didn't have to sit on her own, surrounded by vacant seats. Unfortunately, she found herself alone at a smaller table, everyone else having seated themselves in bunches. The formality of the seating arrangements in the larger hall might have been preferable after all. Knowing no one wanted to sit with her was much worse.

"Do you mind if I join you?"

The elderly woman who had tried to speak for her earlier hovered, her hand on the back of a chair at Raisa's table.

"Please," said Raisa. "I'd be glad of the company."

She introduced herself as Gila and sat. "We all want to come to an agreement," she said.

"As do I," said Raisa. "Both of our nations are suffering unnecessarily."

"The emperor was overjoyed when your king made it known that he was sending you." Gila hadn't brought any food with her.

Raisa finished a bite of hers. "If you don't mind me asking, why send Thane? I'm sure you're aware of his terms."

Gila sighed. "Thane is the most familiar with your kingdom and the history surrounding the rift between our nations. So much so that your king suggested him as the lead emissary." She hesitated, and Raisa put down her fork. Her appetite had disappeared.

"Were you and your emperor aware that he wants me dead?" she said. Was the king aware of it?

Gila met her gaze. "Yes," she said. "We were not aware that you personally would be conducting the negotiations."

"So you thought to negotiate my execution with a third party? Didn't think you'd have to face me?"

Gila drew herself up, and her face hardened. If the king hadn't wanted her to alienate the Empire and get herself killed into the bargain, he had sent the wrong emissary.

Raisa brushed her scales. "Look," she said. "I don't want to die. But I need—my kingdom needs—the magic back."

"As much as I wish things were different, Thane has the last word, and he will not change his mind. Barring a resurrection for his sister, his course is set." Even with the magic, resurrection was impossible. Changing Thane's mind was likewise impossible.

The magic would not return to her kingdom as long as Raisa lived. The king wouldn't be able to break her bond.

Gila finally looked guilty, made her excuses, and left Raisa in peace. The rest of the emissaries weren't avoiding her because she was from the kingdom; they had been squeamish about sitting with a condemned woman the night before her execution.

6

After another interminable evening of bombarding Raisa with images of dead faces, the rays of the setting sun painting them macabre colours, Kalanthi landed on the ledge outside her room. Kal snuffled at the door and nudged it open with her face, her soft nose peeking into where Raisa lay curled on the bed.

"You might as well come in," said Raisa. The images had faded away as Kalanthi came closer to Ferrin Isle, and a little warmth and comfort in this deserted wing would be more than welcome.

Kalanthi squeezed into the vaulted room and slid the door shut with her foot. She curled into a round nook across from the bed that might have been custom-made for dragons and rested her head on her front legs. She blinked slowly at Raisa. This damn dragon.

She was never going to stop imparting her gruesome images. Thane was never going to agree to give their kingdom back the magic, not unless she traded her life for it.

Raisa swung her feet over the side of the bed and wrapped the blanket over her shoulders. She stood and dragged it across the floor to the creature who had been her best friend, all those years ago. She'd never felt as if she belonged, never had a purpose until Kalanthi. *Raisa* had been no one. *Kraisa* was a protector and a messenger, someone who could go places and do things that no one else could do.

Raisa stepped over Kalanthi's tail and snuggled into her huge body. The dragon wrapped a wing over her, and for the first time since the Massacre, Raisa relaxed and dropped right off to sleep, knowing that no nightmares would greet her tonight.

Twenty years earlier . . .

The wind streaked Kraisa's tears back toward her ears. Now she had to tell the king that they were all dead, murdered probably.

Kalanthi landed in the courtyard, and Kraisa slid down her neck by feel, unable to see through her overflowing eyes. She swiped at them and pulled herself together. A tumult echoed from the throne room as she approached. She was ushered in right away and the babble died down. The various politicians', advisors', and aids' stares made her stomach roil.

The king reclined on his throne and motioned her forward. "Another crisis?" he said.

Kraisa stood at the bottom of the steps that led to the throne and stared at the inlaid marble floor. Everyone watched in hushed anticipation.

"I hope you weren't bothered by the storm," said the King.

"It blew us off course, but we made it to Rams Village," said Kraisa, her voice shaking.

"Tell me what you found."

"They—they were gathered in the hall, Your Majesty. The whole village." She cleared her throat. "The bridge was broken, as you thought."

"Will they last until we can get the bridge mended?" said the king.

Kraisa shook her head. "I didn't get a chance to speak to them, sire."

"They're dead, then?" said the king, much too matter-of-fact.

Kraisa nodded.

"Any signs of who might be responsible?"

Kraisa delved back into her training. Dragonriders reported accurately and completely. She closed her eyes. "There were no weapons or blood. The bodies were scattered in the hall, lying as if untouched."

The king's brow furrowed. "Magic, then," he mused. That ruled out the Northern Kingdom.

"The Empire," said Kraisa. A babble broke out again, but the king silenced it with a wave of his hand.

"It seems that way. Thank you, dragonrider. I will see that the Roost gets a glowing recommendation from me. On your skills." His face softened. "I imagine it was a taxing first assignment for you."

"Um, yes." She swallowed hard. "I mean, thank you, Your Majesty."

"You may rest here at the palace should you wish to."

"Thanks very much, Your Majesty, but Kalanthi and I will return to the Roost."

"As you wish." The King's gesture to the door was minute but very clear. The jumble of voices resumed in earnest now.

On her way back outside, Kraisa sent an image of herself and Kalanthi curled up in their den.

Warmth, snuggling, sleeping peacefully. A stuffed animal clutched in a little hand.

Kraisa shuddered. Maybe that last one had been her own memory?

7

Raisa gasped and stretched. Kalanthi rumbled but didn't stir. If she lived to see the sunset, it would be back to the nightmares and the loneliness. The rest of her life stretched before her, plagued by gruesome visions, alone in her cottage, watching those around her suffer from lack of magic, tormented by the knowledge that she could have reclaimed it but was too cowardly.

If Thane required her worthless life in return for lifting her entire kingdom from ruin, it was a small price to pay. Jarom. She took a steadying breath. The light of her life. Her baby. He would be safe with his leatherworking master, and one day, he would understand why she had to do this.

Raisa crept to the huge doors out to the ledge and slid the bar across them. Say what you would about Kalanthi, but she would never *let* Raisa be executed. Hopefully, the doors would hold until it was done.

Raisa grabbed her clothes and slipped into the corridor. As she padded toward the conclave, a voice called from the shadows.

"Trying to slip past someone?" Thane stepped into the grey morning, his eyes burning with a fierce light.

"Yes. My dragon," said Raisa.

Thane fell into step with her.

"She'd never let you kill me."

Thane nodded and grimaced. At least he had the decency not to gloat.

Raisa ducked into one of the last chambers in the wing. In the corridor, Thane turned his back to her but left the door ajar. Raisa pulled on her robes. She rubbed the scales at her hairline. What would happen to Kalanthi when she died? She'd finally get to find a new rider. She could torment *them* with grisly murder scenes.

Raisa pulled the door open, and Thane turned to her and nodded. They fell into step once more.

"I'll need your official assurance that once I'm dead, my kingdom will have all the magic they can buy."

"I already have the paperwork drawn up," said Thane.

"That was quick," said Raisa.

"My terms were always going to come down to this. I just didn't know they would send . . . you," said Thane.

"A life for a life," said Raisa. "You're probably more familiar with history than I am, but aren't you worried this will escalate . . . everything? My son could be a military officer for all you know."

"Your son?" said Thane. He looked at her askance.

"He isn't," said Raisa. "He's just an apprentice leatherworker. No threat to you or the Empire."

"I didn't know you had a son," said Thane. "Is he—will he be taken care of?"

Rage simmered in Raisa's chest. "Suddenly concerned about the consequences of your demands? My losing my life means nothing to you, but my son losing his mother melts your heart?"

"He's an innocent," snapped Thane.

Raisa shrugged. There was no convincing someone who didn't want to be convinced. She'd been innocent too, back before—

Barred door. Tiny opening. No Kraisa.

Kalanthi was awake. There was no blocking out what Raisa was about to do.

"You'll have a distraught dragon to deal with once I'm gone," said Raisa. "Just don't leave her trapped in there. Let her go home."

"You have my word," said Thane.

Twenty years earlier . . .

"Kal, please," said Kraisa. The stone floor was hard and cold under her knees. Kalanthi's head loomed over her.

Glassy eyes, still and silent, dust in a shaft of sunlight.

"Kal, I can't—" Dragons didn't understand words.

A small hand curled around a stuffed animal.

"Just shut up, you damned dragon! Why are you doing this to me? Can you just stop? I hate you!" The image of Kalanthi, riddled with spear holes, tumbling into the ocean, sprang unbidden to her mind.

Kalanthi rumbled and raised her head.

"Kal, I'm sorry— I didn't mean it," said Kraisa.

Kal stalked to the entrance to their den and dropped over the ledge, the beats of her huge wings fading in the distance.

"I can't do this," said Kraisa. "I'm just making us both miserable." Her mentor had told her to give it time, that dragons didn't always know what they were imparting, that the memory would fade eventually. It had been months and nothing seemed at all faded.

Kraisa started to pack.

Kalanthi still hadn't returned when Kraisa left their den, and she scanned the sky as she descended on foot to the pier. When was the last time she'd made this trek? Had she ever? It was a much longer walk on human feet than on dragon wings.

Everyone avoided her as she boarded the ferry. Obviously, she was the only dragonrider aboard. She brushed her fingers over the scales on her forehead and avoided the curious looks of the other passengers.

The ferry pushed off from the pier. Was there such thing as a former dragonrider?

Present day . . .

They stopped outside the hall. The doors stood open, and a few of the Empire's delegates already sat in their seats. A scroll lay open on the table, and Thane waved Raisa toward it.

"As long as the treaty meets with your approval, we can proceed," said Thane.

Raisa sat and slid the scroll closer. She scanned it, trying to take in the words. The essentials seemed to be present. Raisa signed and slid the scroll back across the table. Thane signed without reading it.

A roar shook the high windows, and the floor trembled.

"I recommend we don't delay," said Raisa. "Kalanthi is liable to bring the whole island down around us once she realizes what's going on."

Thane gestured to the head of the room, and the two of them met there. He had no weapon. Did he plan to strangle her with his bare hands?

"It doesn't hurt," Thane said softly.

Glazed eyes staring up, a shaft of sunlight cutting across a throat.

"What doesn't?" Raisa breathed.

Thane laid a hand firmly on her collarbone, and Raisa swallowed against it. Another roar had the delegates glancing nervously at each other.

Clumps of snow drifting gently onto a stuffed animal.

Would Kalanthi not let her die in peace? She was finally about to join those corpses, then she'd be free of their dead-eyed stares.

"I'm going to channel the life from your body," said Thane.

For all she knew, these delegates would dump her corpse in the ocean without a proper ritual, just like the poor souls she'd found on that stormy grey evening . . .

Moonlight shivering over a blank face.

Moonlight. Snow? Those weren't memories of that day. They couldn't be.

"Wait," said Raisa.

Thane raised his eyebrows.

Raisa imagined the island, sun crossing the sky, seasons changing. Would Kalanthi understand what she was trying to find out?

Kalanthi swooping through the night, stars wheeling overhead as she landed on the island. Then her breath puffed out, and her wings stirred snowflakes as she ducked into Rams Village.

Kal had been going back. She wasn't sending Raisa their memories of that day. She had been letting Raisa see through her eyes when she visited the island. No rotting corpses or picked-clean skeletons had ever appeared in the images Kal had imparted, just pristine, untouched bodies. How could they be exactly the same, unchanged, twenty *years* later?

"They're not dead," Raisa breathed. She stumbled to the table and spread both hands on its solid surface. She hung her head, and tears spattered the white marble. How they could possibly not be dead was a question for later. The important thing was they might still be alive.

"What are you talking about?" snapped Thane.

She turned to him and smiled softly into his sharp gaze. "All this time, Kalanthi's been trying to tell me that the Massacre—it wasn't a massacre. Or might not have been. Care to see if we can bring your sister back to life?"

Twenty years earlier . . .

Kraisa craned her neck to look out the train window up at the looming mountains.

"Won't be much longer now," said one of the passengers in the seat behind hers.

"We're almost there?" said his companion.

"We are, but I meant next time we come this way, we'll have to take a bloody horse and carriage."

His companion made a disgusted noise and then tutted. "That child-king is too hot-headed."

Child-king? The king was at least twenty-five, almost a decade older than her.

"Gone and lost us the magic," said the man. "It's only a matter of time before it runs out completely."

Kraisa tuned out the rest of their conversation. She wasn't concerned about travelling this way again. She wasn't going to leave the mountains. They were too high and dangerous for Kalanthi to fly in, and they were far enough from the Roost that she could close down the images her dragon still insisted on sending.

She'd settle somewhere folks were nervous around dragonriders, too nervous to ask detailed questions. She'd imply once or twice that her dragon had been killed, and word would spread that she didn't want to talk about it. Then she'd just be a normal person again. Not a dragonrider, not the one who had killed the magic. She'd live out her days in obscurity.

A child's face, eyes like those of the stuffed animal he clutched, glassy and empty and staring.

This would take practice, but she could do it. She could leave that life behind forever.

8

When Raisa returned to the little room where she'd locked Kalanthi, the door lay flat on the hallway floor, blown off its hinges. Kal's head was wedged partway through the doorway, and her nostrils flared as Raisa approached. She snorfled and then retreated, making space for Raisa to enter.

When she did, their eyes met, and something passed between them that had been missing since that first assignment . . . maybe trust?

Thane followed Raisa through the doorway, and Kalanthi blew a breath over him, the air shimmering with the heat of it. It wasn't fire, at least, but Thane flinched.

Raisa brushed her fingers over the tiny scales on Kalanthi's snout. Explaining to a dragon why she needed to carry another passenger, one who had, not an hour ago, been dead set on killing her rider, would be much easier if only she understood words.

Picturing the three of them flying to the island was simple enough, but how was she supposed to picture improving diplomatic relations between the Empire and her kingdom? She wanted Thane to witness the magic at play, yes, if that's what it was, but they also needed a channeller to identify what was going on and whether it would be possible to fix it. Giving her life for her country was one thing, but if they could get Thane's sister back, clear the Empire's name of the

Massacre, perhaps the king would break her dragon bond after all. Guilt choked her throat. That wasn't the way to convince Kal.

Raisa pictured herself and Kalanthi together, sun moving overhead, seasons changing around them. Kalanthi crooned and nudged her rider with her huge muzzle. All this time, her sweet dragon had just been trying to tell her about the magic. They just needed to do this one last thing and they might be able to free themselves from the shadow of the Massacre forever.

The three of them, Thane and Kraisa riding Kalanthi, landing on the island.

"She'll do it," said Raisa. "Let's go."

"You're sure I can't just use a portal?" said Thane, eyeing Kal nervously.

"You know as well as I do that, without magic, no portals can open in the kingdom. Even if there was magic, there's no permanent portal there, and no one to open the other side. Why do you think they sent me to investigate the island in the first place?"

Kalanthi stalked out onto the ledge, and Raisa sauntered after her. She sighed as the sunlight hit her face. It was possible she wasn't going to die today. She couldn't keep from smiling. Kalanthi crouched, and Raisa leaped onto her back in her usual practised motion and patted the space behind her.

Thane scowled and scrambled up the smooth scales. Kalanthi grumbled as he wedged his foot into her wing joint and hoisted himself over. Raisa patted her neck. She imagined him toppling off Kalanthi's back and made sure the dragon sensed her horror at the prospect.

Kalanthi, gliding smoothly through the sky.

"Thanks, Kal," said Raisa. "Hang on tight, Thane."

Thane wrapped his arms around her waist and pressed into her back. His breathing came in shallow pants in her ear, his chest moving rapidly against her.

"She's going to be nice to you," said Raisa. "No acrobatics or anything."

Thane just grunted, and Kalanthi ran over the ledge. To her credit, she snapped out her wings right away so Thane didn't have to endure that stomach-swooping catching sensation of being in freefall for long, but his arms tightened even more around Raisa's body.

Kalanthi was as good as her word and flew smoothly straight to the Massacre site. Raisa's heart pounded. If she was wrong, they might be about to cause another international incident. Thane would not take kindly to being flown straight to his sister's weathered bones.

Kalanthi had hardly landed when Thane slipped off her back and crouched, both hands on the solid stone.

Raisa chuckled and slid to the ground. The cave mouth yawned before her, and the smile faded from her face. If her hunch was right, they were still in there. The kid with his stuffed animal. All those glassy eyes. She shuddered and strode toward the opening.

Thane gasped from close behind her.

They were just as she'd left them.

The shafts of morning light illuminated the scene much more clearly than Raisa had ever seen with her own eyes. Kalanthi's images hadn't done it justice. At least fifty people lay motionless about the hall. And in the very centre . . .

"Salin!" said Thane. He picked his way past the collapsed bodies to the head of the hall, where a thin woman dressed all in white stood, arms upraised. *Stood.* She was no older than Raisa had been last time she was here, and as unmoving as the rest of the villagers; neither her eyes nor her chest so much as twitched.

"Why didn't you show me *that*?" said Raisa to Kalanthi. "Dead humans don't *stand*, Kal."

Kalanthi just rumbled from where she'd stuck her head in the doorway. She had tried her best to tell Raisa that something was not as it seemed. Dragons just didn't think the same way as humans.

Raisa crouched next to the kid with the stuffed animal. Her hand shook as she reached out. Would he be chilled like a corpse? Warm as in life? Her hand reached his shoulder and kept going. Right through his body as though he weren't there.

"Thane . . ." said Raisa. She passed her hand through the boy and through the stuffed animal he held.

She hurried *through* the other folks strewn about the cave to the head of the hall where Thane stood by his sister, Salin. Raisa tapped Thane's shoulder, and he jumped.

"Look," said Raisa. She reached up and passed her hand through Salin's arm.

Thane snatched her hand back.

"It's magic," said Raisa.

"Salin did this," said Thane. He shook his head. "This kind of channelling . . ."

"What? Are you about to tell me that they're dead after all?"

Thane studied her face. "No. Not necessarily. But I can't reverse it. I can't break it. It would take someone with a talent for undoing spells and reversing magic. I can't think of a living channeller that could do it."

So they *were* dead. Frozen forever in this half-present state of magic.

"Why did you do it?" Thane muttered to Salin.

"What was she even doing here?" said Raisa. "Did the king know she was visiting?"

"She's a channeller," said Thane. "She was off doing her journeyman studies. Thought your kingdom would be a good place to practice."

"Do you think it was a mistake? A channelling gone wrong?"

Thane shook his head. "No, this isn't something she would have done on a whim. This is legendary, a last resort. As I said, no one I know of can reverse it. The upside is that it'll last forever, until someone with the skill comes along."

Legendary magic. She'd gone chasing legendary magic herself. Breaking a dragon bond was no easy feat. Now that Kalanthi had brought her here, had got through to her at last, maybe she wouldn't need to get the king to use his legendary magic to unravel their bond. *Unravel.*

"What about the king?" said Raisa.

"What about him?" Thane gazed at his sister's face, as if trying to read the secrets of her channelling there.

"I was going to ask him to break my bond to Kalanthi if I could get the magic back for our kingdom. There are records of his lineage accomplishing similar procedures."

"You're suggesting that your king could reverse this channelling. All I'd have to do is grant your kingdom's magic back."

"That's right."

"Which is what you've been trying to get me to do from the beginning," said Thane and glared at her.

"Look, I was wrong about what happened here," said Raisa.

"You think that excuses the consequences of what you did? What you put the Empire through?"

"I never accused the Empire of killing these people," said Raisa. "I told the king what I found, and he came to his own conclusions."

Thane rounded on her. "And you think that excuses everything? Your king could have just come here twenty years ago and—"

"How old do you think I am?" said Raisa. She drew herself up.

"I haven't a clue."

"I'm thirty-six years old," said Raisa. She let it hang there, let him work through to the end of the train of logic.

He deflated.

"That's right. I was sixteen when I found this place. I'd just been thrown off course by a storm, I was terrified of being too late, finding whatever the soldiers from the Northern Kingdom left behind. It was pitch black, and I discovered a room full of what appeared to be corpses. It was my first assignment."

Thane ran a hand over his face. "Fine, we focus on moving forward. You think your king can do something about this? Take me to him."

"I can't just—"

"Take me to him so that we can discuss sourcing some magic for your kingdom."

Twenty years earlier . . .

Kraisa crossed her arms and frowned at the tumbledown cottage. The thatching was falling apart, and the whitewashed walls were more of a brown. As she opened the door, a rustling began in one corner, and a small furry creature streaked out the window opening.

The point was, no one would look for her here. No one would know who she was. She'd be the lonely spinster off at the edge of town. This could work. She could block Kalanthi out here. The only alternative would be to break their bond, or try to. Everyone knew the risks that entailed. No, Kraisa would do this. Alone. But at least she was alive.

Present day . . .

For the first time, the king's aid in the palace courtyard looked shaken as he watched them land in the palace courtyard. Dragonriders didn't take passengers, let alone an unannounced emissary from the Empire. Instead of leading them through to the throne room, the man dashed away. His cap flew off and rolled across the flagstones.

Raisa slid down and hugged Kalanthi's muzzle.

"I'll be right back, Kal," she said.

Kalanthi rumbled. Thane hurried down from her neck, and she padded to a corner, turned around twice, and lay down in a heap of scales.

"Should we wait for an escort?" said Thane, as though Raisa would know.

She shrugged. "I know the way, and His Majesty has likely been informed of your arrival already."

They walked side by side into the vaulted marble corridor. Raisa caught Thane's wide eyes as he gawked around the palace. Maybe he hadn't known just how much money the Empire was giving up on principle just to punish her kingdom.

The dishevelled aid stood outside the throne room doors, hands clasped behind his back, bare headed.

"Please, come with me," he said and bowed. He led them around to a smaller door and through a narrow corridor that emptied into an antechamber behind the throne room. The king wasn't risking seeing her in public this time. He stood as they entered, his gaze fixed on Thane.

"Your Majesty," said Raisa. "This is Emissary Thane, from the Empire. He led the negotiations that I was assigned to attend. He and I have discussed a few possibilities of arrangements, but there's something you should know first."

The king's gaze finally flicked to Raisa. "Go on."

"The Massacre was not a massacre, sire. It was a spell. I've seen it myself."

"It's true, Your Majesty," said Thane. "I have extensive experience with channelling, and I assure you, it is magic holding those people prisoner, not the embrace of death."

The king's eyes narrowed. "You would give us back our magic in exchange for restoring your nation's reputation?"

Thane sighed. "We are all keen to end this stalemate. That much the dragonrider and I established. I have it on good authority that you would be capable of breaking the channelling if the magic was restored to your kingdom."

"We can find out what really happened," said the king. He dropped into a chair and steepled his fingers, staring into the fire.

"Yes," said Thane. "And someone from the Empire is also trapped within the magic. It seems she performed the channelling. I . . . the Empire . . . would very much value her safe return."

"It seems I have found myself with a sudden excess of leverage," said the king.

"What?" said Raisa, but Thane's face hardened.

A smile tugged at the king's mouth. "I have within my grasp a valued Empire channeller, an Empire emissary, the only witness to the Rams Massacre, and her son."

Raisa gasped and clutched the chair opposite the king. He had her son?

The king glanced up. "Oh, yes. Didn't I mention that when last we met?"

"Leverage for what?" said Raisa. "We're offering you a way to get the magic back that requires no sacrifice from you whatsoever. Don't you want the magic back?"

"He does," said Thane. His hands clenched into fists at his sides. "It's a question of circumstance. He doesn't want the Northern Kingdom to have it."

"It's not a question of want," said the king, waving his words away. "It is simply too dangerous for the Empire and the Northern Kingdom to form an alliance. I refuse to let the past twenty years of suffering be for nothing."

"It was never the Northern Kingdom pillaging," said Raisa. "You were trying to frame them all along? So when I reported back that Rams Village had been attacked with magic . . ."

"The best laid plans, as they say," said the king. "How could I have known there would be a channeller in that backwater able to defend the villagers? Still, at least your report shattered the fledgling alliance. We don't have magic, but nor do they, and it solidified the Empire as our common enemy."

Raisa brushed her scales. Either he was telling them this because it was common knowledge here among his lackeys, or he didn't expect they would get a chance to repeat it to anyone. Thane must have realized it, too.

"Killing me will ignite our countries into an all-out war. Even you can't want that," said Thane.

The king smiled and Raisa's heart stopped. No one knew they were here. No one knew *Thane* was here. Last anyone had seen, he'd been flying away with Raisa. Who would doubt the king's claim that she'd lured Thane off to kill him?

Fifteen years earlier . . .

Jarom squirmed, not yet in control of his own limbs. He punched blindly for her breast, his tiny mouth opening wide. Raisa blinked and must have fallen asleep for a second because a staring corpse flashed through her mind. She jolted awake when Jarom squawked.

"I'm here, wee one. I'll never leave you," she crooned.

Between the baby and Kalanthi's images, she simply never slept anymore. If only she could break off the connection, get her sleep back ... *Focus.* Her son needed her. She couldn't go off taking risks, even to be free of the nightmares.

Jarom gripped her finger with one fist and nuzzled into her breast. She drew him close, and he latched on, his tiny ears moving rhythmically as he swallowed. Before Jarom, she'd spent her days moping around the cottage. Finally, she had something to keep her going.

Present day ...

"What exactly are you proposing, sire?" said Raisa.

"I'll admit, I *had* hoped to get the magic back and rid myself of the only witness to the Rams Massacre in one fell swoop." He raised his eyebrows at Thane.

Thane shook his head. "I no longer subscribe to that proposal."

The king clucked his tongue. "Your seal on a binding document suggests otherwise."

The agreement they'd signed as assurance that Thane would follow through on his promise after her death. Killing them had no downside for the king, as he had made perfectly clear. No one would ever know what had happened to them.

The aid's hat tumbling in the windy courtyard.

Except Kalanthi. But how could Raisa possibly make her understand *this*? Subtle threats, intrigue, and plots were far outside a dragon's comprehension. And even if she did, she couldn't tell anyone about it; dragons could only communicate with their rider, the one they were bonded to. If Raisa was dead ... Kal would get a new rider. Her pulse settled.

"You've made a mistake, Your Majesty," said Raisa. "I'm not the only witness to the Rams Massacre. In fact, it was my dragon, Kalanthi, who figured out what was going on. You kill me, she gets a new rider and spills all your secrets."

The king went pale and glanced at Thane, who shrugged. Neither of them seemed to know for sure whether she was telling the truth.

The king's eyes narrowed. "What would you have me do then, dragonrider?"

What should Raisa ask for with her *leverage*? She'd come here to break her bond with Kalanthi. She could request that the king break her dragon bond, be free as she'd planned. If she declined now, the king would never entertain so much as the thought of helping her.

Pouncing on the flyaway hat. Snapping it in Kal's jaws and shaking the life from it.

Raisa smiled at her dragon's antics. Thane watched her impassively, but his riveted gaze revealed that he awaited her reply just as eagerly as the king. His sister had been frozen in time long enough. Her kingdom had been without magic long enough.

"I won't manipulate you, Your Majesty. All I ask for is what you promised me. I get the magic back, you grant me a favour. Emissary Thane has agreed to open the magic trade to the kingdom on the condition that you free Rams Village and clear the Empire of wrongdoing. Unravel the channelling holding them frozen, and I will consider that my favour."

The king glanced between Raisa and Thane's set faces, clearly trying to determine whether they were playing him as he'd tried to play them. He scowled. "What choice have you left me?"

"A better choice than you ever gave me," said Raisa.

9

Raisa—Kraisa—met Thane and Salin on the pier. Salin's head was craned up, and she kept pointing at the dragons swooping overhead, oohing and aahing over their rainbow of shimmering scales. Kraisa tried not to laugh.

"Welcome to the Roost," she said.

"Thanks," said Salin. "Where's Kalanthi?"

"Swimming," said Kraisa. "We can join her if you like."

Salin clapped her hands. "Can we, Thane? I know we have serious matters to attend to—"

"I still can't believe you're my *older* sister," said Thane, shaking his head.

"And I can't believe this old man is my little brother, but here we are," said Salin, smacking him on the shoulder. "Is that a grey hair?"

They followed Kraisa up to the lake, high above the dens—they only walked partway; Salin levitated them after a hundred or so steps.

Kalanthi slithered from the water and charged them, stopping just short and shaking the water from her face. Salin shrieked and tried to hide behind Thane.

"I thought you wanted to swim with the dragon," said Thane and shoved her at Kal.

Salin's eyes were huge and round as Kalanthi sniffed her and then crooned softly.

Soon the two of them were swimming together, leaving Thane and Kraisa alone.

"I hear the Empire is doing better," said Kraisa.

"We've worked things out with the Northern Kingdom. We'll have peace for the time being. You're back to being a neutral dragonrider?"

"Neutral, yes. I stay away from my kingdom for the moment."

"You get into the capital regularly to see your son, though?"

"Yes, actually." As long as she stayed well away from the palace, the king let her be. "I'm glad you didn't kill me," said Kraisa.

"I'm glad your king didn't kill the both of us," said Thane and smiled ruefully.

"So am I."

Salin climbed on top of Kal and leaped off her back into the lake, spray flying into Kal's face and making her blink ponderously.

"Thanks for visiting personally," said Kraisa. "I know you could have sent someone."

"Salin would have turned me into a frog or something if I'd refused. Before she became a journeymen channeller, she always dreamed of being a dragonrider."

"Most kids do," said Kraisa. "It's not all swooping through the air and snuggling in a den."

Kalanthi picked Salin up and beat her wings to hover a few feet over the lake.

"Now!" hollered Salin, and Kalanthi dropped her into the water with a resounding splash.

"She's pretty well the same age as Jarom," said Kraisa. "My son. I wish I'd thought of bringing him out here to keep her company."

"Next time," said Thane idly.

He seemed to realize what he'd said at the same time Kraisa did. They smiled at each other.

Kraisa and Thane embracing.

"Incorrigible," said Kraisa. Damn dragon. Kraisa imagined the four of them gathered in their den, eating dinner.

Jarom eating dinner with them all.

They'd need a bigger den.

BLOOD, PAINT, AND STEEL

THE SWORDSWOMAN AND THE VAMPIRE

ELIZABETH F. SHEARLY

CONTENT NOTES

Sexually explicit scenes, blood, being confined, slaying a vampire, magical kidnapping.

Please see the book's web page at www.elizabethshearly.ca for detailed content notes.

1

With her shirtsleeves rolled up, the scars on Amaranth's muscular forearms were obvious. A hundred cuts from a hundred battles. She straightened the chalk portrait hanging on the tavern wall, stepped away, and peered critically at it. The vampire's dark eyes pulled her in as they had in person. She hadn't even spoken to him, and yet it had seemed as though he knew her better than anyone else.

Behind the bar, Olivia wiped her hands on her rough-spun linen apron and planted them on her hips. "Who is he?" she said. "I haven't seen him in my tavern before."

Not surprising. He hadn't seemed the type to so much as enter a tavern like this one. Perpetually smoky air, terse regulars, and cheap local ale didn't do much to recommend the place. He hadn't seemed the type to so much as set foot in their little village either, not without having been compelled by a summoning.

"I don't know his name," said Ama.

"You know him, in the carnal sense?" said Olivia and crossed her arms over her chest.

Ama shook her head.

"I take it you want to?" said Olivia.

Ama just nodded. No sense in denying it. Olivia had set her up with vampires enough times. The tavern owner had an eye for them. She'd been the one to point a vampire out to Ama the night she met this mystery vamp . . .

Ama drained her tankard and clunked it on the bar. The place was packed and rollicking, but somehow, a wide berth always seemed to open around where she sat at the end. Olivia bustled over, her hair afrizz and her apron askew.

"Another?" she said.

Ama grunted, and Olivia waved away her attempt to pay for it. The hero of Griston didn't pay for drinks. When Olivia swapped her empty tankard for a full one, she nodded across the throng.

"In case you're looking for company tonight," she said and was immediately called away down the bar.

The vampire Olivia had pointed out was a baby, all tousled hair and boisterous laughter. Probably younger than Ama. He'd never do on his own, but he had his uses. Ama nursed her last drink of the night and waved to Olivia when it was empty. She crossed through the thinning crowd to the vampire's table, where he was making up some story to a group of wide-eyed youths, hanging on his every word.

". . . and then I snatched it from his jaws!" he said, flashing a smile.

Ama crossed her arms over her chest. "Hey, vamp," she said. "Want to go?"

His Adam's apple bobbed, and his gaze flicked to the door.

"You can come back after," said Ama. "It won't take long."

The vamp's adoring fans had been rendered catatonic with awe at Ama's presence, and she grit her teeth. When the vamp nodded, Ama towed him quickly outside, across the dark square, and into the narrow alley behind her house. It wouldn't do to have someone overhear the summoning.

"Shall I compel you, or do you know the words?" said Ama.

"You mean, you don't want to . . .?" said the vamp.

Ama quirked an eyebrow. "With you? No offence, but you're a little young for me."

"I've never done the summoning before. Compel me?" He swallowed again and his eyes had a puppy-dog quality that left a bad taste in Ama's mouth.

She took his hand so their bare skin was touching and said the words. "Nightwalker, bring forth your sire that I may supplicate myself before their splendour." Whoever designed this particular summoning thought pretty highly of themselves. Ama had never supplicated herself in her life.

A flash of blue light flickered over the baby vamp's face.

"Hey, kid. You summoned me?"

Ama dropped the baby vamp's hand.

"She compelled me," he said over her shoulder.

"And now you know how to do it." The new vampire was older—that's how sires worked—but not too much older than Ama, maybe fifty or sixty. Vampires never looked their age, but with enough experience it was easy to tell. He looked Ama up and down and ran a hand through his hair. In life, he'd probably been a labourer. If he'd been human, Ama couldn't have taken him in a fight without playing dirty. As a vampire, she'd have to play really dirty. Not that they were planning to fight now.

"You want the kid to hang around and watch?" he said.

"No. He has admirers expecting him back in the tavern," said Ama.

"But—"

"You heard her, kid," said the new vampire.

He grumbled but obeyed his sire.

"How do you want to do this?" said the vamp when the baby had ambled out of the alley.

Ama unlocked her back door and led him upstairs to her loft. She strode through the cozy living room into the bedroom.

"Just bite me when I'm coming," said Ama, stripping off her jerkin, shirt, and trousers.

"Right to the point," said the young vamp and stripped.

With any luck, they'd finish up and she'd be passed out in under an hour.

"Just flash your fangs and I'll be good to go," said Ama.

The vamp nodded and pasted on a feral grin. Ama's heart pounded as he ran his tongue gently over the sharp points and then pulled her over to the mirror propped on her dressing table.

"I can tell you want to watch me," he said. So thoughtful.

He entered her from behind, and his fingers dug into her hip, his opposite arm wrapped around her chest. Ama watched him in the mirror as he ducked his head and licked up her neck. The adrenalin pounded through her veins, but not the kind she sought. His shaggy blond head was suddenly her dead husband's, in this room they had shared. Desperate words spilled from her lips, words she'd never uttered on the brink like this.

"Nightwalker, bring forth your sire that I may supplicate myself before their splendour."

The vamp growled, and a flash of blue light in the mirror had Ama blinking to clear her vision. This vamp's sire was old. His dark eyes flashed, though his hands were buried in his trouser pockets, and his slim frame leaned casually against the bedpost. His steady gaze chased the spectre of her husband from the bedroom and anchored her as the delicious heart-pounding exhilaration of being on the brink of oblivion roared in her ears. The blond vamp's fangs finally sank into Ama's throat, and she cried out, focussed on his sire's reflection. The pumps of blood leaving her body faded into the background and Ama floated away.

That had been weeks ago, and Ama figured those dark eyes, that casual stance, the weariness in the sire's face would have lost their allure by now. The chalk sketch in front of her was proof enough that the image could still cut straight through her with longing.

The moment she'd woken up had perhaps cemented her obsession, when she'd come back to herself tucked into her bed. Sometimes, she woke up sprawled on the floor, sometimes deposited on the bed, but never tucked in with a bandaged neck. No one had cared for her like that since she was a child. Not even her husband.

"A drink, Olivia," said Ama and sauntered to the bar.

"It's one in the afternoon," said Olivia.

"Indeed," said Ama.

Olivia shrugged. She'd never deny the hero of Griston anything, as much as she might disapprove. The vampires were proof enough of that.

2

The bell over the gallery door jingled, and Ama glanced up from her latest sketch of her mystery vampire. The newcomer shook the water off his hood, mindful of the artwork that surrounded him on all sides, and pulled it back.

His gaze swept her studio gallery, and Ama held her breath as that dark gaze caught on a portrait of himself. An impressionist interpretation of his casual stance, leaning against the bedpost with his arms crossed, his face blurred enough to not be identifiable. But he could easily recognize the scene. Was he here to tell her to stop displaying portraits of him? Right next to the impressionist work was a detailed portrait. Ama cocked her head. The likeness was reasonable, considering she'd only seen him for a few minutes at the most. Definitely recognizable as himself.

"See anything you like?" said Ama.

"Warren told me about the drawing in the tavern, but not these," he said.

"He probably doesn't know about them," said Ama. "I don't get many visitors."

"You should," said the vampire appreciatively.

"Do you want me to take them down?" said Ama. Not that she would comply, but her curiosity got the better of her.

He shook his head. "I like them. You know my face well."

All she had to do to see it again was close her eyes.

"How about a name to put to the face?" she said.

"Lazarus Rayne," he said.

Lazarus, his vampire name, was a little on the nose. Had he chosen it himself, or had his sire picked it out for him? A sire that would pick a name like that was pretty full of themselves, since the Lazarus in the story had been resurrected by the Messiah himself.

Lazarus moved on to the next piece, giving each a moment's attention, even the few that didn't feature him as a subject. Ama surveyed the sketch on her easel. Her seat was intentionally backed into a corner so that her unfinished work would be obscured from patrons.

This was the first sketch she'd made that depicted her. The younger vampire's head bent over her neck, just fangs and a mop of hair, but her body featured within the confines of the mirror frame. This was also the first sketch she'd drawn from Lazarus's perspective, herself in the foreground and Lazarus in the background, watching her reflection as she was tasted by his progeny.

Lazarus had made it back to the impressionist work that had first caught his eye. "How much for this piece?" he said.

He wanted to buy it? Vampires were not known for their material goods. Any moment, they could be summoned halfway around the world by their progeny, if they had any, and Lazarus did. It wasn't exactly her business, as long as he had the money.

"What will you give me for it?" said Ama. Not that she needed coin. The town treated her to anything she might want or need, her protests casually brushed aside.

He threw out a number large enough to buy her entire studio and the loft above it.

"Done," said Ama. She ducked into the back room to fetch burlap and string to wrap the painting. She spread it carefully in the middle of the floor and placed the painting on top.

"I didn't know vampires had that kind of money," said Ama as she worked.

"You'll find we're as varied as humans, in our way," said Lazarus.

Ama had met plenty of vampires, but she'd never hung around them long enough to find out what they were like. She got the oblivion she needed; they got their blood, and when she passed out, she never saw them again. Her manner always made it clear she had no desire to do so.

The sunlight slanted in the front window across the burlap as Ama tied the string tightly around it. The piece was oil paint on wood, but the texture made it vulnerable to chips and cracking anyway.

"Unfortunate that it must be wrapped. I wanted to continue to admire it," said Lazarus.

"You can admire it all you want when you hang it up," said Ama.

Lazarus nodded noncommittally. "I spend very little time at my home."

Being summoned all over the continent without warning would do that to someone.

"Your payment will be available at the solicitor's office in town," said Lazarus.

Ama checked the wrappings one last time and passed Lazarus his latest acquisition. He tucked it under his arm and stood by the door, making no move to leave.

Should she retreat into the back? Ask him to go? Haul his body against hers? Invite him to join her for lunch?

"Would you like to join me for lunch?" she said.

"Lunch?" He cocked his head, a slight smile softening his confusion.

"The meadow just behind the gallery is a lovely spot to eat on a nice day," said Ama, "and it looks like the rain's cleared up." She gestured to a landscape of the meadow in question, propped in the corner. What the blazes was she doing?

Lazarus's smile made her heart jump in her chest. If her stomach kept feeling like this, she wouldn't be able to eat any lunch.

"Come with me to tuck my new painting away, and we can have lunch wherever you'd like," said Lazarus.

"Sure, where are you staying?" said Ama. She took off her smock, hung it by the easel, and put on her hat. She motioned for Lazarus to precede her out and locked the door behind them.

Ama followed Lazarus as he wove through the crowded square filled with shoppers and merchants opening their stalls now that the sun was out. He pulled the painting tight to his side, carefully protecting it from the bustle. A goat bleated and lunged on its line for a mouthful of burlap, and its owner jerked it away, muttering apologies. Lazarus nodded and walked on. Did he notice the sidelong glances the whole square was sending his way?

Ama fell into step with him as they left the crowds behind, striding together through a winding alleyway, up a few steps to a one-room loft. The place was fairly bare; a dusty locket languished on the dressing table, and a coat much too big for Lazarus hung on a chair back.

"Is this your place?" said Ama.

"No," said Lazarus. He propped the painting against the wall in a clean corner of the bedroom. "As you may imagine, when a vampire is summoned to an unknown location, they often require a place to stay. These places are well known among vampires. We leave one another's things alone"—he gestured to the locket—"assuming that the person who left it was summoned and will return for it in time."

If Lazarus was summoned, he could come back for the painting as long as he left it here.

"Are you summoned often?" said Ama. Her mouth was working faster than her brain today.

Lazarus motioned her out the door again. "I've made it clear to my progeny that I am available if they wish for my aid. As such, I am summoned regularly, yes. Not all vampires are so accommodating. For my part, I do not summon my sire. She does not appreciate that aspect of our abilities."

Another pang hit Ama. She'd been with dozens of vampires, summoned quite a few of them, and compelled quite a few of those summonings. She'd never before stopped to consider whether they minded.

3

The two of them selected food from the stalls in the square. Ama pulled out a coin from her pocket to pay, but the vendor refused her money. Lazarus was one stall over, and she didn't want to attract attention, so she acquiesced without comment.

She and Lazarus meandered to the meadow Ama had suggested. The fresh breeze cooled the sunny day, and Ama spread a blanket on the damp grass. She sat, closed her eyes, and turned her face to the sun.

"Is your coin declined often?" said Lazarus.

"Always," said Ama grimly. "These are stubborn folks. The hero of Griston doesn't pay."

"If there's no changing how they see you, why not leave?" said Lazarus.

She'd thought about leaving so many times, but something always held her here. This was her home, where she'd grown up. Her parents' graves were here, along with her husband's. Her gallery had been her parents' soap shop, and her grandparents' before that. This was where her husband had waited for a decade for her to come home, where she had always thought she'd raise her own children one day. She'd spent so many hours and sleepless nights on the road with her regiment, dreaming of coming back to this place. Up and leaving . . . was impossible.

Ama shrugged.

"Where did you learn to paint so beautifully?" said Lazarus.

"Our regiment got snowed in one winter, up in the mountains. Just happened that a painter was trapped up there with us. No one else was interested, but I took to it. She was happy to teach me, and I was happy to learn. Wasn't much else to do but spar and—" She glanced at Lazarus. Could she say fuck in front of him? What business did a foot soldier like her have with a fancy vampire who'd lived a century if he'd lived a day?

"Do you paint all the vampires you . . . summon?" said Lazarus.

Ama shrugged. "No. I never think of them again."

"I'm the one that got away, then?"

"Could be," said Ama. Her breath caught, and her fingers tingled. "We can fix that, if you like."

Lazarus leaned in close. Ama shivered as he held her firmly by the shoulders and bent to her neck. She tipped her head up to give him access, her heart racing as he came within a hairsbreadth of her skin. He took a long sniff of her scent.

He recoiled, wrinkling his nose.

"What?" snapped Ama.

"You're afraid of me," he said.

Ama snorted. She could count the things she was afraid of on one hand, and vampires were not among their number.

Lazarus crossed his arms. "Your adrenalin is elevated."

"And?"

"The taste is not to my liking," he said.

"Seriously? Blood is blood!"

"Maybe to the untried youth you favour," said Lazarus.

"I'd hardly call . . . your progeny youth," said Ama. She didn't know the blond's name. Heat crept up her chest. She never knew their names; she'd never even thought to ask. But this was the first time she'd been ashamed of it.

"I still think of my progeny as youngsters," said Lazarus with a fond smile.

"Do you see them often?" What were vampire family dynamics even like?

"Not as much as I might wish. My sire is not very welcoming. I appreciate you giving me the chance to spend time with Warren and Matthew."

Ama nodded and lay back in the sun. She put her hands behind her head and closed her eyes, letting the sunlight dance on her lids in blood-red spiderwebs.

So he wouldn't bite her. So what? There were plenty of other vampires out there who would be more than happy to oblige.

4

Ama splashed across the square to the tavern. The sunny break mid-day had been short-lived. She ducked inside and shook the water off her cloak, almost soaked through just from the quick walk. Maybe she could convince the tailor to take some of the chunk of money she'd made today. Either that or she could trek into town where they would be more likely to let her pay.

Ama kept her gaze on the scuffed floorboards or on her banged-up empty stool by the bar as she crossed the tavern. The locals always glanced away and the travellers always stared and elbowed one another. As she sauntered toward the bar, one of the regulars got up from the seat next to hers and stood a little farther down. What, did he think she'd bite or something? Olivia sidled up and plonked her usual tankard in front of her.

"Thanks," said Ama, and she took a long swallow of beer. When she put the tankard back down, Olivia had already retreated to the other end of the bar. Ama tried to catch her eye, but Olivia steadfastly avoided looking at her. She was practically run off her feet. It was probably for the best anyway. If someone was willing to listen, who knew what Ama might say?

Lazarus didn't want her blood. What the hell? At least a dozen vampires had fed on her over the years, and she'd never once had a complaint. The one time she actually cared what this guy thought, and he was disgusted by the scent of her. Come to think of it, why did she care what he thought? Sure, he'd taken care of her when she was passed out, had looked at her like a person, not a walking blood source or an untouchable hero of legend . . . and he'd liked her paintings. Enough to spend a fortune on one.

Meeting him in person had done nothing to break whatever strange hold he had over her. She couldn't alter her body's response to a vampire's bite, even if she wanted to. Who wouldn't get their blood up at the thought of fangs sinking into their throat?

Meeting an opponent on the battlefield was one thing. You might get hurt, sure, might even be killed, but you could do your damnedest to stay alive. When a vampire sucked your blood, you were pinned against them, helpless. Who wouldn't be a little jumpy?

Ama drained her glass and clonked it on the bar again, and Olivia bustled back over. The tavern was overflowing, but Olivia always made time to fill her cup. As she poured, she jerked her chin across the room, and Ama turned.

The vampire she'd been with before, Lazarus's progeny—either Warren or Matthew—stared at her from across the room. If Lazarus didn't want her blood, plenty of vampires out there did.

"Thanks again, Olivia," she said and took the full tankard Olivia slid across to her. Ama gulped some down so it wouldn't slosh as she walked and slid into the seat across from the vampire. "You watching me for a reason?" she said.

"Absolutely," he said. "Want to get out of here?"

He didn't even want to have a conversation first. If she didn't know his name, chances were pretty good that he didn't know hers either. Ama's steady heartbeat didn't speed up, and her body stayed loose. Would you look at that? She felt nothing for this vampire. She studied his face, and he flashed her a little fang. Normally that would set her heart galloping and twist her stomach into knots, but still the thudding of her heart remained steady and even in her chest.

"You're not in the mood," said the vampire, more disappointed than accusatory.

Ama considered asking this guy whether he'd liked the taste of her blood last time, whether there had been anything wrong with it, but he was already scanning the tavern for another target. So, very uninterested in conversation, then.

Damn Lazarus! Somehow, this was his fault. What had this vampire been doing when she'd summoned him? She opened her mouth to apologize but took a drink instead. He could have been in the middle of anything, anywhere. He could have been halfway around the world, for all she knew. How long would it take for him to get back there? Not something she had ever thought of before godsdamned Lazarus showed up.

"Are you Warren or Matthew?" said Ama.

"Warren. My sire really got to you," said the vampire, mirth dancing in his eyes.

"How do you know I'm not interested in you?" said Ama. Could he sense her heartbeat somehow or smell her lack of that gross adrenalin scent Lazarus had seemed to hate so much?

He quirked an eyebrow. "Are you?"

"Not particularly," said Ama. "But how could you tell?"

He shrugged. "When you've done this as long as I have, you can tell." His smile seemed genuine enough. "Besides, last time you were panting for it."

"Thank-you for putting it so delicately," said Ama. A quick glance showed her that she'd caused the folks around the vampire to turn their backs on him. "I'm scaring away your prey."

"Speaking of putting things delicately," he said and grinned at her. Warren was actually a really nice guy, very different from Lazarus. Not that Lazarus wasn't nice, but that was not the first word that came to mind when she thought of him.

"Have a good night," said Ama and stood, taking her tankard with her. "I hope I didn't do permanent damage to your reputation by association."

"Don't worry about it," he said. "I'll lure them back in." He winked at her, and Ama retreated to her corner of the bar to finish her drink.

She wasn't going to stay much longer, but she would at least finish this one drink. Lazarus wouldn't bite her, and now she wasn't interested in a gorgeous, willing vampire? Next time she needed to sink into oblivion, where would she even look?

5

As Ama led Lazarus into the shelter of the trees, he paused, and she turned back. His glance flicked up into their branches, then scanned the undergrowth. A bird chirped and fluttered away, and something rustled on the ground. As Lazarus caught up to her, he tripped on a stone and stumbled.

"How much farther?" he said.

Ama shrugged. "The villagers don't like to see my practice," she said. "Reminds them what I did to get my hero title."

"I'm sure they're thrilled to have their hero consorting with a vampire."

"I doubt they noticed," said Ama. But what if they had?

The trees thinned into a clearing, the earth packed flat from a hundred steps, except where a treacherous root or two poked up.

"Who else uses this place?" said Lazarus, looking around the clearing.

"No one that I know of," said Ama. She could be alone here, thankfully. She limbered up.

"How long has it been since you had a sparring partner? Do I need to fear for my life?"

"I can still pull a punch," said Ama. "Besides, I swore never to kill again, so you're safe."

The dappled light meant that no particular angle would place the sun directly in his eyes, but Ama knew the ground better than Lazarus did. He was a vampire so had no need of leathers. He stripped off his shirt.

"Trying to distract me?" said Ama. She circled him. He was wiry, but vampires' strength and speed didn't come from their muscles. Though the muscles were not half bad to look at.

"As you may have guessed, I am an expert at removing stains, but if I can avoid them, I do."

"Think you'll be the one lying in the dirt, do you?" said Ama. She focused on Lazarus and took a fighting stance. "What if you get summoned?"

"I've been summoned from worse positions, believe me. My eldest progeny—" He broke off as Ama made the first move.

They both landed a couple of light hits in short order. Lazarus was fast, obviously, but he didn't have the battle experience that Ama drew from, which put him at a disadvantage. Ama was already panting. Maybe she did need to find a sparring partner she could practise with regularly.

Lazarus's next blow came out faster than a human could manage. She ducked, too slow, and his fist glanced across her face. Coppery blood filled her mouth, and she spat on the ground. She drove her shoulder into Lazarus. Her dander was up now, and she grinned. His sniff was loud in her ear, and then he twisted her face up and took her mouth with his. He groaned and sucked her tongue. He was tasting her blood—for the first time. And he wasn't pulling away from her.

He broke their kiss. "Fuck, that's good," he panted.

She took the opportunity to punch him in the stomach. He doubled over, but it might have been more from laughter than from pain.

"Now you like my blood?" said Ama. "Or you're afraid you're going to lose, so you're trying to distract me again?" Her smile was probably still streaked red; it seemed to distract him.

"I always knew I was going to lose," said Lazarus.

"Is that why we never talked stakes?" said Ama. She went for him again, but he dodged. Too fast. This match would only end one way: with Ama collapsed on the ground, too tired to chase him around anymore. As long as she played fair.

"What would you ask for if you win?" said Lazarus.

"When I win, you mean?" said Ama. She tilted her head back, let him see the pulse pounding in her throat, and his gaze snapped to it. Which gave her the window she needed. She feinted left. He dodged right, promptly tripped over a tree root, and landed on his ass in the dirt.

"Your fighting style leaves little room for honour," said Lazarus. He collapsed flat on his back. So he was a bit tired after all.

"If I had honour, I'd be dead many times over by now," said Ama. She reached a hand down to pull him to his feet, but he shook his head.

"Allow me a moment to recover, please. Have at least that much honour," he said.

Ama leaned against a tree and looked down at him. His chest heaved, and round white scars showed up in stark relief on the flushed pink skin of his torso. He'd been through something, when he was mortal and could scar. If he wanted to talk about it, he would bring it up.

"Swim some of that dirt off?" said Ama.

He grunted assent and let her pull him to his feet.

Ama led him down the hill to the bend in the river where she normally bathed after her solitary practice sessions. She had won their bout, which meant she could ask him for something. He'd said her blood was good. Why hadn't she demanded he drink from her then? Besides wanting to win. She stripped mindlessly, muscle memory laying out her boots, leathers, and underclothes on the bank, and slipped into the water. She dunked her head under. A thunderous splash indicated that Lazarus had jumped in as well.

She didn't want him to drink from her in the woods, sweaty and grimy from sparring, at least not the first time. She grimaced under the surface where he couldn't see. She wanted the first time to be special? Ugh. She broke the surface, gasped for breath, and clawed for the river bank. She hoisted herself out, dripping, onto the grass. With her back to Lazarus, who was still rubbing at the dirt on his arms, she squeezed the water out of her hair and tied it into a tight bun. If she wanted their first time together to be special, she cared what their first time was like.

Ama's linen tunic stuck to her as she pulled it over her damp body, as did her canvas trousers, but she let her hands work while her mind wandered. She let the familiar motions soothe her pounding heart. She wanted their first time to be special? That meant she wanted more than one time.

Lazarus's hands landed lightly on her shoulders, and she startled.

"You'll take a punch without flinching, but whatever you're contemplating now has you terrified. Care to enlighten me?" said Lazarus.

She rolled her shoulders.

Lazarus took the hint and dropped his hands.

"We should get back to the village," said Ama without turning. She climbed the riverbank back to the clearing, Lazarus at her heels.

"Someone expecting you?" said Lazarus.

No one was expecting her. The gallery could stay closed and folks would hardly notice. It wasn't as if she required regular patronage of her shop.

Why was he even spending time here with her? Surely he had somewhere to be, somewhere that she'd summoned him from those few weeks ago? Or perhaps it wasn't far away, and he'd returned there directly only to come back and find her when Warren told him about her drawing?

"Anyone expecting you somewhere?" said Ama as Lazarus fell into step with her.

"My sire still wants a word. I'm sure it'll keep. A few weeks for her is barely a blink," he said. "Dinner?"

"Sure," said Ama. She already wanted to make their first time together special. In for a penny, in for a pound.

6

Ama picked at her food. Thankfully, the tavern was noisy enough to cut through the awkwardness. Ama caught Olivia's glare from across the room, but Olivia's face quickly smoothed into a vapid smile. Olivia was always setting her up with vampires. Why would she care that Ama was sitting with one now?

"Shall we go for a walk?" said Lazarus. He'd long since cleaned his plate and likely concluded that she wasn't going to eat any more.

Ama nodded and tossed a couple of coins onto the table. Doubtless, they would be returned to her on some pretext in the near future. Ama sighed. Maybe moving away from here was not so impossible.

Starlight sparkled down on them as they crossed the shadowy square. The idea of sitting alone in the still, silent loft she'd shared with her husband repelled her. She steered Lazarus up the hill toward the church spire just visible over the rooftops. He didn't try to make conversation in the quiet night. In a dimly lit window, a face disappeared behind a twitching curtain as they walked by. No one would dare question the hero of Griston and a vampire.

The cemetery was huddled behind the church, and Ama opened the creaky gate to let Lazarus in and latched it behind him. He didn't ask why they were going to a graveyard at night. He was a vampire, after all, not exactly known to be squeamish about death.

Ama and Lazarus meandered between the gravestones, set in rows. Ama didn't have to read the stones in the waning moon's faint light to find her way. Finally, she paused, and Lazarus stood silently beside her. Her parents' gravestone was still easily legible, and Lazarus didn't ask about it. Their death dates were many years ago, and close together, before she'd left town, in fact. Just a year after she'd been married.

Ama mouthed a benediction and paced down the row, her feet heavy. She stared at the ground, no need to count the stones or check the names. She stopped again, Lazarus still by her side. He let the silence stretch on, even though this name wouldn't easily connect to Ama since she'd never taken it as her own.

"The space is for me," she said. Her husband's name, followed by an empty line, then the benediction. She'd be buried here too when she died.

"What took him?"

"Disease," said Ama. The year before she'd returned home. There hadn't even been time to send word. Not that there was anything she could have done, even had she been here. Being at the battlefront had possibly even saved her life.

"I was dying when my sire turned me," said Lazarus. He looked up at the stars now, hands clasped behind his back.

"The scars?" said Ama.

"From bleeding. That's what passed for medicine back then," said Lazarus. Before the magic.

"I suppose being turned could have saved him, too," said Ama, jerking her chin at the headstone.

"Perhaps," said Lazarus. "It's no guarantee."

Ama stared up at the night sky. The clear day had turned to clear night, and the Milky Way splashed across the scattering of stars, stretching off to eternity.

"Why vampires?" said Lazarus. "What draws you to us?"

A shadow flitted across the sky, the high-pitched squeak of a bat fading into the night.

"I've done many things I want to forget," said Ama. "A vampire's bite . . . lets me rest, for a while."

"And the fear? Why do something that terrifies you so much?"

"There's an edge to it that I enjoy, just a whisper of the rush of battle. But you have it wrong. It's not the biting, it's the hold that gets to me. Being pinned like prey doesn't come easily."

Ama had the sudden urge to bare her throat to Lazarus, but the gravestone's dark presence beat into her, and she muttered the benediction and took his hand, instead. She led him away from her husband's grave, her eventual resting place, and out the creaky gate, back down the hill.

"I think I know how we can do this," said Lazarus.

Ama unlocked her door and led him up the stairs to her loft. She threw open the windows, letting in the cool night breeze.

"You've done it before, I take it?" said Ama.

"Please allow me to make a suggestion," said Lazarus. He took both her hands in his. "You fear letting me take from you. Instead, give to me."

"What does that mean?" said Ama.

"I won't bite your throat," said Lazarus.

"If you still refuse to bite me, why are you here?" said Ama. She tugged her hands away.

"I didn't say I won't drink from you," said Lazarus. "Just that I won't bite your throat."

Ama yanked off her jerkin, looped one arm around Lazarus's neck, and pulled him into a kiss. Her heart pounded when his fangs grazed her lip, but it wasn't the rabbit-like patter she was accustomed to. Soon they were undressed, and Lazarus rolled onto Ama's bed on his back. He spread his arms, and Ama joined him there, but he still made no move to take things further.

How long had it been since she'd made love? How long since she'd had no expectation of being bitten? Since she'd been intimate with someone she . . . trusted? She expected the thought to take her spinning off the rails again, but no telltale clench twisted her gut.

She traced Lazarus's scars, and he let her trail her fingertips over them slowly. He'd been vulnerable once, just a mortal like her. He was still vulnerable in his way. If she really wanted to, she could take him down. She'd never fought a vampire before, not for real, but as Lazarus had said, she fought dirty. She fought for survival. Vampires like Lazarus didn't need strategy or training; they relied on their inherent ability to hunt prey. Ama was so much more than prey.

Ama shuddered and took Lazarus inside her. Still, he made no move toward her throat, made no move to take control or to drink from her. The thought of it didn't send her heart racing; she finally understood what he'd meant. She kept moving slowly as she leaned forward a little and brought her wrist to Lazarus's lips. He licked over her scars and kissed them each gently in turn. Ama ground her hips into him and shoved her wrist in closer. He smiled against her arm and grazed it with his fangs, his panting breath hot on the thin skin that was all that separated him from her pounding pulse.

"Drink," said Ama, and that was all the encouragement he needed.

His long fingers gripped her arm on one side and her hand on the other, holding her steady as she kept rocking against him. His fangs seemed to slip gently into her with only a slight ache. It felt different than being bitten on the throat, or maybe the difference was Lazarus rather than some nameless vampire.

Ama came with a cry, and for the first time, as oblivion overtook her, she didn't want to fade into blackness. She wanted to stay here with Lazarus, wrapped in his embrace.

7

Ama painted the same board over and over. A starlit graveyard, a portrait, a still life of an empty room. But a shadowy figure lurked against the tombstones, the portrait had glinting fangs, and a carefully wrapped painting leaned in the corner of the empty room. Lazarus was gone from her life, but he remained etched into her thoughts.

In the evening, when she might otherwise have crossed to the tavern for a drink or two, she would huddle in her studio, painting, preparing boards, or mixing paints. She kept the gallery door locked, even in the daytime. She found food on her doorstep once or twice a day. The last thing she needed was for Olivia to try to set her up with a passing vampire; the thought held no appeal for her, not anymore.

At dawn, she would slip out her back door and march to the clearing to practise, the forms the only thing that let her escape her thoughts. Perhaps she was simply immersed in thoughts of Lazarus there, under the dappled morning light, where they had first begun opening up to one another, where they had first kissed and he'd first tasted her blood. Lazarus had no gravestone for her to haunt, so perhaps that place was the closest she had to a monument to him.

She painted over the empty room, started again. The sketch she'd been working on when Lazarus first came into her gallery lay in a roll in the corner. She stretched it out on her easel. She'd never finished it, but perhaps it was enough to base a painting on. Inside the mirror's frame, her naked body was stretched taut from Warren's bite, Lazarus's gaze pinning her from the background, belying his casual pose.

At the end of the week, when it was finished, she'd made her decision. She searched for a place in her gallery to hang the painting, but it seemed wrong to share it so publicly. She carried it up the stairs to her loft and methodically hung it on the bedroom wall, a moment frozen in time. She couldn't stay in Griston.

The next morning, when Ama came back from her practice, she unlocked the gallery door. She put the wildflowers she'd gathered in a jar beside her easel. She prowled the room and rearranged her paintings. She pulled out a small portrait of Lazarus, his face shadowed. It didn't capture him, at least not anymore. She set it on her easel and painted the flowers over it, his face gradually disappearing behind the little pops of cornflower and buttercup.

She left it on her easel to dry and stood in the middle of her gallery, Lazarus's portraits staring at her from all sides. She'd have to pack all this up. She grabbed the nearest portrait and ran a hand down the rough edge of the painted board. Lazarus, or a version of him, stared back at her. She tore open the back door and flung the painting into the dingy alley. Tears pricked her eyes, but she blinked them away as she gave in to the satisfaction of ridding her gallery of his face. She'd lost him, and she couldn't do anything about it but forget.

Once her gallery was all landscapes and still lifes once more, she brushed off her hands and strode across the square to the tavern. One last portrait remained to be exorcized.

The moment she came through the door, Olivia spotted her.

"Ama!" she called. "Where have you been?"

"Here and there," said Ama. She strode to the drawing and lifted it off the wall.

"He left you, did he?" said Olivia. "I thought as much. That's why I turned that other one away. We don't need a vampire hanging around bothering you."

"What other one?"

"The nervous one," said Olivia, waving her hand dismissively. "He's been asking for you, but I put him off."

Ama's stomach clenched. "Which vampire."

"The skinny one you left with that first night. That one's sire, or progeny, or whatever," said Olivia and waved to the portrait tucked under Ama's arm. "Don't worry. I turned him away. Told him you had no interest in getting caught back up with them."

Ama clenched her fist. "Where is he?" Matthew knew she wasn't interested in his bite, so what did he want her for?

"How should I know?" said Olivia. "Probably been summoned halfway across the continent by now. You know how they are."

Ama took a deep breath and let it out. It would not do to punch the tavern keeper. She spoke through gritted teeth. "If he comes back, you direct him to me. Understand?"

"But Ama," said Olivia. "You know what people were saying. A night with a vampire is one thing, but they aren't for settling down with. I mean, you of all people, with a vampire?"

Ama's teeth ached, she was clenching her jaw so hard. She turned and left the tavern before she could do anything she'd regret.

She might be able to find Lazarus. She might even be able to get him back. If she wanted him back. Vampires could be summoned, that was part of the deal. They could disappear at a moment's notice, despite your careful plans. Like her husband had. If she found Lazarus, if they did build a life together, how could she ever relax knowing that?

She laid the portrait on top of the others in the alley. She could throw away as many portraits as she wanted, Lazarus was entwined in her thoughts now, and there would be no extricating him. Her husband was dead. She couldn't do anything about that. If there was a chance she could track Lazarus down, the only reason to refuse would be out of spite, or out of fear.

She turned on her heel and emerged from the alley and climbed the hill to the vampire haven.

8

"Victoria, his sire, has some plan to keep from ever being summoned," said Warren. "I guess Lazarus's vow isn't enough anymore."

Ama had found Matthew wringing his hands in the little one-room loft, the painting Lazarus had bought from her still propped in the corner. Once she'd determined that Warren had been taken and that Matthew had forgotten how to summon him back, compelling him was a simple matter. Warren had appeared in a flash of blue light.

Now they sat together on the bed, Matthew's head in his sire's lap. Ama sat across from them in front of the dressing table.

"She's sealed him up so he can't be summoned," said Warren.

"Pretty careless of her not to do the same to you," said Ama.

"Last she knew, I had no progeny," said Warren. "Besides, now that she has Lazarus, she's done with me."

"You know where he's being held?" said Ama. Lazarus had been summoned and was being held captive. This she knew how to handle.

"I can take you there," said Warren. "It's only a day and a half away."

"Great, let me get ready, and we'll leave today," said Ama.

"We're just going to storm the place?" said Matthew.

"Not you, young one," said Warren. "Stay here. I'll be back for you."

Matthew struggled to his feet. "Like last time?"

"You know how to summon me now," said Warren.

"But Victoria has that sealed room—"

"I'll take good care of your sire," said Ama and left Warren to placate him.

They'd have to make camp overnight, but otherwise the journey to Lazarus shouldn't be arduous. Ama arrived back at her little apartment, everything she needed to pack bouncing around in her head.

She hauled the carved wooden trunk out from under her bed and ran her hands over the dusty top. She unlocked it and lifted the lid. Ama's hand shook as she traced the embossed leather of her scabbard, worn but well oiled and only a little dull from sitting in the dark for so long. She swallowed and wrapped her fingers around the scabbard and belt. The hilt . . . would wait. She laid out her armaments on the bed: sword and sword-belt, dirk, light mail. She'd have to do without a shield. Her old cracked one had been abandoned before she even reached home. The chances of having to fight blade to blade with someone were low these days. Victoria might have hired out-of-work mercs to guard her keep; they'd work for room and board since the war ended. Maybe she would scrounge a shield from somewhere along the way.

The easiest way to carry all this would be on her body, since they had no horses, nor was she any good at riding one. She slid the mail on over her leathers and strapped the sword-belt to her waist. Her stomach was tight as she descended from her loft. The feel of her gear dragged her into the past. The last time she had worn this, she had found out her husband was dead. She'd wandered into town, brash as anything, thinking she would come victoriously home and he would sweep her up and they'd make room in the loft for all her painting supplies, settle down, make a life together, a family.

Warren waited for Ama in the square. She locked the gallery door.

"Ready?" she said to him.

He glanced over her weapons and nodded.

"Lead on," said Ama.

Mercifully, Warren didn't insist on nattering while they walked; unfortunately, Ama's thoughts had free rein to run wild in the silence. The two of them passed farmers' carts and other travellers, their pace set partially by their stamina and partially by urgency. They had lunch as they walked and kept on until the sun dipped low.

"Where should we stop for the night? Unless you want to keep on?" said Warren.

"Vampires don't need sleep?" said Ama.

Warren shrugged. He was worried about Lazarus as well. As much as Ama might want to keep going, she would be much more useful if she was well rested when they confronted Victoria.

"I know a spot," said Ama. She had patrolled these roads often enough. The campsite might not be well maintained anymore, but it would serve them.

Ama lay for a long time, watching the stars wheel overhead.

"You really care about Lazarus?" said Warren from the darkness.

She grunted. She did care about Lazarus, even beyond having him pop into her head constantly. No one else had shown an interest in her life, in her thoughts, her feelings, since she'd come home.

"But not about me?" said Warren. After all, he had drunk from her. Gods, she had no idea what he'd even been doing when she'd summoned him that first time.

"I'm sorry, Warren," said Ama. "I didn't treat you like a person."

"Par for the course," said Warren. That only made it worse. No wonder Lazarus had chastised her for painting all vampires with the same brush.

Ama sighed. "Exactly. I'm sorry. What were you up to when I summoned you?"

"At the theatre, watching a play. I do wonder how it ended," said Warren.

"Which play?" said Ama.

"Something about a prince switched at birth. Lots of ribald humour and a mysterious old man."

"A comedy, then? It would have ended with everyone getting married and living happily ever after. Probably no deaths, but you never know."

"Seen a lot of plays?"

"They used to put them on to entertain us when we passed through towns. Keep us out of trouble, I think," said Ama. Trouble usually meant carousing in the tavern, breaking into a crypt, or tormenting the nearest . . . vampire. As a senior foot-soldier, Ama had put a stop to such behaviour when she could, but never out of concern for the vampires. Discipline in the ranks was paramount, and such antics did not endear them to the local populous or make for a cohesive regiment.

Ama must have dropped off to sleep, because the next thing she knew, birdsong had awakened her, and the soft light of dawn filtered through the trees. She shook Warren gently awake, and they continued on their journey.

Midmorning, they reached Victoria's tower house.

"I've been here before," said Ama. "I didn't realize you meant Amherst Castle. It didn't belong to a vampire then." The tower house was surrounded by a bawn wall. There would be no sneaking past the guardhouse that stood sentinel at the only entrance.

"Victoria's been living there a couple of years. She has some plan for it."

"Where is she keeping Lazarus?" A regular cell wouldn't be able to keep him from being summoned. What exactly would it take to keep him trapped?

"A mural chamber without windows, off the kitchens. An egress of some kind is necessary for the summoning to take, though it can be small. Even a keyhole would do."

Victoria probably prepared a room specially to hold a vampire.

"Why go to so much effort to keep him trapped?" said Ama.

"She's been trying to block summoning for almost as long as she's had progeny. Lazarus is the last of them," said Warren.

"What happened to the rest?" said Ama, but she already knew the answer.

"She killed the rest," said Warren.

"Why not kill Lazarus too, if she wanted him gone?" said Ama. Victoria had killed all of her progeny but hadn't the spine to finish what she'd begun.

"He's her favourite," said Warren. "I think she tried and lost her nerve. Besides, who would challenge her for him? This way, she gets him all to herself."

Ama would challenge her for him. She traced the grip of her sword lightly. Whether she was ready or not, she was going to have to break the vow she'd made all those years ago not to kill again.

9

Two guards were dicing in the entryway when Ama sauntered up. Warren sulked in her wake, still not convinced that this was going to work. Ama had brushed him off.

"Morning!" Ama called.

Both guards gave her an assessing once-over, lingering on her sword. The large one with a jovial face jerked his chin at Warren.

"What's he doing out?" he said, but he seemed more curious than accusatory. Was he talking to Ama or the other guard?

"Got summoned. Coming to check on his sire. What do you mean out?" said Ama.

"He can bugger off, unless he wants back in a cell," said the second guard, scowling.

"Back in his cell? He's supposed to be a prisoner here?" said Ama.

"He was. Getting him back is outside of our agreement with the lady," said the jovial guard. He shook his dice cup and rolled.

"Can I have a word with her?" said Ama. She leaned in closer to the guards, away from Warren. "How badly does she want this vamp back?"

The jovial guard shook his dice cup and rolled, then groaned and passed it back to the scowling one.

"Look, at least let your lady know we're here," said Ama.

Warren gripped her arm, but she shook him off. The larger guard didn't look up.

"Right, one of us goes up to the house and you gang up on the other one," said the scowling guard.

"Nah," said Ama. "I don't need to draw either of you away." She loosened her sword in its scabbard. The hilt felt far too comfortable in her hand.

The jovial guard resignedly picked up his shield, and Ama moved in. He swung a dirk at her before she took in what he was doing. But her instincts stood her in good stead; she dodged back, whipped her own dirk out, and swung it toward his face, trying to get a few seconds to draw her sword. Her dirk thunked into his shield, and Ama let it go. The rasp of her sword leaving the scabbard raised the hair on Ama's arms. This fight might go her way: her sword versus his dirk and shield.

The scowling guard, however, did draw a sword, finally losing his scowl at the chance to do violence. Ama retreated a pace and almost had her face bashed in by the other guard's shield until Warren loomed over the sword-wielding guard's shoulder and ravaged his neck. The guard dropped his sword, staggered back a step, and crumpled to the ground. The other guard retreated a pace, his back to the guardhouse. Warren wouldn't get behind him, and Ama's sword would be severely hampered by the close quarters.

"Even if you get past him, you're not getting Lazarus," called a light voice from high overhead. Ama stepped back and craned her neck up. A pale figure stood on top of the wall.

"You don't think so?" said Ama.

"Victoria," hissed Warren.

Victoria looked down on them with a tight smile. "Run along," she said. "I'm not going to kill him, Warren. You can call off your hound."

"Looks to me like your guards are sorely lacking, my lady," said Ama. "Are you in the market for a new hire?"

Victoria's eyes narrowed and flicked to the man lying unconscious on the ground.

"Ama!" said Warren. "You're paid up until the end of the day! You can't just—"

"You heard the lady," said Ama. She sheathed her sword. "We're not getting in. End of the day or no. How much will you give me for returning your prisoner?" She grabbed Warren's arm roughly. He could have thrown her off.

Instead, Warren swore a blue streak and took a swing at Ama for good measure. She dodged it easily. He could have at least tried a little harder to hit her. Victoria was already suspicious.

"Come on inside, Ama, was it?" she said. "Bring him."

"Amaranth, yes," said Ama. Something about her name in this woman's mouth curdled her stomach.

The jovial guard produced a length of rope, and he and Ama tied Warren up. His resistance was obviously token, but hopefully, Victoria wouldn't notice. The guard led them into the keep.

This tower house was much like all the others Ama had frequented over the years, if a bit emptier. The two guards on the gate seemed to be the extent of Victoria's defences. A handful of servants looked up when Ama and Victoria passed the outdoor kitchen on their way to the tower entrance, but the tower itself was still and silent. Ama eyed the murder hole overhead, but Victoria led them straight through the lobby and upstairs. Their footsteps echoed up the spiral staircase as they climbed to the indoor kitchen.

Victoria led the way to the window embrasure and swung one of the two doors on either side open. She gestured at Warren.

"I'm sure you're happy to be home. Your progeny will likely summon you again, but until then, I can't have you trying to free your sire."

The other guard stepped back and crossed his arms over his chest. He gave Ama a little nod. She was supposed to lock Warren up? She shoved him none too gently, and he stumbled into the cell. This one had a narrow arrow slit that let in a modicum of light. The one opposite must be the sealed cell Warren had mentioned.

Ama didn't bother to untie Warren's wrists. Showing any solicitude would only raise Victoria's suspicions. The guard nodded to her again and ambled off, no doubt back to the guardhouse. Ama shut the door with a thud, barred it, and followed Victoria up another couple flights of stairs to the hall.

It too was empty. The benches were pushed into the long table, and the lord's chair sat vacant. Victoria swept to it, skipped up the two shallow steps, and perched on the throne. Pulling out the bench on her own would just make Ama look silly, so she leaned against the table and crossed her arms.

"You look as though you mean to negotiate," said Victoria. "I'm a vampire, you know."

"I know," said Ama.

"You'd work for me?" said Victoria.

Ama shrugged. "Why not?" She paced to a tapestry and examined it. The merc who only cares about the money angle was probably the safest option.

"Aren't you curious about Lazarus? Why Warren hired you to get him out?" said Victoria. "Aren't you concerned I'm keeping him against his will? I'm sure Warren told you stories."

"Not especially," said Ama. "Lords and ladies have their games and their secrets. I have my sword." She patted the pommel at her hip. If it took her some time to find Lazarus and get him out, it wouldn't be the worst thing in the world. Since he wasn't already dead, chances were Victoria would keep him that way.

Victoria flashed her some fang. "I'll tell you what. You took my guard out of commission. He'll be out for eight hours? Maybe ten? You replace him overnight, then run back to whatever hole you crawled out of. I'm sure Warren won't be far behind you."

"Done," said Ama, hiding her sinking feeling behind a brusque exterior.

Ama pretended to haggle over payment in good faith, and they swiftly agreed on a sum (was that really what mercs were accepting these days?). Victoria dismissed her to the kitchens to have her lunch. No particular duties were assigned, so Ama ate and wandered down to the guardhouse.

The scowling guard was still out cold, and his partner had simply left him there in the dirt.

"How long you known him?" said Ama and jerked her chin at the prostrate guard.

"Been working here together half a year," said the guard. "You play dice at all?" He grinned.

"A bit," said Ama. Games of chance did little to ease the boredom of long hours on guard duty, but if it would endear her to this guy, she'd play.

"She's got him locked up, they say," said the guard as he took his roll.

Ama's heart leaped, but she kept her hand steady as she took the dice cup from the guard. "Who's that?" she said.

"His name's Lazarus. Vampire," said the guard. "I fool around with a kitchen wench, and she takes him food, sometimes. Says there's no windows, not even a slot in the door, just a little antechamber. She opens it and leaves his food, and then he opens the other side once she's gone. Never even sees him. Could be dead, only the food keeps disappearing. Sometimes Lady Victoria goes in. No one else."

Playing dice always made the gossip flow. "Why's she keep him like that, you think?" said Ama.

"No clue," said the guard. "Maybe he wronged her somehow. I try to keep on her good side, leastways."

So summoning Lazarus was out of the question, unless they could pinpoint the exact moment Victoria opened the door to his room, and she would need Warren to do it. Ama tried to keep her face neutral. She only had a few hours to figure this out. They wouldn't get Victoria to let them in here again.

10

Ama crept up the stairs. The last rays of the sun had just disappeared from the sky. With any luck, the passed-out guard hadn't woken up yet. Hopefully, he'd remain that way until they were long gone. The other guard stood watch in the guardhouse, and Victoria had gone off to bed—at least, the light in her window had flickered out.

This was Ama's chance, and she wouldn't get another. She crept across the deserted kitchen to the window, one barred cell door on either side. She dragged the bar off Warren's door with a thunk and ducked out of the embrasure and scanned the shadows. They were still alone. No one would come in here except to see Lazarus. She dragged the door open, and Warren slipped through.

"Stand watch," said Ama. "I'm going to get Lazarus out."

Warren slunk to the stairway.

Ama crossed in front of the window, lifted the bar across the door, and swung the outer door open. Just as the guard had said, an inner door had been put in place in this chamber, so even now, Lazarus was locked in. The inner door was also barred from her side, making it impossible for Lazarus to open, but nothing stopped Ama from doing so. Her heart raced. She could get him out, right now.

Ama put her shoulder to the bar across the door, and lifted it out of the hooks, and then slid it to the ground. She pulled the inner door open slowly. A sliver of light from the cracked door was the only illumination inside. Was Lazarus even in here, or was it all a trap?

Ama heard a sniff.

"Ama," said Lazarus, his voice tight.

Sheets rustled and then bare footsteps padded across the room. Victoria's face loomed out of the darkness, and Ama pulled her dirk, but she wasn't fast enough. Bruising fingers groped for her arm and held the dirk away from Victoria's body. Ama drew back and punched her in the ribs. Victoria was likely more surprised than hurt, but her grip loosened enough that Ama could shove her into the cell.

Lazarus slipped past her, and together they slammed the door in Victoria's face and hoisted the bar back into its hooks.

"Let's go," said Ama.

A resounding thunk hit the cell door, and Ama jumped back into the window embrasure.

"She'll get through eventually," said Lazarus as he helped her bar the outer door. "She's stronger than I am."

"It won't be easy to get out of the keep. There's just the one gate with a guard on it," said Ama.

"We'll manage," said Lazarus. He was even paler than before. He'd been shut inside for a week with not even a window. Could he fight? Had he had enough food? How strong was he? He would have to be strong enough.

They hurried to the stairs.

"Are we going to make it?" said Warren.

The rhythmic thunking of Victoria trying to break free was interrupted by a loud crack, then started up again. She'd made it through the inner door already.

"As long as Victoria doesn't join the fray," said Lazarus.

"Then let's get going while she's still trapped," said Ama.

They pounded down two flights of stairs to the lobby. The door to the yard stood open, and Lazarus slipped through, Ama close behind. Warren yelled from behind her, and Ama whirled around. A tangle of limbs flailed on the lobby floor. Victoria had pounced on him through the murder hole overhead.

Lazarus gripped her arm, and Ama turned back to the yard. The guard on the gate must have heard the commotion because he jogged across the yard toward them, dirk in hand.

Ama drew her sword. The hilt in her hand soothed her nerves. She really should have scrounged an old shield from somewhere. She pulled her dirk in her right hand, more to fill it than because she thought it would be useful.

"Let us through," she called to the guard.

His face was set, all trace of jocularity gone. Ama went for him with an overhead swing. He would be too slow with his shield. Ama hesitated. She'd vowed never to kill again, and this guard was just doing his job. That was all the time he needed to block her stroke.

Lazarus dove at his middle and knocked him to the ground. He pinned the guard and drank, and the guard was out cold in a moment.

"Go!" Lazarus shouted.

Leaving Warren behind was a bad idea. Victoria would use him to summon Lazarus, and they'd be back to square one. Speak of the devil.

Victoria had Warren by the throat and, in a graceful gesture, lifted him off his feet. Her meaning was clear. Run as far as you want. It makes no difference while I have him.

Lazarus crouched into a fighting stance beside Ama, and Ama raised her sword. Victoria paused. She had eyes only for her progeny.

"I can't let you go," she said to Lazarus.

"I can't stay," he said.

Lazarus's pained expression jolted through Ama. He wasn't going to kill Victoria. It would have to be her. Ama recoiled from the thought. Killing Victoria was the only way to end this. Ama raised her sword.

"Run!" shouted Lazarus and grabbed Ama's arm.

"Lazarus! We have to!" snapped Ama, trying to shake him off. But he'd seen something she hadn't: the scowling guard had emerged from the tower, a crossbow aimed right at them. They'd missed their chance.

11

Ama turned and fled, right on Lazarus's heels. With Warren in Victoria's clutches, he could be summoned back at any moment. What was the use in running? Predictably, no one chased them. Once they were out of sight of the walls, Ama stopped and sheathed her weapons.

"Do you have a plan?" Ama said.

Lazarus wrapped her in his arms, but she pushed him away.

"I could have taken her down," she said, but was that really true?

"I know," said Lazarus.

"She had you trapped in a windowless box. Is that how you want to spend eternity?"

Lazarus wasn't even listening to her. He brushed a stray lock of hair out of her face. "You came for me," he said, the ghost of a smile on his face.

"And seems like I'll have to come for you again pretty soon, only this time, they won't just let me on in."

Lazarus sighed and looked down. "I don't want to kill her," he said.

She rested her hand on the pommel of her sword. "I don't want to kill, either. We're out of options." But if they went back, they'd still be overpowered with that guard plus Victoria.

"We?" said Lazarus. He shook his head. "I can't ask you to kill for me. I just wanted a few moments to say goodbye before I'm summoned again."

Summoned. That was it.

"Lazarus, you summon her first," said Ama.

"Why would I summon her?" said Lazarus.

"It will give me the time I need to take her down before she realizes what's happened."

Lazarus knit his brow. "I swore I'd never summon her."

"And I swore I'd never kill again," said Ama. "She won't stop coming after you."

He took a deep breath.

"We have to do this before she summons you," said Ama. "She won't wait long."

He closed his eyes, and a tear trickled down his cheek. If only she could spare him this . . .

Ama snatched his hand in one of hers and gripped her dirk in the other. "Nightwalker, bring forth your sire that I may supplicate myself before their splendour."

Ama slit her eyes against the flash of blue light and brought her dirk up. She wrapped an arm around the materializing figure's body and pulled Victoria to her chest. She brought her dirk to Victoria's throat, but before she could slice, Victoria jerked, and a warm red stain bloomed under Ama's hand. Victoria's eyes rolled back. Lazarus's face was set and streaked with blood. A thick branch stuck from her chest. Lazarus was strong. Ama sheathed her dirk as the light faded from Victoria's eyes, and she lowered the vampire's corpse to the leaf-strewn ground. Lazarus knelt on Victoria's other side and tenderly brushed a lock of hair out of her face.

"You did it," said Ama.

"It was the least I could do. I couldn't have you breaking your vow for me," said Lazarus.

Once again, Lazarus proved that he cared for her. She helped him keep his vow, and he did the same for her. It wasn't charity, it wasn't pity, he knew her integrity was important to her, and he wanted to support her.

"I'm going to leave Griston," said Ama.

Lazarus looked askance at her. "Where will you go?"

Ama shrugged.

"There is an empty tower house close by," said Lazarus. "As Victoria's only progeny, it belongs to me now. You're welcome to join me there."

"You want to live where Victoria had you imprisoned?" said Ama.

"I have more good memories there than bad. I stayed with her for almost a year before she imprisoned me," said Lazarus. "Plus, it has a handy room for when I don't want to be summoned."

Using his prison to their advantage? It would be nice to have somewhere Lazarus would be safe, where he could stay with her and Ama would know he wouldn't have disappeared by morning.

"There's more wall space for your art than in your loft," said Lazarus, a touch of anxiety creeping into his voice.

Ama nodded and gave him a light smile across the body of his sire. "Let's go rescue Warren from our guards," she said.

12

"That looks lovely," said Lazarus from the doorway to their chambers.

Ama smiled and climbed down from the scaffolding. They stood together and surveyed the nearly completed murals covering their bedroom walls. Ama had left space to hang her paintings, and her self-portrait from the night they met already graced one end of the room.

"Has it started?" said Ama, wiping paint onto the smock she wore over her clothes. "Yes, but Warren is greeting the guests. There's no rush," said Lazarus.

Ama shucked off her smock, pressed her body to his, and pulled him into a kiss. After a moment, he pulled away, smiling down at her.

"I'm not sure we have that much time," he said.

"Later then," said Ama and gave him one last peck on the lips. She took Lazarus's hand and led him up to the hall.

Warren greeted them as they entered. He'd decided to stay on with them and seemed to like the idea of having a room in the house where he could go to avoid being summoned.

Ama's easel stood in a corner. She didn't mind folks wandering in and out while she worked, as long as they didn't comment on her work in progress. The impressionist portrait of Lazarus that he'd bought from her hung over their ornate chairs.

Folks had started filtering in for their family gathering. Not something vampires did, historically, but Lazarus wanted to be closer to his progeny than vampires normally were. He wanted a family.

She threaded her way to the head of the room, up the two shallow steps to her seat, made in the likeness of Lazarus's big chair. Soon, the benches on either side of the long table only had a few seats free, and Ama smiled. Their first family dinner was in full swing. Lazarus chatted with one of his progeny and laughed suddenly at something they said. Ama startled and then smiled. He'd been doing that a lot more lately.

Warren brought his progeny up to the dais to greet Ama, and the three of them shuffled their feet at his side.

"Nice to see you again, Matthew," she said to the baby vamp she'd met before.

He glanced at Warren, who gave him an encouraging nudge. "Nice to see you too, my lady," he said.

The others introduced themselves and one of them even settled nearby to chat with Ama.

Not every single relation was here; some had declined the invite, and some had not been found in time, but perhaps someday they could build relationships with all Lazarus's progeny.

Soon, this little family would be scattered to the four winds again; only a few would choose to stay like Warren, but they would always know that they had somewhere they could come home to, someone who would help them if they needed it, someone who would one day mourn their passing and remember them fondly.

HE'S DEAD AND CAN'T HELP HER—
UNLESS SHE BREAKS ALL THE RULES

A PENTAGRAM OF CANDLES AND SPECTRES

ELIZABETH F. SHEARLY

CONTENT NOTES

School bullying.

Please see the book's web page at www.elizabethshearly.ca for detailed content notes.

1

"Please fetch five candles from the cupboard at the back of the class," said Cindy.

The student scampered to the storage unit while the rest of the kids fell silent. Five candles meant invoking a ghost.

Her runner dumped the candles on her desk, and Cindy thanked them as they settled back in their seat. She stood the candles in a pentagon on the floor at the front of the class and clicked her electric lighter to get each one burning.

A whisper slid through the classroom as Cindy finished off with the candles. She took a deep breath and closed her eyes. The tug of the veil urged her across, but instead, she reached across the veil and grasped Pauline's hand. The old woman grasped hers in return and allowed herself to be towed across the veil. The students fell silent. Cindy opened her eyes. Before the class stood a translucent old woman beaming at them.

"Good morning, Ms. Flivor," said Cindy. "Thanks so much for joining us today."

"Thank you for having me, dear," said Pauline. Despite her wispy appearance, her voice retained a teacher's no-nonsense intonation.

"Class, please welcome Pauline Flivor, activist and former teacher here at our very own Landon Sikes Public School," said Cindy.

"Everyone has been looking forward to hearing your story, as always."
Cindy smiled and gestured for the spectre to proceed.

"I'm happy to hear my audience is interested," said Pauline. "Before
I begin, let me get to know all of you a little better. Who here likes to
invoke spirits across the veil?"

A few hands went up. At this point, most of Cindy's students
didn't have enough experience to know for sure.

"And who among you likes to walk the spirit realm and convene
with us that way?"

A few more hands shot up. It was the more common way to com-
mune with the spirit world.

"And who likes to do both, like Ms. Dawson?" said Pauline, gesturing to Cindy.

This was the most numerous group. It was good for eight-year-olds
to keep their options open.

"Thank you, everyone, for participating," said Pauline. "I was one
of you in that first group when I was young; I found that I preferred to
invoke across the veil rather than travel there myself. You should know
that there is nothing wrong with either way of doing things or using
each method in different circumstances. Back when I was teaching
here, the school board and many parents—your great-grandparents
that would be now—disagreed with me. They believed that spirits
should never be drawn to your world, that crossings should only occur
in one direction: from the land of the living to the spirit realm, never
the other way around.

"Today, I'm going to tell you the story of Ms. Dawson's grandmother Frances, someone who greatly favoured invocation. In fact,
she had real trouble crossing the veil at all."

Cindy had heard this story a dozen times; every year, in fact. Pauline
had tutored children who had trouble crossing the veil, until the

school board and the parents forbade her methods because they involved invoking spirits. She had left the school and worked to change perceptions of people like her. After a lot of hard work from many people, now folks can cross the veil or invoke spirits whenever they please.

The story was tailored to her class of eight-year-olds. No doubt the entire tale wouldn't be appropriate for them.

The bell rang, and the kids packed up for the day. A few straggled behind to ask Pauline more questions, but soon Cindy and Pauline were alone.

"I think that went well," said Pauline.

"Yes, thanks so much for coming," said Cindy. She picked at a hangnail.

Pauline smiled. "There's something else you want to talk about."

Cindy flushed. "Once a teacher, always a teacher, eh?"

Pauline just waited for her to explain. One of the candles flickered, but they were far from burning out and inadvertently banishing Pauline.

"The story you always tell my students," said Cindy. "How did it really happen?"

"We would need bigger candles if you want to hear the details," said Pauline.

Cindy held her gaze. "I do." She looked down. "How did you know it would be worth it? That what you were doing would really help?"

"I didn't," said Pauline.

When Cindy looked up, Pauline was smiling softly at her.

"Call on me again when you have a bit of time," said the spectre.

"Tonight," said Cindy firmly. "Thank you."

Everything was ready. Cindy had picked up a dozen candles on her way home, and she'd set up six around her living room. Invocation had never been her strength, and more candles helped. She could always set up a second ring if the first started to flag.

Cindy lit the candles and popped across the veil to find Pauline, who was ready on the other side. She waved through the mist, took Cindy's hand, and they crossed back to Cindy's living room together.

Cindy collapsed onto the couch, and Pauline conjured a wingback chair inside the circle of candles. She sat and conjured again—yarn and knitting needles. After a few moments of clicking away, she spoke.

"All the tests showed that Frances had a strong connection to the veil. Yet her partner, Grace, was running circles around her..."

2

All the tests showed that Frances had a strong connection to the veil. Yet her partner, Grace, was running circles around her. Grace huffed for the third time while she waited for Frances to cross over. Frances gripped her candle in her lap so hard that her knuckles were pale.

"I'm going again," said Grace finally. "You're just sitting there."

Frances pounded her candle on the table, and her eyes shone with tears.

"Frances," I said, "to me."

She shoved out her chair and stomped up to the front of the class. The other students who weren't presently travelling beyond the veil pretended not to watch her. I pitched my voice to be just between the two of us.

"Is something wrong?" I said. Maybe she was distracted, or perhaps someone close to her had recently passed forever to the other side.

She shook her head.

"No recent deaths in the family?"

Another head shake.

"Not even pets?"

"No, Ms. Flivor. There's no reason. I just can't do it," said Frances.

"I'll come by your house after school," I said. "We'll get you sorted out."

I let out my breath and went back to marking tests. I'd never seen a case quite so severe as Frances. The last thing I wanted was to have to fail someone so talented. I'd tutored students before, privately, until they got the knack of crossing the veil. I had no more than a passing acquaintance with her parents, and no idea whether they would approve of my methods.

Children this age were not supposed to invoke, you see, it was considered advanced, the country of adults, despite the very real fact that some children, myself—and I suspected Frances—included quite naturally lean towards invocation and away from performing crossings. I found using invocation very effective as a stepping stone to making that first crossing.

For the most part, parents were glad to have their children pass, regardless of method, but in the preceding years, I think we had all felt a change in attitude among parents. But I'd be damned if I'd give in to the pressure and let a child fall through the cracks in my class.

After class, I tidied the classroom and stacked all the candles neatly in the supply cupboard. I gathered up the candle stubs from around the room and packed them into my bag. They wouldn't be missed, and I could melt them down and reuse them. In those days, we had to be creative to get around the single-purchase limit.

I paused and hefted a half-burned candle. I needed to talk to Landon, but crossing the veil would knock me sideways for at least half a day, and I had tutoring with Frances tonight. I'd have to risk bringing him to me instead. I locked the classroom door, pulled down the shade, and then laid three partly used candles out at the front of the room. Enough for a simple invocation, and pulling him through was always simple for me. He always seemed to be standing ready when I reached across the veil. My heart in my throat, I pulled my matchbox from my pocket, struck a match, and got two of the candles lit before it singed my fingers and I had to strike another for the last candle. The smoke curled up into the still air.

The veil bulged and shifted. I reached through in a smooth motion and pulled Landon through to me. I couldn't feel his body against mine, more's the pity, but he used my aura to right himself and conjured a chair from the ether.

"Hey, Paulie," said Landon—Dr. Sikes—and crossed an ankle over the opposite knee.

I stepped out of the triangle and pulled up a chair myself.

"Today was the day, eh?" he said.

"You saw them, did you?" I said, and I couldn't keep a note of pride out of my voice.

"A number of us come to watch the newbies every year," he said. He took off his glasses and polished them on his shirt. I suspected it was out of habit, though I'd never asked whether his glasses got dirty in the spirit world.

"And cheer them on, I hope," I said.

"We don't interfere," said Landon. "Especially me. Can you imagine crossing the veil for the first time and coming upon someone like me?" He grinned.

From anyone else, this would be the height of arrogance, but Dr. Landon Sikes was a household name, no matter what household you were in, whether bogeyman or avenging angel.

"I'm sure I would have heard all about it," I said. "From both the student and from you."

"Any little rabble-rousers this year?" said Landon. The children who begged to invoke a ghost on their first day were Landon's favourites.

"No," I said. "There have been fewer every year. Since you died, at least. And I understand why. It's getting . . . It's not safe for us these days."

He sat forward, rapt. "Not safe how?" said Landon. He'd lost all trace of his easygoing demeanour.

I sighed. "Not safe like if anyone walked in right now, I could lose my job."

Landon's eyes narrowed. "No one likes to hear that they died for nothing, Paulie."

"Not for nothing," I said.

"Just tell me what's going on."

I sighed. This wasn't his problem. The dead were supposed to be at peace. "They twist your words, Landon. They cherry-pick. I can't correct every single person."

"Tell them they can come find me any time," said Landon.

"They don't want to find you, and they don't want the truth, Sikes," I said.

"So they're the same as they've always been. Afraid of ghosts," said Landon.

I shook my head. "I never thought they'd go this far," I said. "Frances is talented. Very talented. But she can't cross the veil. I'll work with her, use your stepping stone technique, but it will probably never be easy for her. And if her parents don't approve of invocation, that'll make it all the more difficult."

"Just tell them the truth about their daughter," said Landon.

I shook my head again. "You have a lot of faith in people."

"Yup," said Landon and stretched his arms up over his head. "That's probably what got me killed." He grinned.

"All the same, I can't just out her to her parents," I said. "Not without asking her first."

"So ask her," said Landon.

"I'm tutoring her later."

Landon's eyes lit up, and I chuckled.

"You can wait on the other side of the veil in case she makes it through. Or you can hang around so that she can practice invoking you."

"You don't think seeing Dr. Landon Sikes would spook her?" He flashed that grin again.

"I think she's made of sterner stuff than that," I said. "Though your face might scare her off."

"Come now! I'm a renowned stunner!" said Landon.

I swallowed hard. He was. He had been. But he was dead.

"Hey," said Landon. He brushed a hand through my aura. "I'm right here."

The candle remnants around Landon had burned down low, and he would be gone in a minute. This wasn't how our meeting should end.

"Stop that," I said. "You're mussing my aura." I waved a hand through him.

"I am doing no such thing," said Landon and crossed his arms over his chest. "I am straightening it. Any fool can see that."

"Don't give me that," I said. "Since when does my aura need straightening?"

"Since the weight of the world landed on your shoulders, Paulie."

"Seeing kids struggle always weighs on me," I said.

"No, it's not seeing them struggle, it's having to stand by while they struggle, being ordered not to teach them when you know your method works," said Landon. "I'll be there to help."

One of the candles flickered and guttered out. I snuffed the others and put them away, singing my finger on the hot wax. I couldn't leave them there to be found, as evidence that I'd been invoking spirits in my classroom.

I sucked my throbbing finger. I would need fresh candles for tonight; Frances would have better luck with them. The stubs from today's practice would serve well enough for my own purposes, but they would take time to prepare. Someone would notice if I took candles from the classroom. That sort of thing was closely monitored back then. Besides, Frances would get better use out of my fresh candles than I would. I had four hoarded at home, and I still had my week's credit, so I could pick a fifth up on my way.

3

"It's natural to be afraid to cross the veil," I said. "Especially when you're like me and you have to enlist a spirit to pull you through."

Frances sat on her living room floor in the circle of five candles. One had gone out, and I rummaged for a match to get it going again. Her parents had waved us in here and shut the door. They hadn't asked for details of the lesson, and I hadn't offered any.

She'd managed to get Landon across the veil on her first try and managed not to faint at the sight of his ghostly form. He'd sworn up and down that he hadn't helped her, except by standing still and not resisting the pull. Now I was encouraging her to let Landon tug her across. Sweat gleamed on her brow, and her ragged panting filled the stuffy room. I didn't dare open the door or windows. Her parents might be willing to countenance invocation if it would help their daughter be "normal," as long as they could claim ignorance after the fact.

I held the match carefully to the wick and waited for it to light. As soon as it took, Landon was back.

"You're getting good at that, Frances," he said.

She shrugged. "It's super easy."

"Not for everyone," I said. I caught Landon's eye. I'd only ever crossed the veil with the help of people I trusted from the other side.

Landon, another student in my class, had been the first to realize that invoking my grandmother and getting her help would finally let me cross for the first time. My own teachers had been too busy deriding mt failures to make any such realizations. I was unwilling to let Frances suffer that way. But according to Frances, she hadn't had a recent death in the family, so our options were limited.

"I want to try again," she said.

"Maybe Landon isn't the one to help you," I said.

"What?" said Frances.

"Is there anyone else beyond the veil that we could ask?"

Frances worried her lower lip. "My aunt . . . but she would tell my parents!"

"Tell your parents?" said Landon.

"If I invoked her. She'd tell my parents what I'd done," said Frances.

"And what would happen then?" I said, dread creeping through my chest.

"They'd throw me out," said Frances, without hesitation.

"That's a trifle dramatic, don't you think?" said Landon.

I shook my head at him from behind Frances's back. "That's fine, Frances. We'll keep working this way."

Landon nodded and popped out of existence, ready to connect with Frances on the other side of the veil.

Three knocks rent the air. Frances twisted and stared at me beseechingly. Five candles. Two people. No spectre, thankfully, but there was no denying what we were doing. The door handle was already turning, and loud voices made their way through the dense wood.

Then abruptly went silent as the door swung slowly open. Frances went pale, and stared at her equally flushed mother, who took in the circle of candles with her daughter smack in the centre. Terror overtook her shock. She snatched Frances bodily from the circle.

"Mum, I told you—"

"Not that you would be holding a seance in my house! If anyone found out—"

I planted my fists on my hips. "That's going too far. Part of learning about the veil is invoking willing spirits. It's but a step on the road to one day crossing in turn."

She pushed Frances behind her. "When Frances told me her teacher was coming to tutor her, I assumed she meant an education professional, not a ghost-whispering charlatan. Get out before I report you."

I picked up my bag as calmly as I could. Five candles were still planted on the floor, but they were too hot to move, and this woman wasn't above making good on her threat. I'd seen the fear in her eyes. I'd have to leave the candles behind, and I couldn't help my glare as I passed her. It would take me weeks to scrape that many candles together again.

I gave Frances a soft smile, but I didn't dare talk to her now. I didn't want to make things worse for her.

***

I pulled the drawer from my desk, dumped it across my bed, and rifled through the jumble of candle ends for something that would support a crossing. I snatched up the largest one I could find—still only as long as my thumb—and jammed it into a holder. There's nothing worse than returning from across the veil to wax-seared fingers, and this stub wouldn't last me more than twenty minutes.

I flicked a match and set the thing burning. Reaching for Landon, I let him pull me across to the other side. I had no choice.

His shocked face greeted me. "Are you sure, Paulie?" he said.

"I don't have long," I said. "Just didn't want you to worry."

"How long?"

"No more than twenty minutes," I said. "Frances's mother couldn't tolerate our lesson after all. She called it a goddamned seance."

Landon grimaced. "I've been discussing it with everyone over here." In the spirit world. "Tell us how we can help."

I shrugged. "I don't know yet. A *seance*. Do they even—"

"No, they don't know what it really means. It's been a long time since spirits and mortals ripped each other across the veil without permission. I'd be surprised if anyone over there remembers. Plenty over here do, of course."

"Of course," I said and took a deep breath. If Frances's mother didn't report me, it would be okay. It would all be okay. Sure, Frances might not ever learn to cross the veil . . . and life would keep getting harder for people like her. People like me.

"We'll help," Sikes was saying. "Just say the word."

"When I figure out how to fix the world, I'll let you know," I said bitterly.

"For now, just focus on yourself," said Landon. He watched me intently from beneath a furrowed brow.

"I—" My stomach was ripped from my body as I jerked across the veil. The guttered candle fell from my tingling fingers, and I stumbled to the bathroom to vomit. When I was a teenager, I could weather the crossing much better, but by the time I hit my thirties, my body refused to be ripped back and forth that way. I just wasn't built for it. Tomorrow, the hangover would be hellish.

4

I trudged down the hall, heading back up to my classroom. I hadn't had any lunch, but I also wasn't remotely hungry. My stomach was still punishing me for having crossed the veil last night. I opened the door at the bottom of the stairwell and paused.

"Here, ghost whisperer," said a student's voice from the top of the stairs, out of sight. "Have a bunch of candles. You'll need them to make your circle."

A squeak preceded the thump of candles hitting the floor. I let the door click shut behind me, and my own footsteps echoed up the stairs as I climbed to the landing and turned the corner. Three of them stood frozen opposite Frances. Five candles littered the floor. One rolled off the top step with a clunk.

"Candles are restricted to classroom use only," I said.

Of course, Grace was the one to talk back. "What are you going to do about it?" I could practically see a slur on her lips, but even she didn't have the guts to go that far.

"Tidy those up and get to class," I said, letting my anger turn my voice hard. Singling Frances out in this moment would only make things worse for her.

When the afternoon bell rang, Frances dawdled with her things, and I stayed at my desk. Her friends left her there, so either she'd already told them she was staying, or they weren't very good friends.

"Shut the door, please," I said, without looking up.

Frances shut the door and scuttled to the front of the class. She stood rigid by my desk as I finished another pile of marking. "About today in the stairwell," she said. "It wasn't— They weren't—"

I held up a hand. "You don't have to explain it to me, Frances, unless you want to."

She sighed and ducked her head. "I was supposed to be talented," she murmured. "I can't even cross the veil." She locked eyes with me, equal parts rage and terror flashing in their depths. "It's true, what they called me, isn't it?"

"Ghost whisperer?" I said. I held her gaze and quirked an eyebrow. "You successfully invoked a spirit on your first try, so yes, it would seem to be accurate."

She tapped her foot.

"Would you like to try invoking again?"

She shook her head. "I just wanted to tell you . . . My mum . . ." She swallowed.

"She doesn't want me tutoring you anymore," I supplied.

Frances spoke to her shoes. "She told the principal. She said they're going to surprise you with an inquest. She wants them to fire you."

I knocked on the principal's door, he called for me to enter, and I shut the door behind me. I didn't need all of reception to hear me get chewed out. Or fired.

I sat across from George, on the edge of my seat, and folded my hands in my lap.

George took off his glasses and rubbed a hand over his eyes.

"Get on with it, then," he said.

"I walked in on a bullying incident today. Grace Jones and a few other students. I'd like permission to suspend them, or at least Grace."

"You can understand my position," said the principal, as though I had been privy to the entire conversation he'd clearly been having in his head all day.

"What position is that?" I said.

"Now, Pauline, I think you know," said the principal. "If word gets out that you're a . . . you know . . . I wouldn't be able to retain you on staff."

"That I'm a what?" I said. Maybe if he said it out loud, he would realize how he sounded.

"A ghost whisperer," he said. "A spectre summoner. An invoker of phantoms. All right?" He scrubbed his face with his hands. "One of your bully's parents is already breathing down my neck. And he's on the board."

My stomach clenched. One of Grace's parents was a school trustee?

"I have his word that he won't take it further as long as you keep your . . . proclivities . . . to yourself," said George. "As Dr. Sikes said, our activities beyond the veil are no one's business."

"You must know Landon didn't mean—"

"Pauline, please. Don't say anything I have to fire you for. You're a good teacher, an excellent teacher! I would hate to lose you over something so silly."

"You're right. It is silly that anyone would believe invoking spirits is dangerous. I've helped numerous children do just that, and they are all perfectly fine. Just yesterday—"

The principal deflated. "Pauline . . ." he said and closed his eyes.

"I couldn't just watch Frances suffer. She's amazing! She summoned a spectre on her first try, George. Her first try *ever*," I said.

"You know I've had to open an inquiry into your behaviour? Every action you have ever taken—every action I've ever taken—will be judged completely out of context," he said.

"You and I both know that I was helping that kid," I said. "Can't you just say you're taking disciplinary action and let it go?"

"It doesn't matter what we know, Pauline," said George. "It's not about the kid, it's not about us. They want to make an example of you, and of me if I stand in their way. What happens to the school if I'm replaced by some fanatic? I toe the line to protect kids like Frances."

"You'd see her, what, fail out of school for her own protection?" I said. I smacked a hand on his desk.

"Sneaking around her house after school to have her invoke ghosts was for her protection?"

"Sneaking? You make it sound illicit! Her parents were fully aware that I was there *tutoring* a student, a very common practice among teachers, George. I was trying to do what I always do. Give her the tools to pass."

"And? Did you?" said George and refused to meet my gaze.

I straightened and leaned against his desk. "I've never seen someone quite so . . . ghost-inclined. *I* was my most stubborn case until yesterday. Did you know crossing the veil makes me physically ill? As in, when I come back, I turn myself inside out vomiting for half a day."

"I didn't," said George.

I shrugged. "Maybe once someone she loves crosses over, she'll trust them enough to let them pull her through. That's the only thing that worked for me. For now, her only option is drawing phantoms through to this side."

George straightened and put his hands in his pockets. "I think you should be less worried about Frances's future and more worried about your own."

I collapsed back into my chair. George had stood by me, until now. "You're not going to defend me," I said. My roiling stomach was caused by equal parts veil-hangover and our conversation.

George shook his head and motioned me to the door.

5

When the bell rang the next morning, the dread started in my gut. The missing students were probably just dawdling. I watched five minutes tick slowly by while the students who were present became increasingly fidgety. Finally, I took attendance. Frances was among the missing, as was Grace. A full third of the little desks were empty today. Frances's warning twined with George's. They were going to make an example of me.

I taught the class as usual. If the remaining students understood why their classmates were missing, they didn't let on. They were a little quieter, perhaps, a little more restless.

At the end of the day, George came to see me.

"I've done all I can, Pauline," he said, hovering in the doorway. "They wanted me to pull you from the classroom immediately."

"Hence the missing students," I said. Those kids were missing school for my principles. "When's the inquest?"

"Next week, but—"

"Move it up, as soon as possible," I said.

George blanched. "Don't you want time to prepare? I know a lawyer who—"

"That won't be necessary. Let's not have these children missing any more school than they already have. I won't leave my classroom until the inquest is dealt with, and these parents seem content to keep their kids home as long as I'm here. So let's just get the whole thing over with, shall we?"

George nodded, croaked out tomorrow, and hurried away. I snapped the door shut behind him. I needed to talk to Landon. Halfway through ramming things into my bag, I paused. My candles had been abandoned at Frances's house, and I couldn't even buy one until next week. I hadn't had a chance to melt down my pile of stubs. One candle wouldn't be enough; crossing the veil tonight was not an option with the inquest tomorrow.

I fiddled with my chatelaine and eyed the cupboard at the back of the class. I couldn't help a furtive glance at the door as I crossed the classroom. The click of the lock turning over seemed to reverberate more than usual. Four would be enough. Gathering them under my arm, I secured the cupboard doors again.

My bulky bag would give me away; the candle outlines were not subtle once I had the thing closed, but what were they going to do? Start an inquest? Fire me?

***

I wasn't drunk. Not so that it would matter. I'd just dulled the edges a little bit. The stolen candles burned in the corners of the room. I wanted a bit more space for Landon and I to talk. The usual tiny circles were fine for a quick conversation, but this wasn't going to be quick.

I sat on my bed and reached through the veil for Dr. Landon Sikes. His spirit always felt to me like sunlight filtered through trees, like a comfortable chair in the usual spot. I pulled him across. He glanced around the room, then made himself a chair, flipped it around, and settled with his arms draped over the back.

"I haven't been in your bedroom for a while," said Landon. He waggled his eyebrows, but his heart wasn't in it. "What's wrong, Paulie?"

I sighed. "How can I possibly survive an inquest? I'm going to say too much and get myself fired."

"How should I know? I said too much and got myself assassinated."

"If you're trying to be funny—"

"Look," said Landon. "I'm not the one to ask about these things. I am far too principled for this life. I think I proved that when I did that week-long hunger strike across the veil in our misspent youth."

"A lot of good it did," I said.

"Don't say that, Paulie. We made a difference. The backlash just means it's working."

"Backlash. Like when I cross the veil and spend four hours tossing my cookies," I said.

"I don't think—"

"You know what the worst part of the inquest is going to be? When they quote you. Out of context. Why did you even say, 'Our activities beyond the veil are no one's business'? Or 'Anyone should be allowed to cross the veil or not as they choose'?" I raised my eyebrows at him. I actually wanted an answer. But it wasn't fair to loose my anger on Landon.

"They're getting good at twisting my words," he said.

"You're telling me."

"So prove them wrong."

I prowled around the little room. "Remember that time you said it would be chaos if there were ghosts floating around everywhere? What were you thinking?"

"They're still bringing that up? You know I took that back!"

"I know that, Sikes. Do I ever know that. Try telling them." I topped up my glass of wine.

"All right," said Landon.

I put down the bottle and turned slowly to look at him. "What?"

"All right. I'll tell them," he said, totally in earnest.

"You're not serious."

"Invoke me during the inquiry. If they come at you with any Dr. Landon Sikes quotes, draw me in, and let me speak for myself."

"Are you aware of how quickly that would get me fired?"

He smiled softly. "You got caught teaching a student to invoke a phantom without their parents' permission. Paulie, I'm pretty sure you're getting fired either way."

"I know. I suppose I've just been lucky until now." I shook my head. "When they implemented the single-purchase law, I was sure it would be temporary."

Landon nodded. "It will be. History will look upon this as a dark time, but a finite one, Paulie. We'll make sure of it."

"Fine. If it comes to that, I'll invoke you. Now, shoo. I'll need these candles."

Sikes stood and nodded. "Knock 'em dead, Paulie," he said. The chair disappeared, and he flashed me a grin and walked straight through the closed door.

Landon's flair for the dramatic could certainly come in handy at the inquest. That would be as good a reason as any to invoke him. I snuffed the candles.

6

The inquiry was not going terribly well. I sat beside George in the front row. A dozen or so parents had come out to tell stories about me and to rant and rave about ghosts and the danger they posed to society. Only one parent had stood up to defend ghost whisperers, and had been booed, talked over, and then asked to leave.

The final parent was having their say. "I'd like to quote Dr. Landon Sikes, an invocation activist, as I'm sure you all know, and a ghost whisperer himself. He said, and I quote, 'If every ghost whisperer were allowed to draw spirits through the veil, it would be chaos. We have to make sure we set limits on when and how many ghosts can be brought over. That means restricting some folks from invoking.' End quote. Evidently, even the most avid supporter of the right to invocation knew that it was dangerous and needed to be restricted.

"Dr. Sikes also said, 'Anyone should be allowed to cross the veil or not as they choose.' Those who don't like to cross the veil, no one is forcing them to do it. Just don't cross if you don't want to!"

A murmur of assent swept the onlookers, and a few members of the board nodded sagely, as if this were good advice. Never mind that something as simple as a middle-school essay would be impossible without consulting spirits, let alone daily life as an adult accessing everything from directions to law records.

As a teenager, I called on my grandmother almost daily. I asked her for the family pastry recipe, how to manage my finances, what my mother looked like as a baby . . . They were all talking as though consulting ghosts were possible to opt out of and still live a full life. No one had any rebuttal at all.

Grace's father, Trustee Jones, stood on the dais, behind the long table of nodding school board members. "In light of the arguments presented here today, I move that so-called ghost whispering should not be taught, or indeed referred to at all in our school, except in the context of historical events, in which case, it should only be taught to students old enough to grasp its dangerous nature."

I shot to my feet. George tugged on my arm. I shook him off and strode forward to the podium.

"Members of the school board," I said. "I dissent. As a trained educator, I believe it is important to honour students' strengths and weaknesses. This isn't always a matter of choice or preference. Why, Dr. Sikes himself said, 'For those who cannot cross the veil, the ability to call to phantoms is of the utmost importance to their lives and livelihoods.' I don't think it can get any clearer than that."

"Ms. Flivor, I think we all know about your biases." His mouth twisted on the word. "You would have us believe that your . . . seances . . . are helping our children learn."

I glared at him. Calling a ghost across the veil had nothing to do with possession or demons. Nothing. And his little smirk said he knew it. I gripped one of the candles in my pocket. "Please explain to me how invoking a spirit across the veil in a candle circle has anything to do with a seance."

He waved my words away. "Next, you'll be calling for exorcisms on children when they want to cross the veil like normal citizens," he said.

I gritted my teeth, and my voice came out as a growl. "Trustee, I can't emphasize enough how utterly you have mischaracterized my position—"

"You were a friend of Dr. Sikes? Correct?"

"Yes, he and I—"

"He would be ashamed and horrified at your suggestions here to-day. Did he not say that seances were a blight upon the past? Exorcisms were a barbaric practice?"

"Trustee, you are the one who brought up—"

"I don't think I want you teaching my child, Ms. Flivor," he said. "I'll do you the courtesy of not enquiring further into the candles that are missing from your classroom. Regardless, I speak for all the parents here when I say—"

I pulled a candle from my pocket, jammed it on the front of the podium and stood the other two on the floor behind me. Before anyone could stop me, I had them lit and stepped out of the way as Landon hopped through the veil.

***

I retreated a step and crossed my arms over my chest. My heart hammered. I'd invoked a spectre in the board meeting, in front of people who thought doing so was akin to holding a seance.

Landon spread his hands on the podium. He couldn't actually touch it, of course, since he was ephemeral, but he was nothing if not familiar with capturing the attention of an audience. He surveyed the board and then the spectators. They had come to watch this drama unfold, so at least I was giving them a show.

"I understand—" said Dr. Landon Sikes. He turned to the trustees. "I understand that my words have often been quoted by this board, and this gathering." If we'd been alone, Landon would have said something like I know I'm utterly quotable, but please see if you can't restrain yourselves, and flashed a mischievous grin. As he surveyed this room, his eyes were flinty. "I am here today to set the record straight."

Someone at the back cleared their throat, and everyone turned to look at them. They froze and huddled in on themself, waving the attention away. Every eye returned to Landon.

"I have maintained, throughout my tenure, that there is nothing wrong with invoking willing spirits." He locked eyes with Trustee Jones. "Nothing." The board member beside Jones fidgeted. "Early in my career, I believed that all movement through the veil in either direction should be monitored, but in my later years, I realized that there was no reason to do so, no call at all to regulate traversals through the veil either for the living or the dead." His gaze swept the room again, and he did allow his expression to soften now. "I understand that I have been out of the conversation for several years. If anyone can explain the reasoning behind restricting the invocation of spectres, I am of course willing to listen. But I must insist that you provide a logical progression for your arguments. I am, after all, a logical person."

No one in the crowd moved.

Jones sat back and crossed his legs. "I should think it was obvious," he said.

"Then consider me to be very dense," said Landon cheerfully. "Please, if you wouldn't mind enlightening me?"

"Anyone with common sense can see that this"—he waved in Landon's direction—"is not natural. If we allow people like Ms. Flivor to commit such flagrant acts in our very meetings, it will only escalate from there. As harmless as something like this little . . . show . . .

may seem, it will do nothing but incite our vulnerable children into dangerous activities, as I have already stated."

"You have stated that, yes," said Landon. "I see no evidence of it."

"You wouldn't," said Grace's father. "You said yourself that you have been absent for years. Plenty of reliable experts agree that pulling spirits across the veil leads to other, more dangerous, activities. I don't feel it's a productive use of our time to engage in such petty showmanship as Ms. Flivor and Dr. Sikes have initiated here today. I move that this meeting be adjourned until order can be restored."

"I see no lack of order," I snapped, gesturing to the silent audience.

"There is also the matter of freedom of movement for the spirits," said Landon.

Jones beckoned a squire and whispered something to him. The squire bustled toward the podium. Toward my candles. I stepped into his path as Landon soldiered on.

"I have consulted with a number of spirits across the veil, and we are all agreed that our ability to cross should remain unimpeded—"

Landon broke off. I turned. He was gone.

In his place, George held a snuffed candle, a tendril of smoke rising from the blackened wick. George shook his head sadly, dropped the candle, turned his back, and left the chamber. Wax spattered the tile.

"There, now," said Trustee Jones. "We shall adjourn to determine the curriculum changes that will be necessary going forward. I don't think we need to deliberate for me to say that, Ms. Flivor, you are no longer needed as a teacher under this board."

7

"That's it?" said Cindy.

Pauline had broken off and knitted two full rows before Cindy had lost her patience.

"That's it," said Pauline. "I never taught with that board again."

"What did you do?"

Pauline shrugged. "This and that."

Cindy sighed. "Was this supposed to be helpful?"

"You wanted to hear the whole story, dear. The rest of it isn't very interesting. All drafting petitions and advocating for legislation."

"So you're saying that as a teacher, I can't do anything?"

Pauline put her knitting aside, and it vanished. "Did you expect a step-by-step guide to equity?"

Cindy flushed. "No, of course not."

"You have so many options," said Pauline, more gently. "So many that I didn't have. If you're looking for permission to try something new, permission to take a risk, then you have mine."

Was that what she'd been looking for? Cindy had always kicked the can down the road, been too busy with her teaching to really focus on extracurriculars, or that's what she'd told herself.

"Plenty of parents would support you, these days," said Pauline. "And so would Landon and I if it comes to it. We have inquest experience." Pauline fought back a smile.

"Very reassuring," said Cindy with a snort. But it was, a little. So many options stretched out before her, events, projects, and a club she'd always wanted to start. A ghost whispering club. She took a lavender candle from her shelf. She had plenty to share with the kids that needed it most.

HER CASTLE
HER HOWL
HER PACK

ELIZABETH F. SHEARLY

CONTENT NOTES

Torture, claiming bites, sexually explicit scenes.

Please see the book's web page at www.elizabethshearly.ca for detailed content notes.

1

"There!" Faris gave the bow one last tug and wrapped her arms around her daughter. Michaela was too old for it, but she leaned into the embrace, anyway.

"What if I don't like him?" She stared out the narrow window frame, and Faris followed her gaze out into the misty distance, over the unending sea of rustling leaves, just unfurled. Here and there, a dark conifer stood out against the pale new growth.

"Don't worry about that, Junebug. Dad and I will take care of it." The breeze licked a strand of her daughter's hair loose, but Faris didn't pin it back.

"We need him to secure the outpost against the forest." The heavy thunk of an axe rhythmically chopping wood floated up to punctuate Michaela's words.

Sandrel shouldn't have mentioned the possible advantages of the alliance to their daughter. *Too late now.* "We have so many options to keep the forest in check. Forcing you to marry someone you hate isn't one of them."

Michaela sighed.

Faris gently turned her daughter so that they were face to face, but Michaela's eyes remained downcast. "I'm serious, Ela. You tell us if he turns into a dipshit when we're not around. I'll have your dad sic the dogs on him."

That got a chuckle out of Michaela, but it died too quickly. She smoothed the front of her dress. "What if he doesn't like me?"

Not like my daughter?

Ela's frown melted into a half-hearted smile; Faris's eyes must have visibly flashed their rage. Still something Faris couldn't control, even after all these years.

"Dogs get sicced on him. Got it." Ela's smile faded, but the frown didn't return. It was something, but Faris's rage didn't abate.

Ela was really asking: *What if he finds out I'm a wolf shifter and thinks I'm a disgusting beast?* That was a distinct possibility. *I'm sure he's not like that*: her daughter would immediately see the comforting words as the lie they were. If the new Lord of Aran River Keep was a raging bigot, Sandrel would probably brush it off. He'd think that Lord Heinrich would come around, once he got to know Michaela. But Sandrel would never go so far as to force the marriage. He wasn't like their parents . . .

Faris's first glimpse of her human betrothed had been at the front of the empty temple, waiting to be joined. Sandrel had been as large as a wolf shifter from home and had caught her gaze to give her a reassuring, if slightly tense, smile.

None of her people had come with her across the sea, so Faris was accompanied by a grizzled woman with an axe on her hip—Julia—who stood silently by as if to head her off if she bolted. But one look at Sandrel and her wolf had—thankfully—given a yip of approval.

After the short ceremony, they'd taken a hired carriage straight to her new home. Julia and her counterpart, a greying man with a quarterstaff—MacIntosh—rode up top, leaving her alone with her new husband. They didn't speak on the journey, except for the few times that Sandrel drew her attention to landmarks they passed.

The carriage had lurched to a halt, and Sandrel hopped down, the tension that had characterized him from the moment they met nowhere in evidence. Someone had called to him, and he'd hollered back, letting out a boisterous laugh. His sword had tapped at his leg as he'd turned back to her, amusement still alight in his previously stoic dark eyes.

"Welcome home," he'd said and handed her down from the carriage.

She had craned her neck to take in the outpost, which stretched up to a tower three stories high. Sandrel had watched her, giving her a moment to absorb her new home.

She'd pasted on a smile. "It's lovely."

The windows up higher were mostly small—probably to keep anyone from falling out. Shifters lived sensibly on, or sometimes under, the ground, but her brother's words had come back to her: *They'll treat you like a beast unless you act like them.* She'd squared her shoulders and prepared to climb the wooden stairs up to the entryway.

"Come in with me, my wife." Sandrel had extended his hand, palm up, and waited. He wasn't trying to make her roll over. Shouldn't he be cementing his dominance over her?

She'd put her hand in his large, warm palm and let him lead her through their cozy kitchen where something at least smelled good enough to eat, not like the fare on the ship, thank the gods. The thought of eating that gruel for the rest of her life had almost made her jump overboard.

Sandrel wasn't stopping for food, though. She gripped his hand more tightly as he led her up a twisting stone stairway, the arrow slits showing the ground retreating below them. He had continued through a doorway—there were windows in this room as well, big ones—and as she'd retreated into the most solid-looking corner, he'd shut the door. The look her new husband had turned on her was familiar to both her and her wolf, who had immediately tensed to spring, to pounce and pin him beneath her—

But he was a human, and humans didn't want beastly wives. They wanted refined ladies, and that's what Sandrel expected from her, a lord's daughter from across the sea. Faris tamped down her wolf, locked it away. Sandrel must have seen some shadow of its longing, though, because he'd stalked toward her slowly.

"I'm not going to hurt you, wife."

"Please, call me Faris." They may have been married by his standards, but they were not yet properly mates. To become mates, she'd have to sink her teeth into his thick neck, bite down until the taste of his blood filled her senses, and—

No, that could never happen. She would never let it happen. The very thought of his reaction—fear, anger, disgust, rejection—had her clamping down ever harder on her wolf.

"Faris." He was close enough now to brush her hair off her neck, and she shuddered. His marking her was somehow just as tantalizing, despite the thought having repulsed her before now—before Sandrel.

"Not the neck, please."

He nodded. "Anything else I should know? I'm not familiar with . . . your culture."

"Just treat me like one of your women."

"Except for the neck?"

"Except for the neck."

He wove his fingers through her hair and brought their lips together. She relaxed into his touch; she wouldn't betray the secret that led to her exile by taking control now. If Sandrel had discarded her as Martin had, she would have been truly alone in a strange land of humans.

All these years later, Sandrel still hadn't rejected her, and her hold on her wolf remained iron clad, never once slipping, especially not with Sandrel.

Ela was well practised in the same art—she'd never even shifted—and she could handle Lord Heinrich in the same way.

Faris kissed Ela's forehead. "Let's get down there. I bet Lord Heinrich and your father are already getting on well."

Michaela smoothed her dress again and nodded, taking a deep breath as if she were about to jump off the tall rock at the lake.

Faris ushered her out before taking a deep breath of her own. The new lord was a complete unknown. He could just as easily install a new outpost lord as he could agree to ally with them in marriage.

2

Revellers already lined the long tables set out for Lord Heinrich's welcome feast when Faris and Ela entered. Lord Heinrich and Sandrel had their heads together, but when they caught sight of the two women over the gathered folks, they both stood. Sandrel was a head taller than Heinrich and twice as broad. He'd been working here on the edge of the forest since before Heinrich existed, and it showed. The young lord ran a smooth hand through his wavy hair and looked down his nose at them.

Faris held Ela's fingers firmly around her arm and guided her up onto the dais. Faris shot Sandrel a smile and bowed her head in a curtsy that Ela echoed. When they rose, Sandrel extended his hand to Faris, but Heinrich just jerked his head at them. Was he trying to bid them come closer?

Whispers flowed through the room behind them, their people forming their own opinions of this new lord of Aran River Keep. The old lord had hardly given them the bare necessities, absorbed as he was in women and drink. It was a wonder he'd died without an heir, though he'd never had the stones to actually choose a wife. Heinrich wore a plain black doublet, brocade though it may be, and a simple silver pendant that marked him as lord of the keep. No rings adorned his fingers, no circlet on his brow. No sword at his waist, either.

Still holding Ela firmly to her, Faris circled the table and stepped onto the dais to take her husband's warm hand. Sandrel clasped Ela's shoulder briefly and guided her around to face her suitor.

Faris took a moment to survey the court gathered before her. Most were artisans and guild members from the outpost or those visiting. Many were farmers or woodcutters, men and women who had taken her in without question when she'd arrived, Sandrel's new wife from across the sea. Yes, they would have opinions about Ela's suitor. A few unfamiliar faces greeted her, men Lord Heinrich had brought with him for protection, their arms marking them plainly. Doubtless, Heinrich had never been this close to the forest before. Faris stepped around Sandrel and focused on her daughter.

"Lord Heinrich, may I present Michaela Lunala of the Gantry Forest Outpost."

"My lord." Ela's voice was barely more than a whisper, her eyes downcast. Thankfully, a hush had fallen over the hall, and she didn't need to repeat herself. A log fell in the fireplace.

Heinrich didn't hide his perusal: his gaze raked her body from her scuffed shoes to the strand of hair that had come loose from its net. Maybe Faris should have pinned it back when she first noticed it. Wishing wouldn't do any good now.

"Delighted," said Heinrich. His accent was as circumscribed as the rest of his appearance. He lifted a hand and waved, earning a quirked eyebrow from Ela, but before she could speak up, a man from the court below strode to his side. "Now that I've seen you, I can deliver my terms."

The man handed Heinrich a folded parchment and shouldered his way back down to the floor. Faris's wolf bared her teeth at him, and Faris didn't blame her: the way he fingered the pommel of his sword when he looked at Ela was equally unsettling to wolf and woman alike.

Heinrich held the parchment out to Sandrel, not sparing a glance for Faris at all. "I'd like to officially request your daughter's hand. Here are my terms. I trust you will find them to be fair. If at all possible, an agreement will be in place before Earl Anders's tournament."

Sandrel took the parchment and broke the Aran River Keep seal. Faris stepped to his shoulder to read it, Sandrel angling the page toward her. Heinrich cleared his throat but wisely didn't comment.

If the two of them had been any other outpost lord and lady, they would likely have had to admit to being illiterate. Sandrel having ended up here as punishment, a younger son of some far-off lord, and her having come from across the sea, the eldest daughter of a wolven lord herself, they were not the typical woodcutters' offspring one would expect to find as Lord and Lady Forest Outpost.

The agreement was standard. Dowry terms, alliance terms . . . lupine heritage. Her stomach dropped, and she swallowed to keep the bile from climbing her throat.

> *Should the Lady show any signs of her lupine heritage*
> *(or progeny likewise), she shall at minimum be returned*
> *(no dowry to be repaid) or, if no other viable progeny*
> *have been produced, disposed of that the Lord may be*
> *free to enter into a new arrangement.*

Faris clenched her fists and squeezed her eyes shut. They would be glowing gold, what with the way her wolf was demanding she rip out Lord Heinrich's throat. *Disposed of?* Her daughter? Her chest rumbled with a growl, and she started as Ela's hand firmly turned her toward the glass window behind the dais. The snapping of the wolf in

Faris's head nearly drowned out Ela's comment about her mother not being used to reading or some other bullshit.

"What the hell is in that contract?" Ela hissed at her, once they were a few paces away in the window nook. The breeze on Faris's face reassured her that her back was turned safely to the room. She opened her eyes.

Ela had gone pale, but her own eyes flickered with sparks of rage, her wolf responding to Faris's in sympathy. Surely Sandrel wouldn't shackle Ela to a contract she clearly had not a single hope of fulfilling? Faris had taught her daughter everything she knew about keeping all signs of the wolf inside her under wraps; even so, there were facets that no one could control.

At a tearing noise, they both spun around, heedless of the risk of revealing their wolf natures to Lord Heinrich, whose back was thankfully turned to them. Sandrel was facing them, though, and he took in the barely contained rage in his wife and daughter before he spoke.

"While I appreciate the time you've taken to bring us this arrangement, my lord, I'm afraid I must decline in the strongest possible terms." Sandrel kept his voice steady, but the rough edge of the final words was evident, at least to Faris.

"Surely you'd like a few days to consider my offer? Until the tournament, perhaps? I think you'll find that I've taken your proximity to my keep and your sterling reputation into account in my ... *reasonable* dowry request. Not to mention the bloodlines of all involved. You come from such an illustrious house. As does your lovely wife." His derision bled through on the last words, but thankfully, he didn't deign to glance at them. Faris's wolf was snarling, hackles raised.

"I will not repeat myself," said Sandrel, his voice finally rising. "You and your men are no longer welcome here. My people and I would be happy to escort you out if you've forgotten the way."

A cacophony of scraping drowned out Heinrich's reply as everyone in the hall stood. Heinrich turned to the two shifters on his way to the floor, his icy gaze taking in Ela, her hands on her hips now, the sparks still dancing in her flinty eyes. Faris looped her arm through her daughter's and stood by her, meeting Heinrich's gaze. His lip curled in a sneer, no doubt quite aware that her glowing eyes were a sign of her *lupine heritage*.

Heinrich leaned in, and a flash of red from the stained glass high in the windows splashed across his cheek. "It's a pity," he hissed, "that your little outpost will be overtaken by the forest so quickly without my support. No matter. I can reclaim it once the monsters have eaten you all."

Sandrel loomed over his shoulder, and Heinrich scurried away. The three of them watched as he beckoned his men, and they all filed out of the hall. Their clatter faded, and in the silence, their people turned back to their lord and lady.

So many people to protect. Perhaps Ela was thinking the same thing, because she furrowed her brow and turned to Sandrel, but he hushed her.

"Not here, either of you."

He was right. They could discuss *lupine matters*—she shuddered at the phrase—in private.

3

They'd explained the contract to Michaela as gently as they could. There was no sense in shielding her from what was likely to be a very gruelling marriage process, judging by this first foray. Ela immediately tried to insist that they let the clause go, but surprisingly, Sandrel was adamant that they would not accept a whiff of bigotry from any prospective marriage candidate. Michaela had flounced off to her tower, no doubt certain that with her parents' decree she stood no chance of ever marrying. Which left Faris and Sandrel in the Lord's Chambers, the wide chamber they used for family only. No one would enter without permission, especially not after that display downstairs.

"She's right, you know," said Faris. She watched her people through the wavy glass windows as they wandered out from the feast and back to their work.

"Is she?" The hard edge that had disappeared when Sandrel was talking to his daughter reappeared.

"You're not going to find a suitable mate who doesn't care about her shifter side."

"You found me, didn't you?" He leaned back in his wide chair, but his feet were planted as though he was ready to spring out of it.

"You were hand-picked by my father. You can't lock her up forever. Having you reject every suitor out of hand for making a comment about lupine this or that is no way for her to live."

At her words, Sandrel finally got to his feet and stalked around the low table to where she was standing by the window. "And you would accept that for her?"

Faris purposefully took a step back when all she wanted to do was get in his face. "If it meant that she lives a real life? Of course I would. She wants to get married, have her own household. Can't you see she's tired of living under us?"

"So you would sell her off to a man who threatened to kill her—*kill her child*—if their eyes so much as shine?"

She turned away. "That's . . . not all being a shifter is, you know."

"No?" He laid a heavy hand on her shoulder. They had never explicitly talked about her shifter nature. Not like this. There had been some discussion at the beginning about what chance their child stood of being a shifter. Sandrel hadn't seemed put off at all when she'd told him that shifters' babies were always shifters themselves. His warmth pressed against her back. "I'd like to see more of what being a shifter is." His low voice growled into her ear, and her wolf responded in kind, hackles raised, ready to meet his challenge. As usual, she fought down her wolf. But he'd said he wanted to see. He snaked a hand around her waist and pulled her hips back against him.

"Sandrel, you don't know what you're asking for." She wanted to pull away. Of course, she'd fantasized about giving in to her wolf with Sandrel, but she wouldn't be able to stand seeing that look in his eyes, the look Martin had given her all those years ago when she'd tried to claim him. And make no mistake, her wolf wanted to claim Sandrel. She could show him just enough to intimidate him into leaving her wolf be. Prove to him that he wouldn't like the wolf part of her. The alpha part.

She turned in his arms. "Here," she said, running a finger down the side of her neck, "kiss me."

His eyes widened, but he obeyed. Sandrel bent and nipped her skin where her finger had rested. A shiver of desire worked its way down her spine. She clamped a hand around his wrist and twisted it behind him as she pressed her body against him, snarling, panting. He buried his free hand in her hair, his eyes alight with desire. She wrapped her other hand around the back of his neck and dragged his face down to hers. He met her in a bruising kiss that left her wolf even more ravenous than before. *Shit*, her wolf was too near the surface. She never acted like this.

She pushed the wolf down and wrenched her fingers apart to release his wrist. But . . . he wasn't pulling away. His newly freed arm wrapped around her waist, and he pulled her to him.

"I think I like your wolf." He didn't give her a chance to answer as he took a turn devouring her mouth.

When they finally broke apart again, Faris panted. "You might like her now, but as I said, you don't know about shifters, Sandrel."

"I want to," he said, kissing down her neck again, and she let him. "Tell me."

A howl tried to work its way up her throat, but she clamped down on it. They didn't need the entire outpost to know that they were, what? Making love? They were man and wife; they had a child, for gods' sake. No, she didn't want them to know about her wolf; those that didn't already. She didn't want them to know how volatile her wolf was, how *dominant*.

Just Sandrel, just within this room . . . She tore at his clothes, unlacing his doublet, his flies; he spun her again and worked her laces loose enough to slide off their clothes until they stood, he in his shirt and she in her chemise.

"You really want this?" said Faris. The wolf still snapped inside, and Sandrel was eyeing her bare legs as if he wanted to eat her up. But shivering here in her underwear, those other eyes came back to her.

Martin, his wolf and hers practically panting for each other, their bodies pressed together, finally about to mate, then her wolf howled, snarled, went for his neck . . . and he'd ducked out of the way, looking down at her as though it were *she* who'd betrayed *him*. *Alpha*. The worst betrayal a female shifter could visit on her mate.

"Faris," Sandrel whispered. "Fuck, I want you so much. You know, your wolf has always called to me. But that's not the look of someone who wants to be here in this moment. Where are you gone off to?"

"I'm not going to bite you." Was she saying it for his benefit or her wolf's?

To his credit, he didn't recoil or blanch. The only sign of his surprise was a lifted eyebrow. "Bite me where?"

"What?" *That's* what he was worried about?

"Where would you bite me?" Somehow, his eyes still snapped with desire.

No, he couldn't want that. "A claiming bite is on the side of the neck or the shoulder."

His breath went a little ragged, and the pulse beating in his neck sped up.

Or maybe he could? "You'd . . . like that?"

He rumbled in his chest, a sound so like a growl that her own howl tried to make its way up her throat again. "You're damned right I would."

They had to slow down. This was all going too fast. She had never let her wolf into the bedroom at all, let alone let it take over. She shook her head. "Not now."

"Fine, not now. No claiming bite today, if you don't want to. But someday?"

Faris trailed her fingers down the side of his neck, and he tilted his head to give her access. He wasn't trying to placate her. He actually wanted it. He wanted her mark on him, for the world to know that he was hers, forever.

Her entire body shuddered. She took a deep breath, threw back her head, and howled, the force of it making her back bow, her body shake, and her throat raw.

When she snapped her head back down, he was on his knees before her. He pushed her into the chair at her back and hooked one of her knees over his shoulder, then licked up to the apex of her thighs. She gathered his shirt, and he drew back to yank it over his head and toss it on the floor where the rest of their clothes were strewn, then buried his head between her legs again.

Sandrel had done this many times before, but never before had she felt like an alpha being worshipped by her mate. She hooked her other leg over the arm of the chair, and he wrapped his arms beneath her hips. Faris gathered a handful of his hair in her fist, and growls bubbled up through her chest as she ground herself against his mouth and finally tipped over the edge. She barely took a moment to indulge in the aftershocks before sliding her chemise over her head and toppling him backwards to the rug. She ended up full-length beside him, his hardness pressed to her hip.

He slid his knees between hers and nestled his hips between her thighs. Normally, she'd let him. She'd take whatever he gave her, soft and gentle or urgent and rough, but not today. Her legs wrapped around his waist and flipped them so that she sat astride his hips. She ground her wetness along his length, and he grinned up at her.

"I'm starting to really love your wolf." His grin widened; her eyes had flashed golden, no doubt.

Sandrel snaked his hands up to her hips, but she grumbled and clasped his wrists in one of her hands. He raised his eyebrows as he tugged and found that he couldn't get free. They had never discussed her shifter strength, and she'd been careful to hide it from him as much as she could. And so they'd never discussed pinning.

"Is this all right?"

He chuckled and thrust his hips up to meet her. "More than all right."

She used her free hand to line them up and took him in one stroke. She howled again, this time triumphant. Her mate was hers and hers alone. He would always be hers. No one could take him from her. Anyone who tried would end up gutted and hung from their walls. She was strong, she was fierce, and none could best her. She rode him, rolling her hips in time to his thrusts, and finally, the moment arrived. That one glittering moment. Maybe if he hadn't tilted his head just so, exposing his pulse to her, maybe if she hadn't lost herself so completely . . . his voice was so quiet that she was practically reading his lips:

"Please," he breathed.

"Please what?" Her words were almost cruel, with an edge of velvet.

"I want you to claim me." His voice was stronger now, a rumble deep in his chest.

She froze. *You're forgetting I said no claiming bites.* That was what she should say. But she didn't want to, couldn't make the words come out. Claiming him would make it obvious that she was an alpha, at least to anyone who knew a thing about shifters. It would be humiliation for him to carry her mark. That was what she'd always been taught. But what did it matter here? No one even knew what shifters were. He wasn't ashamed. He wasn't lowering himself.

He writhed beneath her, thrusting up as she held still.

She had to make him understand what he was asking for. "The mark won't fade."

He made that grumbling growl again. "Damn right, it won't. If it does, you'll mark me again."

Her whole body shuddered, and her hips jerked into motion again, gradually finding her rhythm as she rode him, this time releasing his wrists and bending forward. "Everyone will know," she breathed in his ear.

He thrust up to meet her, staccato jerky thrusts.

Fuck! She bent to his neck, her wolf urging her to sink her teeth into the skin beneath his ear, where everyone could see. She had the presence of mind to lick down to where his neck curved into his shoulder, opened her jaw wide, and sank her teeth into his flesh. Her whole body tightened, and with a few final snaps of her hips, she crested and came apart.

He groaned and pounded up into her once, twice, and stilled.

Faris licked Sandrel's wound, helping it to close over. For the first time, perhaps in her whole life, her wolf curled up, tail over nose, and slept.

4

The rest of the hall was empty but for two maids scattering fresh rushes over the floor and chatting quietly. Sandrel sat at the table against the wall, beneath the dark torch brackets. When MacIntosh and Julia arrived and set the torches aflame, Faris scattered their map pieces on the table, and they silently righted them all and placed them proper distances apart. Sandrel pulled Faris into his lap, and Julia gave her a sardonic look.

If Faris had thought marking her mate would put distance between them, she was dead wrong. Sandrel didn't seem to want to let her out of his sight. His doublet more than covered the mark, but not only had the entire household heard her howls, his changed demeanour was apparent to anyone with eyes.

While she'd always been included in discussions about the outpost, Sandrel had not always pulled her onto his lap and pinned her to his chest as he was doing now.

"Without supplies from Aran River Keep, our own will run dry before the harvest." Captain MacIntosh shook his mane of salt-and-pepper hair out of his face and eyed his lord and lady but said nothing about their semi-compromising position.

Faris peeled Sandrel's arm away and leaned over the map covering their table. "What about the summer crops?"

"We'll have quite a time keeping the fields cleared without support." Julia, in charge of the efforts to keep the forest at bay, stood with one hand resting on the head of her wood axe. She was right. No matter how many trees they felled, how many saplings they pulled, the forest seemed able to take over land, inch by inch, overnight.

"We need help," rumbled Sandrel.

"And we can forget about getting any from Aran River Keep," said Faris. Their list of possible allies was short, but it did exist. For now. Lord Heinrich had no doubt already begun turning everyone within his reach against them.

"Perhaps someone further afield?" Captain MacIntosh gave them a significant look. He was well aware of both Sandrel's and Faris's family connections.

Faris shook her head. "Neither my family nor Lord Sandrel's are likely to come to our aid. As you might recall, 'Good riddance' was the blessing given at our wedding."

Sandrel squeezed her leg. "There may yet be a way to secure aid. Earl Anders's tournament at Castle Redcliff will be a chance to drum up support for our cause, show any potential allies that we are capable and that any supplies they provide will be put to good use."

"Not to mention undermine Heinrich's efforts to paint us as incapable of holding the outpost," said Faris.

"I think we're all aware Anders wants the match between Ela and Heinrich to go forward," said Julia.

"Anders can find another way to ingratiate Heinrich to the people of his earldom," said Sandrel.

Faris cuddled back into his arms. "And you'll tell him that if he presses you?"

"Without hesitation." He kissed her.

MacIntosh struck his quarterstaff on the floor. "Very well, Julia and I will hold the outpost while you are away, never fear."

Sandrel would enter the tournament, win as usual, and prove their strength, while Faris worked behind the scenes in the salons and gardens to garner support through the women's influence over their powerful husbands. That's how they'd always done things, and it hadn't failed them yet.

5

"Horses hate me," said Ela, her mount dancing beneath her. Sandrel chuckled and sidled his mount up next to hers. He soothed her horse as Faris trailed them down the narrow road between the hedgerows. Ela might have Faris's wolf nature, but she had Sandrel's single-mindedness. It had been no trouble at all for her to convince her parents to bring her along. If she found a suitor at this tournament, someone she was interested in, then they might widen their net of allies. Faris and Sandrel had opted not to mention that avenue to Ela, but she'd come to them herself with it, in the end, and they'd both been equally unable to turn her down. Ela was grown and fully capable of making her own choices about such things. Not that either of her parents would allow her to enter into an unhappy arrangement simply to secure the future of the outpost.

Ela tried to imitate the cooing sound Sandrel made to her horse, and the beast tossed its head and nickered. Faris patted her own mount's neck. She'd made her peace with Stalwart long ago; it was a sign of the control she had over her wolf that the horse was calm beneath her. Ela hadn't ever had a chance to make peace with her own: Ela never even shifted, let alone learned to work with her wolf side. They should practise, one day. Then again, Faris herself would need to shift, something she hadn't done since arriving on this continent. Letting the wolf take over would mean handing it the reins and standing back to see what it would do, and there was no telling what that might be. Letting her wolf goad her into claiming her own husband was one thing, but shifting entirely? Her wolf had been caged so long, it would no doubt go into a frenzy with freedom. Not that it would hurt anyone. Unless they tried to hurt her or her family. Or threatened to.

A vision flashed of her wolf ripping Heinrich's throat out, blood filling its mouth, tearing into his belly, his entrails steaming in the morning chill. Yes, her wolf would certainly make that a reality if Heinrich was around. Threatening her child had been very foolish, proving unquestionably that the man had no experience whatsoever with shifters.

Before her, Ela had succeeded in calming her mount, though it still blew out a breath in protest, which Stalwart echoed.

"Hey, now, don't go getting ideas," she muttered to him. Best to save the visions of gruesome murder by wolves for another time when she couldn't be thrown by a jittery animal ten times her size.

They joined Kingdom Road about midday, and their pace slowed considerably as they slipped into the flow of carts and foot traffic on their way to watch the tourney. A few folks spotted Sandrel and waved—he'd won three of the last four tournaments, and he had plenty of admirers. Enough, in fact, that they could have forced their way through the throng—indeed, they pulled to the side of the road a few times to let other lords pass before they reached Castle Redcliff.

The walls were lit by the slanting late-afternoon light, pennants snapping from the ramparts as the evening breeze picked up.

"There's ours!" Ela pointed like a child, and Faris and Sandrel shared an indulgent look. They came to the tournament every year, but this was the first time Ela had been here since she was a child, opting in her teenage years to stay home and mope about the outpost.

Indeed, Gantry Forest Outpost's silver tree on a field of green floated over to the left, alongside Aran River Keep's twisting river on a black ground. The blue of Rockery Island, the greens of a few forest outposts further down the border: Shield, Margin, Tompson, Grant. Then, the red of Castle Redcliff itself, its banner so large it barely flapped in the light breeze. There were a dozen, all nearby settlements that attended the tournament every year. The intention was to strengthen ties, and this event was ostensibly to welcome Lord Heinrich to the earldom.

No matter what Lord Heinrich might want, Earl Anders would not deal gently with infighting between his sworn men. The tournament itself served as an outlet: wrestle your enemy to the ground and release any tensions between you to clear the air and work together once more. Lord Heinrich was new to the Redcliff Earldom, but he would be expected to take his place among the lords of the territory. Marrying Ela had been a part of that, but he could find another way.

They rode through the wide archway under the outer walls with the rest of the crowd, which dissipated as they ventured toward the castle. Their habitual inn stood in the shadow of the castle's walls and always welcomed them; it was good business to house the tournament champion.

They walked their horses through the open innyard doors and dismounted. A farrier kept shop on the other side of the yard, and a ringing of hammer on anvil and waves of hot air from the forge greeted them.

A groom, not even old enough to shave, popped out of the inn, already apologizing for the wait, but Faris waved him away. She led Stalwart to a stall in the inn's stables and cared for him herself.

Once the horses were situated, they just had time to change for the welcome feast. Faris dressed herself and slipped into Ela's room to help her on with her dress.

"I'll keep my eye out for likely allies," said Ela. "Anyone who can help supply the outpost is a candidate."

Faris paused. Had she really taught her daughter to be so mercenary? She resumed buttoning the back of her bodice. "Remember to look with your heart as well as your eyes, Junebug."

"Of course." But her tone was far too dismissive for the gravity of a marriage alliance commitment.

She spun her daughter so she could look her in the eyes. "Really, Ela. If we wanted to shoehorn you into an unhappy marriage for security, we would have accepted Heinrich."

"I know."

Faris sighed and dropped her hands from Ela's shoulders. Her honourable streak could rival her father's.

A tap on the door made both of them turn. Sandrel.

"We're ready," Faris called.

Sandrel eased the door open. The way his face lit up when he saw them would never get old.

The feast was to be in the castle itself, and they joined the stream of merrymakers crossing the castle keep's wide flagstones, torches lighting their way to the huge oaken doors, thrown wide for the occasion.

Heinrich's broad-shouldered glowering man loomed from the shadows. "A word?"

Ela shrank against Faris's side.

Two other knots of people had stopped in the keep, their laughter floating on the evening breeze. No one would remark on them chatting with their neighbours before the feast. Faris nodded, Sandrel a solid presence at her back.

"Thank you, Sepp." Lord Heinrich melted out of the shadows before them. Northern lords were so dramatic. No wonder Sandrel had been eager to escape to the outpost.

"Lord Heinrich, good to see you here," said Sandrel.

"Indeed. At our last meeting, I offered you a few days to consider my proposal, and I'm honouring that gesture now. Announcing our engagement tonight would be ideal, if you're amenable. The entire tourney will be a celebration of our alliance."

How could he possibly have misconstrued their refusal? Faris didn't even try to keep the impatience from her voice. "Lord Heinrich—"

"Do keep in mind that I have avoided sharing any information that might harm your family's—or the lady's—reputation. If you refuse me, I will have no such compunction."

Ela's grip pinched Faris's arm, but she continued, "Lord Heinrich. I'm fairly sure we made our position clear at our last meeting. Now, shall we go in together as neighbours and enjoy the feast?"

Heinrich whirled and stalked across the flagstones alone, his heels clicking, and disappeared into the castle.

"Mum . . ." murmured Ela.

"Just keep your head," said Sandrel and kissed Ela's forehead.

"But he threatened to badmouth our family—"

"Faris!" called a voice from behind her.

Faris was already putting on a smile as she turned to Lady Ellory of Margin Outpost. They wouldn't have any time to talk among themselves tonight. Their focus would be on gaining what allies they could—and keeping the ones, like Ellory, that they already had. Heinrich would make even that perilous.

6

This was it. As predicted, Sandrel had dealt efficiently with all comers, throwing them to the ground without much trouble, toying with some before going in for the kill—metaphorical though it might be. Faris's wolf grinned, tongue lolling. Her mate was the strongest here, the one who would triumph over all others through brute strength. He used plenty of cunning as well, but his thick shoulders and solid thighs were all her wolf was concerned about.

Lord Heinrich sat across the ring from Faris and Ela. Instead of entering the tournament himself, he had nominated a surrogate and, thus, sat unmussed and prim among the spectators. A canopy shaded them, but left the afternoon sun glistening off Sandrel's forehead. His shirt clung to his back, making his rippling muscles visible as he'd thrown all comers to the ground. Heinrich's substitute, Sepp, was in much the same condition after his last match. They were the only two left. Sepp approached the stands where his lord sat, and Heinrich bent to mutter something to him. Sandrel turned to Faris and gave a salute, his grin sparkling and making her grin in return. She blew him a kiss, and he winked back, and butterflies filled her stomach, still, after all these years.

"Mum, stop. You're grown adults, not teenagers." Ela elbowed her and glanced meaningfully at the young man sitting next to her, heir to some other outpost.

Faris just laughed. Win or lose, everyone could see that Sandrel was fighting his own battles, not sitting comfortably in the stands while someone else took on his work for him. That would be enough to gain them allies aplenty. The feast tonight would determine once and for all who they could name among their supporters.

Ela bent to whisper so her companion wouldn't hear. "You're not worried about the rumours?"

Sandrel and his opponent bowed to one another, Sandrel with a flourish, the other man with but a tilt of his head. Always playing the crowd was her husband. He might run a tiny outpost now, but he'd been raised in the backbiting courts up north.

"The rumours about what?" said Faris.

The two men in the ring circled each other. Sepp grabbed him by the collar, and Sandrel slipped out of the other man's grapple.

"The shifter ones that Heinrich started."

Sepp tried to lock Sandrel's arm but got a handful of shirt instead, and Sandrel slipped away again. Heinrich's man made a dodge of his own, but Sandrel pinned one of his arms, and they teetered, almost off their feet.

"Junebug, they can see that none of it is true. They've spent three days with us. They know that we're shifters, but we have comported ourselves as refined—"

The crowd roared as Sandrel shouldered Heinrich's man to the ground, but still Sepp had a handful of his shirt, and the force of Sandrel's blow tore it at the collar so it hung off him.

A ripple went through the crowd, a hush falling, filled with whispers. Ela's companion turned to them, wide-eyed. Sandrel spun, his victory not having been met with the uproarious cheers he'd become accustomed to. There, for all to see, was the still purple-and-crimson bite mark on his shoulder. Not something he could have sustained in this tournament as no weapons were involved. No, the crowd was turning from Sandrel to . . . Faris.

Heinrich's smug smile imprinted itself on her, and Faris clamped her eyes shut, but it was too late. Her eyes had flashed out her rage. Heinrich had instructed his man to reveal her claiming bite: Sepp hadn't grabbed Sandrel's shirt by accident; he'd been intending to tear it away. He probably hadn't even cared whether he won or lost, as long as he revealed the *barbarism* of the shifter Lady of Gantry Outpost.

The crowd murmured again, and Ela gripped her arm. Her suitor's mumbled excuses and retreating steps penetrated Faris's rictus. She couldn't keep her eyes shut; she had to see what was going on. The moment her eyes fluttered open, Sandrel held her gaze and jerked his ruined shirt over his head. He wasn't scrambling to cover her bite; he didn't even look ashamed. Her husband stalked toward her, and Faris's wolf paced in its cage. She stood, Ela's hand falling away, and stepped forward on numb feet to meet him at the rope dividing the ring from the spectators. His palm on her lower back was firm, and he drew her to him and kissed her, taking his time so that there could be no mistake. He was not ashamed of his shifter wife; he was claiming her just as surely as she'd claimed him.

Faris burrowed her fingers into his hair and pulled him to her, her wolf revelling in this display of possession.

Finally, they broke apart. Faris danced her fingers gently over her bite on his shoulder, and he shuddered, his smile sharp.

"Unless you want to give them a proper show, I suggest not doing that again."

Faris bit down her wolf howl. Claim one another for real in front of the entire earldom? No, that would only prove Lord Heinrich right. Such things were not done in polite society.

"Tournament champion," said Faris.

"Only because you weren't entered. I'm beginning to think you could take us all down." Sandrel's smile still played over his lips.

"Now, that wouldn't be very ladylike of me."

Sandrel's laugh seemed to break the spell over the silent crowd, and they cheered. For the moment, the tide of public opinion had turned in their favour. Once the reality of that claiming bite sunk in, their acceptance was far from assured.

The victory feast in a few hours would be their last chance to cement their alliances. They meandered back to their inn, half the people they passed stopping them to offer congratulations. Ela barely spoke, her eyes glittering with her pent-up rage. Clearly, she didn't approve of her parents' public antics, but what had been the alternative? Hiding the bite? Lying about it? *Not biting him in the first place.* That was how they had survived in this world until now—

Ela made to flounce off to the inn by herself, but Faris gave Sandrel one last kiss and trailed after her. There were those who would try to retaliate against Sandrel for their defeat, and Ela wasn't prepared to shift and defend herself as Faris would.

All she got for her trouble was Ela's door slammed in her face once they arrived safely at the inn. Faris extracted a promise from Ela to scream as loudly as she could if anyone so much as knocked on her door, and then she retreated to her room to change.

By the time Sandrel made it back, Faris had already dressed. She stood by the window, letting the breeze dull her anxiety, while Sandrel splashed into his bath by the fire, the silence stretching between them until he was done.

"I still don't regret it." Sandrel stood, dripping, and plucked the sheet from the rail by the fireplace.

"How can you not? Our people are in danger. If Lord Heinrich ousts us and sets up some distant cousin from up north to combat the forest . . ."

Sandrel wrapped his arms around her, and she pressed her ear to his bare chest, letting the rhythm of his heartbeat soothe her. His voice rumbled through his body to hers.

"He would need support from Earl Anders to oust us without repercussion."

"And the earl will be swayed by his outpost lords and ladies, the very people Heinrich is winner over." She pulled away, and he squeezed her shoulder before sorting out his clothes.

"They've known us for years. Heinrich is a stranger."

His smiling eyes tried to tell her everything was going to turn out. They would gather allies at the feast; Sandrel would be celebrated as the winner of the tournament; Ela would find some young, ambitious lad to moon over; and they would ride home tomorrow with the assurance of allies by their side, no matter how Lord Heinrich tried to bring them down.

Faris shook her head. "You're naïve."

Sandrel's eyebrows practically got lost in his hairline. "I've lived longer than you have."

"But you've never lived as a shifter, Sandrel. We may have put them off baying for blood today, but we haven't changed their minds. Seeing my mark . . ." She ran her fingertips over his shirt where the mark lay hidden.

He rumbled deep in his chest. That growling sound that called to her wolf.

"My wolf loves that sound."

"Why do you think I make it?" He smiled down at her, gazing at her lips. Trying to distract her.

She pulled away and paced back to the window. "It's not just me at stake here, my love. It's our people, our daughter. How many men out there would let a woman claim them?"

"More than you might think." He pressed up behind her and rested his chin on the top of her head.

"You are biased, Sandrel." But she smiled in spite of herself.

Their window overlooked the inn's courtyard, smoke from the farrier's forge marking a trail that reached up to the rooftops only to be whisked away by the evening breeze. The rhythmic tapping of his hammer was reminiscent of the constant axe and saw noises of home. Distant chatter and laughter drifted over the castle wall—the feast was already beginning, and everyone would want to enjoy this last night of revelry.

Ela's suitor had rabbited at the very sight of the bite mark Sandrel bore. At best, it would scare off the weakest prospects and draw in those, like Sandrel, who weren't intimidated by a wolf shifter. If any such suitors existed. Faris relaxed into Sandrel's arms. Best to get this feast over with, see what they could salvage, and get back home.

A horse screamed, and Sandrel's arm tightened around Faris's waist. Two black-cloaked figures crossed the courtyard below them, the glint of metal at their sides. Faris took a deep breath, the scent of blood filling her nostrils as the figures looked up and their eyes met. Sepp. He muttered to the figure beside him, and they disappeared into the inn below.

"They're here for us," said Faris.

"Either way, better to disappear."

The drop from their window would be too far to fall; besides, they had to get Ela. Faris cracked the door, the jingle of Sandrel buckling on his sword-belt the only break in the quiet. The deserted hallway led to the stairs, but that was where their attackers—if indeed that's what they were—would come from. Faris crept into the corridor, Sandrel at her heels. She tapped once on Ela's door and tried the handle. Locked. *Good girl.*

"Michaela, open up." Faris didn't raise her voice; Ela's shifter hearing would pick it up easily, attuned as she was to her mother's timbre. The lock clicked over, and the door swung open.

"Mum? What's going on? I heard a scream. And the smell . . ."

Faris ducked inside. Sandrel followed and turned the key.

"We have to leave, Junebug—" She turned to Michaela.

Ela was shivering, panting, her eyes glowing softly in the dim lamplight. The scent of blood wafted through the window.

"Oh, Ela, your wolf wants to take you. She wants to keep you safe." Faris took her daughter in her arms and held her close. She looked over Ela's shoulder at Sandrel, who had his ear pressed to the wall. They could wait until the men were in her and Sandrel's room—no doubt that's where they were headed—and try to shut them in, but Faris hadn't pulled the key from the door on their way out, and Sandrel hadn't stopped to do it either. They could duck into the hallway, but Ela's growling whines would not go unnoticed. The men would be on their heels the moment they stepped through the doorway.

Faris peered out the window again. No human could make that jump unscathed, and they couldn't leave Sandrel behind. Even a shifter, especially one as inexperienced as Ela, would have trouble landing it. At least, in human form.

"Ela, I want you to give in to your wolf."

Michaela went rigid in her arms and pulled away. "What? No! You always told me not to shift. I've never—"

"I know you've never shifted before, Junebug, but this is life and death."

Sandrel held her gaze. "I'll hold them off."

"You will do no such thing. I didn't give you that bite just to abandon you at the first opportunity. If I wanted to fight, you think I'm not capable of handling myself? What happens if we kill those men? You think we'll get support from any of the other lords then? No. We're running, my mate." Her wolf had its hackles raised, ready to pounce. Faris bodily turned Ela around and pulled the end of her laces, efficiently loosening them enough for Ela to pull off her dress. A sharp rapping on the door made Ela start, her whining growing louder.

Sandrel was already working on Faris's laces before she even finished with Ela. Danger pounded through her veins, the thought of finally shifting whipping her wolf into a frenzy. She had to focus. Plan first, shift after.

"I'll shift first. Ela, follow me over. Sandrel, you'll have to ride. I'll take you out the window, though."

"Take me out? I'm twice your size, my love."

"Not in my wolf form," said Faris and let her wolf take her. She staggered sideways and caught herself on the dresser, sending the entire oval mirror crashing to the ground. Shouting sounded from the other side of the door as her wolf took over. In a flash, Ela had shifted as well and tumbled out the window.

The door splintered, and Sepp and the other man came through, training a crossbow on Sandrel. Her mate. Her wolf acted before she could rein it in, clamping its jaws on the man's arm and shaking the crossbow out of his grip to clatter onto the floor. Sepp shouted something, but Ela's yip from the courtyard below had Faris wrestling to control her wolf. *My family.* Sandrel was leaning out the window, and Faris snapped down at him. He stared up at her wolf, wide eyed.

But when she ducked her head, he didn't hesitate to grab fistfuls of her fur and hold tight as she wriggled through the open window and landed softly on the ground beside Ela.

Her daughter froze, snout lifted, nostrils working. Faris sniffed the air herself, the rich scent of blood filling her entire being. Sandrel let her go and pounded into the stable, Faris at his heels. A horse whinnied and a bang and crack on the wall to Faris's side told her they had to get out of here. The horses were spooking, and they'd hurt themselves trying to kick down their stalls.

Sandrel stood rigid, looking down into a stall at the end. The whole place reeked of blood: the horses had already been spooked *before* two giant wolves showed up in their midst.

Stalwart lay in a dark shining pool. When Faris poked her head around the door, he tried to raise his head, and he whickered, most likely in terror, the only sound he had the energy to make.

"They're all dead," said Sandrel. "Besides, no horse will run alongside you two. Go on. I'll find my own way."

Faris growled at him and jerked her head toward her own back. No self-respecting shifter, let alone an alpha, would ever allow a human to use them as a mount, but leaving her marked mate behind was not an option even her wolf would consider. Sandrel ran a hand up the side of her neck, and she crouched lower, trying to urge him on board without words.

He grabbed handfuls of her thick grey fur again and hauled himself all the way up this time, swinging a leg over. Faris jerked her head at Ela, and they padded back into the courtyard. Sepp held the crossbow out the upper window, but they were already moving too quickly, and the bolt he shot thunked into the wood of the stable wall behind them. Faris growled and snapped at him and then turned tail and shot out of the courtyard into the town proper, horses rearing and screaming all around, Ela panting at her tail. Sandrel's breath was smooth in her ear, and the feel of his knees squeezing her behind the shoulders was comforting as she ducked through the main gates and across the fields surrounding the castle.

They couldn't go home, not right now. They would be followed, probably by castle guards after that little escape, and bringing the guard straight back to their outpost would endanger their people. A few allies had stood by them, even knowing all these years that Faris was a shifter. Seeing it with their own eyes, however, was completely different, and it was likely that an armed mob would be gathered to follow them. Which meant that they would endanger anyone they came in contact with . . . that is, if the people they came in contact with didn't simply shoot them on sight.

There was only one place monsters could go to regroup: the forest. Faris veered right, toward where the trees loomed in the growing shadows, strange and dark and somehow alive.

7

The two wolves padded through the surprisingly thin under-growth, Faris slightly ahead carrying Sandrel. Even Lord Heinrich's men wouldn't follow them in, let alone those more familiar with the forest, but as soon as they emerged, they'd be in danger again. Now that they'd provoked the ire of the lords, it would be difficult to quench.

Faris's wolf panted, picking up on her distress, and Sandrel smoothed a hand through her fur. Could they stay in the forest, at least for a while, until they came up with another plan? As long as her family remained nearby, they'd be safe from the forest's monsters; she could take anything that attacked them. But they had no supplies. Sandrel was in his shirtsleeves and breeches, and in a couple of hours, come nightfall, he would be freezing. Ela had only just shifted for the first time, and she'd be itching to return to her vulnerable human form, but she had no clothes at all.

Faris sniffed the air and caught a hint of . . . something. Earthy and deep, something familiar that called to her.

"Keep a weather eye for bears," said Sandrel. "There are scratches on that tree, and I noticed some a while back as well."

Bear.

Faris loped to the tree his weight had shifted toward as he'd pointed, the scratches clear even to her wolf eyes, the scent of bear filling her nostrils. But it wasn't just a bear. A bear shifter.

The trail wasn't exactly fresh, and Faris was very rusty on her tracking, but they were definitely moving toward the bear shifter. Not that they could be sure of their reception, but if it was between an angry human mob and an unknown bear shifter living deep in the forest . . . She followed the bear shifter's trail.

The scent of shifters grew as they progressed deeper into the forest, and not only bear: badger, crow, even squirrel, fox . . . was that a hummingbird? But no flash of a tail or call of a bird caught Faris's attention until a bonfire flickered through the trees. The scream of a blue jay made Sandrel jolt on her back.

"There's a settlement in the forest," he murmured.

Faris just carried him closer. Ela's head hung between her shoulder blades, either from exhaustion or from wariness. The undergrowth was minimal everywhere in the forest, but the ground around the bonfire had been swept clear of fallen branches and leaves. The surrounding trees cast iron-black shadows that could be hiding anyone.

Sandrel slid off Faris's back and approached the fire beside her. He shivered and stretched his hands toward the flames, while Faris lifted her head and sniffed the air again. Fox shifter.

Ela yelped, scratching at a tree trunk. A tree trunk that was so close to its neighbour that not even Sandrel would be able to pass between them, let alone a wolf. In fact, were all the trees closer together? Where was the space they'd entered through? The trees closed in, pushing them towards the firepit, and Sandrel cursed and kicked dirt onto the fire, to no avail. Faris shifted, shivering from the cold sweat that suddenly coated her back.

She knelt by Ela, who was still in her wolf form, on her belly in the dirt, her side pressed to the uncompromising trees.

"Shift, Junebug. Shift and we'll climb." The tree trunks reached smoothly up into the darkness, not a branch in sight. Barely enough space remained to keep Ela's paws from being singed. She needed to shift, but with the flames so close, she wouldn't be able to.

A fox shifter had been nearby; she'd scented it. If they were still about, maybe they could do something.

"Fox! My daughter doesn't know how to shift! Stop this!"

Ela whined and curled her paws under her belly. The trees didn't retreat, but they halted.

A little red fox slipped between two trunks and shifted.

The young fox shifter retained the fox's red hair, cut shaggy around his face, and he gathered clothes from behind him to pull on: a tunic and breeches, homespun but clean and well mended. He rummaged in the gap again and pulled a bag through, which he tossed to Faris, who drew out similar garb and yanked it on.

Sandrel drew his sword and levelled it at the erstwhile fox, who raised his hands and stepped back.

"You've trapped us here," said Faris.

Ela still shivered against the tree trunks hemming them in.

"Is it true she can't shift?"

Faris laid a hand on Ela's quivering shoulder, and she whined. "It's true."

"We don't mean you harm."

"The fire notwithstanding," said Sandrel, but he lowered his sword.

Ela panted, fully whining now, her snout an inch off the ground, shoulder blades sharp in the air. Faris laid a hand on her muzzle.

"Let the wolf go, Junebug. We're safe here."

Ela whined again.

"She's never shifted before?" The fox shifter watched her, and the fire lit his face in stark profile.

"It's her first time."

"I'm happy to lend a hand, if you like. The first time can be hard to manage, especially if you're grown. I've helped a few before, when they come to us as adults."

Ela lay down and belly crawled toward the fox shifter. Faris bit back a recrimination. This was not the time for a lecture on dominance structures. Her daughter was clearly suffering, and anyone who could help was welcome.

The fox shifter crouched before Ela, who had rolled onto her back before him. Sandrel put an arm around Faris and gathered her close, either for comfort or to keep her from fighting the boy away from their only daughter's show of submission.

"There now, you're safe, little wolf." Ela's wolf form wasn't as large as Faris's, certainly, but calling the huge black wolf before him *little* was absurd.

She whined and licked his hand.

The fox shifter stripped again, shifted, and the little fox nuzzled Ela. She sniffed him, rose to her feet, shook her entire body, and touched noses with the smaller fox. In a blink, the two of them regained their human forms, their hands clasped between them. The two breathed in tandem for three breaths, eyes locked.

Her stark-naked daughter held hands with a strange naked man in the middle of the forest. Faris snatched up a long tunic for Ela and threw it over her head. When Ela dropped the fox's hands, he seemed to come to his senses and pulled his own clothes back on, then cleared his throat, glancing at Sandrel and Faris.

"Thanks for your help," Sandrel said.

Faris stepped forward. "Yes, thank you. We don't currently have anywhere to go." There was no sense in hiding anything from this shifter. They needed his help, and if he wasn't willing to give it, better to find out now.

The fox shifter flushed and waved away their thanks. "Call me Peter. And you are?"

"Lord and Lady of Gantry Forest Outpost."

Peter's face darkened. "Outpost."

If this shifter lived with others in the forest, could they be the "monsters" said to inhabit the forest? If that was the case, no one here would be inclined to help them.

"Come on." Peter turned away and marched out of the clearing. "Biyana wants to talk to you." The trees had silently resumed their positions, ringing the fire.

Sandrel raised his eyebrows at Faris, but it was no surprise that the shifters' leader already knew that they were here: she'd smelled more than one bird among the shifter scents. Someone had no doubt already reported their presence back, most likely to the bear shifter, which must be this Biyana. Hopefully, the fact that they were shifters in need would outweigh any potential animosity from their status as Lord and Lady Outpost.

They followed Peter over the crest of the next hill to a larger clearing dominated by a tree as big around as Gantry Outpost. An opening split its side, and firelight poured onto the bare ground before it. Turf houses dotted the clearing, but none of the shifters Faris could scent were in evidence.

Peter brought them into the tree through the huge archway, big enough for a bear, and Faris paused. Dozens of shifters were gathered here, all staring at them. Faris adjusted her borrowed tunic and kept her chin up as Peter introduced them around the entire room. The shifters nodded to them, each in turn, no one making a move to establish any hierarchy between themselves and the newcomers. Not yet, at least. A firepit crackled in the centre of the hall, and a deceptively small woman, considering that she was likely the bear shifter, Biyana, sat on a high seat overlooking the entire room. Finally, they came to stand before the bear shifter.

"You've marked your human mate, but he has not marked you," said Biyana.

Faris recoiled a step. Shifters were known for their straightforward natures, but how could she even see the mark through Sandrel's shirt? And why would a human mark a shifter? And an alpha no less. Such things weren't done . . . still, to bear Sandrel's mark . . . the idea was unsettlingly enticing.

"Don't look so shocked. You'll find we don't stand on ceremony here. And you, young one. How was your first shift?"

"Um, weird," said Ela, eyes fixed on the ground.

Peter took a single step toward Ela before he stopped himself.

"I understand you're looking for sanctuary here. We have a policy of taking in all shifters. Normally, we would be reluctant to take in the man, but he is marked, and by an alpha, no less."

Sandrel should probably have been surprised, looked angry or betrayed. They'd never discussed her alpha status, not even during the marriage negotiations so long ago. But Sandrel just glanced at her questioningly. Maybe he didn't know what her status as a female alpha meant among wolf shifters? Then again, the woman sitting before them was an alpha, there could be no mistaking that. And yet, she led these forest shifters.

Biyana gestured to a tall woman, who hefted a full deer carcass onto the floor between Biyana and Faris.

"To seal our bargain, would you do the honours?"

In spite of herself, Faris's mouth watered. She hadn't eaten organ meat since leaving her childhood home. Humans didn't, as a rule, and ladies even less so. The large woman glared at Faris and pulled a dagger but flipped it and handed it to her hilt first. Faris took it and gripped the hilt. Shifting to rip into the deer's entrails would be so much easier . . . but perhaps that was the idea.

The heart would be what Biyana wanted to share with her, no doubt, nestled safe in the deer's ribcage. Her wolf jaws could crack through bone like kindling, but right now, her human self didn't have jaws, claws, or even have shoes on. She turned to Sandrel.

"Your boots, please, my mate." She waited for him to pull them off, hopping on one foot and then the other. Faris stepped into them. The huge boots were still warm from Sandrel's feet, and she could barely walk in them, but they would protect her from being ripped apart by bone splinters. She lifted one foot, careful to keep the boot on, laid it on the deer's chest, and stomped with all her weight. The ribs cracked under her heel, and steam rose gently from the deer's gaping chest. Faris fell to her knees, the warm scent of blood and giblets sending her wolf into a near frenzy inside her. But she didn't shift.

Faris clutched the borrowed dagger, made a few precise cuts, and lifted the dripping heart free, warm blood coating her hands. Their human teeth wouldn't be able to bite pieces off the tough muscle, so Faris sliced a sliver of the meat and held the rest out to Biyana to do the same. Biyana's knife flashed, and the two women bowed their heads over the kill and ate of the deer's heart flesh. Their pact was sealed.

Faris's wolf was desperate to howl, circling and growling inside her, but laying any kind of claim to this shifter pack would mean challenging a bear—suicide. This was an alliance between Biyana's pack and her family.

"You and your family are under our protection for the time being," said Biyana. She wiped her knife and sheathed it.

The big woman, only slightly less dour now, took her dagger back, and Faris laid the heart back in the deer's ruined chest cavity.

"Thank you, Biyana," said Faris. "We'd appreciate a few days to decide on a course of action. Our people are awaiting our return—"

"Woodcutters." The whisper was behind them but easily loud enough to carry across the room.

Biyana gave the whisperer a glare over Faris's shoulder. "We discussed this. We will not hold your woodcutter status against you, as you will be considered shifters first, as are all members of our community." She seemed to emphasize that last bit for the benefit of the whisperer. "Unfortunately, we don't have a few days. The men seeking you have—" She swallowed. "Have started a fire at the forest's edge. If we don't stop them, our forest could be in danger."

"We've just run all the way from Castle Redcliff. My daughter—"

Biyana held up a hand. "One day to rest and take part in the planning to defend our community tomorrow morning. We will do nothing tonight. By nightfall tomorrow, we will defend our home. Rest, everyone, and prepare for council tomorrow."

The babble breaking out behind them made Faris flinch. She was so on edge. Sandrel put an arm around her again.

As they trudged toward the door, good-natured snapping and growling made Ela start, and Faris turned with her to watch the other shifters. A badger, a crow, and a dog tore into the deer carcass still lying on the ground. The crow grabbed a chunk of liver and flapped up to a high ledge, leaving the others grumbling below. Ela swallowed and grimaced, no doubt torn between human disgust and wolf longing.

Peter approached them bashfully. "Might I show you all around?"

Sandrel shot Faris an amused look. The boy was already smitten with Michaela, and if her wolf's behaviour toward him was anything to go by, she wasn't opposed to his feelings. After all, they had gone to the tournament hoping to find Ela a suitor that she cared for. Why stand in the way of her budding romance? They needed to talk about her first shift.

Faris turned Ela away from the spectacle in front of the throne. "A person's first shift can be . . . overwhelming. How are you doing, Junebug?"

Her eyes were fixed on the ground. "My wolf is really strong."

"Yes, I could see that."

"How do I . . . fight her? Now that she's out."

Faris took both of Ela's hands, not unlike the way Peter had held them after their shift. "It's more about learning to work together, rather than fighting." But even as she was saying it, it rang false to her. What had she been doing all these years but fighting against her wolf? Especially with Sandrel.

Ela nodded, but she still looked miserable.

"Maybe someone here will teach you, Ela," Sandrel cut in.

The hopeful look on Peter's face made Faris fight back a smile. "I would be more than happy to teach you how to work with your wolf . . . Ela?"

Their eyes met, and the ground beneath Faris might as well have tilted over. The moment hung there, the precipice between teenage Ela and grown woman Michaela. Sure, she had been grown for years, but suddenly, Faris could feel it: nothing would be the same between them anymore. Ela's childhood self who ran to her momma for help was fully gone, like the last thread being snipped on a new dress. No longer a project but a beautiful, functional garment in its own right.

Faris tried to smile as the lump rose in her throat, and she just gestured Ela silently to go. Her daughter's eyes shone with excitement; she must have been hiding her desire to learn more about her shifter side for years, and Faris had certainly never encouraged her to explore it.

Sandrel kissed the top of Faris's head. "She's off."

Gone forever. Her baby had flown the nest.

8

The council had lasted all morning, and Faris itched to leap from her chair and prowl back and forth. Sandrel put a hand on her knee under the table.

A crow shifter had spent the night eavesdropping all over Redcliff. Heinrich had used his man's injury to stir up a mob, just as she'd feared. The crow shifter didn't know exactly who had sided with him, but his survey of their encampment indicated that more than just his own me burned the forest.

"It's our forest, and we will protect it the way we always have. No need for you to get involved." The crow shifter probably meant well. He was probably trying to protect them, but all the same, the white-hot rage bubbled up in Faris's chest.

"I am perfectly capable of participating in the defence strategy. We brought the mob down on the forest, and I won't sit by helplessly as others fight." Sandrel's heavy hand on her leg gave her the confidence to keep on. "I have my daughter to protect, and my people. Once they tire of trying to smoke us out of the forest, where do you think they'll go next? Gantry Outpost has no defences, not from the kind of attack Heinrich can now bring to bear."

Biyana's eyes flashed. Maybe Faris shouldn't have mentioned the outpost. Beating back the forest, as outposts were wont to do, was not popular among these shifters. "And you, man?" Biyana knew Sandrel's name well enough; she chose to belittle him by drawing attention to his humanity.

"I have my sword. I can fight as well as anyone."

"Against your own people?"

"They are willing to slaughter us, murder my daughter. Lord Heinrich and those who stand with him have no place among my people."

"Alpha, I must protest!" Another shifter, a wide-shouldered woman, smacked her hand flat on the table. "If humans die, who will be blamed? They'll use it as an excuse to raze the entire forest!"

Biyana lifted a hand and closed her eyes. The shifters' chatter abated. She steepled her fingers and took a deep breath before answering. "The immediate threat is undeniable. Our first priority should be to stop them burning our forest. Once we have the fire under control, we can decide how to handle our visitors. As it stands, they have offered to make themselves useful." She fixed Faris with an alpha stare that had her wolf's hackles rising. "As Faris stated, their daughter is here as well and will remain under our protection until we deem it safe for her to return to your so-called outpost."

The threat was clear enough. They'd use Ela as a hostage if it came to that. They would tolerate no double-crossing from the interlopers.

"Thank you, Biyana," said Faris. *Alpha* stuck in her throat, and she couldn't bring herself to say it. This was why female alphas such as Faris were not tolerated at home; they found it impossible to bend the knee to anyone else and could never assimilate into the hierarchy as a docile mate.

"Be ready at full dark." The shifters would have no trouble seeing in their animal forms, and the humans would be all but blind. "You are all dismissed to prepare for the coming confrontation."

Faris bowed her head stiffly, and she and Sandrel retreated. Ela had gone off with Peter this morning, and it was well past time to check in with her, make sure the other shifters were treating her well.

After parting ways with Sandrel, who was going in search of a cuirass, she followed her daughter's scent to the outskirts of the settlement. Peter had gone with her. Faris had had little time to assimilate his scent markers, but she could pick them out as long as few other shifter scents were present.

Their voices carried to her through a copse of scrub, laughter and the low murmur of their voices floating up from a dell. Faris peered through the leaves and caught her breath at the tableau before her.

Peter and *her* Ela were stark naked, holding hands, as they had when she'd shifted last night, eyes locked in concentration.

"This time, just relax," said Peter. "You don't have to fear your wolf. She wants you safe. She doesn't want to keep you a wolf forever any more than you want to remain a human woman forever."

"Right," said Ela and took a deep breath, then sighed it out in a huff.

Peter held her gaze as he shifted into his fox form. He hopped on his back legs and chased his tail in a few circles before Ela followed him into her wolf form. Her hackles were raised and her body tense as a warp thread. Peter bounded back and forth in front of her, and she bowed into a play posture, then shook her entire body and chased her tail in a circle, some of the tension draining away.

Faris's heart pounded as she waited for the moment that her daughter tried to shift back. Had they been at this all day? Was Michaela so determined to master her wolf form this quickly? Had Peter been so patient with her for hours on end?

Peter led the way again, leaping into the air and shifting back into human form, landing lightly on his feet. He spread his arms wide and gave wolf-Ela a challenging look. Ela reared onto her back legs, hopped once, and then shifted, toppling to her hands and knees on the leaf litter.

Peter let out a whoop and hauled her to her feet as Ela threw her arms around his neck. They seemed totally unaware of their nudity—for a moment. As they stared into each other's eyes, Faris drew back, and when they kissed, she turned tail and ran.

That was not in any way her business. Faris's eyes clouded with tears as she stumbled back to the main settlement, blundering around the huge central bonfire and into the now-empty meeting hall. She scrubbed a hand over her face. Michaela had been magnificent, shifting at will in only one day. No doubt Peter was a good and dedicated teacher. Still, hadn't it been only weeks ago that Ela had been tottering around on the floor babbling to herself? No, that was silly. Michaela was old enough to take a mate; they'd all been planning as much when they had met with Lord Heinrich. If the shifters here really were representatives of the forest, a match between one of them and the outpost would actually be far more advantageous than marrying some outpost lord, since the forest itself was the biggest threat to their people. And the love in Peter's eyes when he looked at Ela was a mirror to Sandrel's when he looked at her.

As long as the mob from Redcliff Castle didn't take it upon themselves to capture Gantry Outpost as the more accessible option compared to the forest itself.

Defending against the mob was the priority now. Her daughter was safe and perfectly content with Peter. She and Sandrel would make their way to the front lines with the rest and—gods, it had been a long time since she'd so much as sparred. What if her reflexes were dulled? Her wolf had been penned up for decades. Ela was not the one she should be worried about now; she should be worrying about defending herself—and her husband—in the coming battle.

Faris followed Sandrel's scent to a little turf house where he was muttering over a cracked set of leathers with the broad-shouldered shifter. Sandrel and the shifter each cradled an epaulette in their lap, and between them sat a bucket of tallow, the rest of the set piled at their feet.

"A few hours should do it," said Sandrel. "As it is, it'll be more hindrance than protection. I can't fight if I can't move."

Faris picked up the chest piece. A crack split the piece roughly from hip to navel. She held it up and tapped it, giving her husband a pointed look.

"I know. It'll still be better than nothing," said Sandrel.

Faris sat herself across from the two of them and started working a handful of tallow into the chest piece.

"Where did you get these? Are they yours?" said Faris.

"My mate's. He was human." Her tone didn't invite conversation.

"I'm sorry," said Faris.

The shifter tended the leather with reverence, and as she cocked her head to bend over her work, the dappled light from the window fell on her neck. She was marked. Had her human mate marked her? Humans thought marking was disgusting, revolting…didn't they?

Sandrel doesn't. Would he be willing to mark Faris? She shivered and pressed her legs together. *That* wasn't a reaction she'd ever had to the idea of a mate marking her.

Sandrel ran a hand over the last piece laid out to dry and nodded to the shifter. "Thank you once again for this."

She shrugged. "No one else is looking to use them."

"Nevertheless, I'll be back before nightfall to get sorted."

Faris and Sandrel let themselves out of the little house and wandered toward the bonfire.

"Ela and Peter . . . have formed an attachment."

"I'm glad." Sandrel stared into the fire.

"Glad?"

"She'll have someone to stay with her."

In case the two of them didn't return.

"We'd better shake some rust off, then," said Faris. "I haven't fought in my wolf form for far too long."

Sandrel brushed his hair back and patted the pommel of his sword. "This is what you'll be up against."

Most of her sparring experience was against other shifters, not men with swords and axes. "Want to give me a lesson? I promise not to gut you without your armour."

"Very reassuring. Let's find somewhere quieter, though."

They found themselves a clearing similar to the one that Ela and Peter had been using to train, on the far side of the settlement. They cleared the ground of sharp sticks and rocks, leaving softer leaf litter in case either of them took a tumble.

"Shall we begin with avoiding strikes?"

"Sure," said Faris, stripping off her clothes.

Sandrel's gaze raked her body, but she shifted before they could get distracted. Coming home to their people, to their daughter, was the highest priority now. Sandrel drew his sword, and they practised dodging various strikes, disarming, and simulated Faris attacking vital organs.

Faris got inside Sandrel's guard and jumped, both her front paws hitting him square in the chest. He took two steps back, overbalanced, and fell on his ass. Faris stood over him, panting into his grinning face.

"You're going to be fine, my love. You can take those lordlings down, any one of them." He left his sword in the dirt to stroke down her furry side. She shifted and landed on top of him, completely naked, of course, his hard length already beginning to throb against her thigh.

"Do we have time for some recreation?" she growled.

Sandrel didn't answer, just flipped her and pressed his hips between her thighs. She arched up into him. She could flip him back, but something had been nagging at her.

"Biyana seemed surprised that you hadn't marked me," said Faris.

Sandrel froze, tension in the line of his body.

She kept on. "Is that something that you might want to—"

Sandrel cut her off. "Yes, very much."

She chuckled.

"You would accept my mark?" Sandrel sounded like he had when he'd shown her Gantry Outpost for the first time. This was important to him.

A shiver worked its way up her spine. Before she'd left home, before she'd known that she was an alpha, it had been expected that she would mate and be marked, as was customary among their people. She'd never been able to understand why the concept revolted her so much, at least not until Martin, when it had all fallen into place. Alphas marked; they didn't get marked. Every wolf shifter knew that.

But they weren't with wolf shifters now.

And she wanted that from Sandrel. She bared her throat to him. Once he marked her, they would truly be mates, having claimed one another in a way that felt *right*. "Yes, please."

Sandrel's hands shook as he pulled his shirt over his head and tossed it aside, then stood and tugged off his breeches. He stalked back to Faris, and as soon as he was within reach, grabbed her ankle. She kicked instinctively, but he held firm, kissing her ankle, her calf, up her leg to her thigh, and then around her hip and up her stomach.

She huffed a disgruntled sound, and he grinned up at her. "Is there something you'd like?"

"I'm the alpha. You're supposed to obey me."

He chuckled. "I'm going to mark you. I think I'm the alpha today."

At his words, heat pooled in Faris's core, and she wriggled beneath him where he pinned her to the soft ground. She had felt nothing but rebellion at attempts to dominate her, not unless she caged her wolf in tightly. It wasn't caged now. It was panting, practically rolling over. Was this what non-alphas felt when an alpha commanded them?

Sandrel gathered her wrists in one hand. Faris could probably break his grip easily . . . but she didn't. She tugged lightly, just to feel his fingers tighten. He bent his head and licked up the side of her neck, and she twisted her head, trying to give him even better access. They only needed one more thing.

Faris turned back to him where he nuzzled her throat. "Howl," she murmured.

He pulled back, watching her quizzically. "Howl?"

"That's right. If you want to do this properly . . ."

"I do." He arranged her wrists over her head and lifted himself on one elbow.

Sandrel's breath expanded his broad chest; he threw back his head, and he howled, the sound echoing to the far corners of the forest, letting everyone know that he had chosen his mate.

Faris shivered again and spread her thighs for him. He lined himself up and plunged inside, letting out a feral growl as they mated, Faris meeting every one of his thrusts, wrists still pinned above her head. She arched, trying to get his mouth, his teeth onto her neck.

He dipped his head, kissed below her ear, and bit down. She let out a strangled snarl, and his bite loosened. Then he was kissing her, the rich taste of her blood mixing on their tongues. They came together as he lifted his head and howled once more, this time in triumph. She was his, and now everyone would know it just by looking at her.

A lightness buoyed Faris's chest as he collapsed onto her, a weight lifted that she had been carrying so long she barely noticed its presence. Her wolf didn't understand marriage vows or declarations of love. It didn't understand caring and gestures of affection, but this her wolf understood. Damn her father and his pack; she and Sandrel were properly mated now, after all these years. Now and forever.

9

They made a strange battalion, to say the least. The broad-shoul-dered shifter, an elk, as it turned out, led the way, followed by the other large creatures, a cougar, a moose, and a bull among them. The smaller animals followed, with Biyana in bear form in the rearguard. After the third time Sandrel stumbled and cursed in the darkness, Faris took him onto her back, ignoring the baleful looks from the other shifters. His leathers hadn't been made for him, and though they were softer with their recent oiling, they were by no means supple.

By the time the woody scent of smoke reached them, Faris's skin twitched, and she shuddered with the instinct to distance herself from the forest fire as much as possible. Sandrel stroked her neck as if she were a skittish horse, and she nearly shook him off in indignation, but her mate's touch seemed to calm her wolf, so she allowed him the indulgence.

The bird shifters had formed a scouting force above the trees; Biyana had ordered them to keep well away from the pillar of smoke in the distance where the forest remained smouldering. The glow from the forest's embers finally reached them in slashes through the curtain of the wide tree trunks; thankfully, Michaela was safe at the settlement. Peter had looked Faris right in the eye, bowed his head, and sworn that he would keep Ela safe. It had to be enough, since neither Sandrel nor she were willing to stay out of the coming battle.

What little underbrush there was in the forest suddenly gave way to blackened ground, equally charred stumps dotting the smouldering field. It wasn't possible that the trees had burned to nothing. Sandrel leaped from her back and climbed onto a stump—cleanly hacked through. Of course they had harvested the valuable wood before lighting the forest on fire. The lords could always be depended upon to be economical.

The canvas tents that presumably housed the lords and their troops snapped in the breeze that picked up as the shifters skirted the burning ground. The force divided, the shifters sneaking toward the tents in twos and threes. Sandrel followed Faris to the closest tent, and she motioned him around the back. She sniffed as he got into position, nothing but ash detectable in the air, and she shifted impatiently before bursting in the front. Faris took in the empty bedroll as Sandrel came slashing through the back of the tent. No one was there.

How could it be empty? Was this not where the forest-burners were sleeping? Faris scented the air, unable to catch a whiff of human over the all-consuming woodsmoke odour.

Sandrel cursed fluently under his breath. "Where the hell are they?"

The shifters' forces were scattered, a handful at each tent, spread across the field, the burning forest at their backs, ready to be picked off or driven into the acrid, burning smoke.

Faris caught the glitter of metal over Sandrel's shoulder and yipped a warning. He got his arm up in time and caught the blade on his vambrace, knocking it aside as he swiped his pommel sideways into the attacker's temple. The man's groan was echoed by yells and cries across the camp as the shifters were ambushed, fighting back with more alacrity than their attackers had anticipated.

Faris whirled, pouncing on an unfortunate woman before she could stomp a badger into the ground. The badger was on her in another second, and the woman's shriek echoed among the other cries and curses of the humans—mixed with fewer yowls and screams from the shifters, but still too many.

Faris bounded around the tent toward the clang of metal that could only be her husband in combat with another human. As he came into view, Sandrel grunted and doubled over. *Fuck, Sandrel!* She leaped onto his attacker's back, knocking him to his face in the dirt, and raked her claws ineffectually over his chain-mail shirt. Ripping his throat out would do the job, but the more of the humans they killed, the stronger the human argument for eradicating shifters would be. They had all agreed to primarily defend themselves. She settled for cuffing him across the back of the head.

Sandrel fell to one knee, his breathing harsh. *Shit.* How badly hurt was he? Faris nuzzled him, the familiar tang of his blood filling her wolf's senses. He pressed a hand to the crack in his cuirass, blood leaking between his fingers. His opponent must have got lucky. He should climb on her back so that she could bear him to safety. She knelt before him.

He waved her away. "Deal with the rest of the men."

"Deal with us? Why, Sandrel, if I didn't know better, I'd think you were a traitor."

Heinrich. Faris stalked to a position between the two men and lowered her head, growling.

"Ah, the guard dog. You should know that after you maimed my man, there have been calls to remove you from Gantry Outpost. Along with anyone loyal to you, of course."

The entire outpost was loyal, after all the years that they'd worked together to keep the place running. Lord Heinrich wouldn't stoop to massacring everyone, would he? Maybe not, but he surely wouldn't hesitate to turn them out with nothing.

"Then again, if you and your lupine companion here were tragically killed in combat, there would be no need to brand you a traitor."

"Faris!" Sandrel's cry was too late. Heinrich's distraction had allowed an axe-wielder to slip up behind Faris, and the axe blade was already sweeping down in a wide strike that would take her head right off her shoulders. The whistling was already too close. She would never be able to dodge the blade in time, what with Heinrich's having drawn her attention. Still, Sandrel tried to rise in her defence, his hand pressed to his gaping side.

A snarl made Heinrich's head snap around, and a black streak of fur tackled the axe-wielder to the ground, its teeth ripping into his throat, the scent of blood enough to slice through the smoky air. *Ela?* A thud had Faris turning: Sandrel sprawled on the ground, limp. Heinrich pulled a dirk and advanced on her husband, and Faris lunged, her shoulder popping as it plowed into his middle. She clamped her jaws on his wrist to keep him from stabbing her, but he just laughed, took the dirk in his other hand, and plunged it into the rough fur of her shoulder.

Faris screamed and whimpered, her blood running cold as an almost identical scream sounded from behind her. *Ela!* She hauled her body around to see Ela struggling to untangle herself from a net that had been thrown over her, two men even now pulling it tight. Faris struggled up on three legs, letting go of Heinrich's arm and limping toward her daughter, but Heinrich wasn't done. He plunged the dirk into her haunch and twisted.

Faris screamed again, agony shooting through her shoulder and her hip, making her totter on the spot. Heinrich raised the dirk again—and a growling fox pounced on his face. Peter tore at his throat, and Heinrich screeched and freed the dirk from Faris's flesh to club him with it. Peter fell to the ground, limp. Heinrich sneered, then glared into the darkness. Faris's vision blurred, but she could still make out what he'd already grasped: dozens of glowing eyes shining from the darkness in a semicircle around the three men and their wolf captive.

Heinrich's snarl was worthy of a shifter. He motioned to his men, who hefted the net between them, Ela still struggling inside. *No! Someone, pounce!* But none of the shifters came forward to help. After all, what was Ela to them? A woodcutter, the kind they hated.

Biyana growled from the darkness, and Heinrich startled and retreated to the wagon.

He probably thought he was speaking too low for Faris to hear, but her wolf's ears were more than keen enough to pick out his mumbling. "If I'd known getting the wolf woman to marry me would be this much work, I never would have agreed to Earl Anders's terms. This backwoods lordship isn't worth half so much trouble."

Heinrich was still planning to marry Ela.

Faris's daughter was slung into the wagon in short order, and they were off.

Faris trembled and collapsed.

Ela.

10

Faris came to staring up at the stars. The bonfire crackled beside her, and she was back in her human form, wrapped in a blanket.

"Where's Sandrel?" she said, trying to sit up. Her shoulder and thigh were stiff but only radiated a dull ache. *Ela.* "We have to go after my daughter."

Peter stared into the bonfire. He hadn't moved when she'd stirred or when she'd spoken.

"Peter, where's my family?" Sandrel couldn't be dead. He'd been injured, sure, but not mortally. Then again, humans were fragile creatures... "Peter!"

"Your husband is still out," said Peter, finally. "I shouldn't have brought her. I'm sorry."

Sandrel was alive. The knot in her stomach loosened a fraction. "What's done is done. But you're right, you should have kept her safe, as you pledged to me. Now all that remains is for you to make amends."

"Amends?" Peter's gaze finally slid to her.

"Sandrel is in no fit state to come with me. You will."

Peter's gaze remained vacant. Had the blow to his head affected him so? He finally looked down and shook his head. "I'll be no help to you. I'm the one who put Michaela in danger."

"Peter!" snapped Faris, and he jumped. "If you and Ela hadn't arrived when you did, I would have been decapitated, without a doubt. Heinrich would have slit my husband's throat. Yes, you are the one who put my daughter in danger. All the more reason for you to help get her out again. Or would you rather I go alone with no support? After that debacle, how likely do you think it is that anyone else here will join me?"

"I—"

"Now take me to my husband. I want to see him before I leave."

Peter nodded, head still bowed. Faris pulled on the tunic and breeches laid out nearby and followed him across the hall and up the back steps to the dais, then through a curtain into Biyana's private chambers.

Her husband had been bundled onto a cot. Biyana crouched beside him.

"He is stable, Faris. But he will take weeks to heal."

Faris knelt beside Biyana and took Sandrel's warm hand.

"I see you finally exchanged marks. That's perhaps what saved him."

"What do you mean?"

"Your blood. He tasted it when he bit you. It's likely some of your shifter healing abilities were extended, however fleetingly, to him."

Her shifter blood. She traced the mark on her neck, still a raised scar despite her healing powers. She brushed Sandrel's grey hair back from his face. "I'm going to get her back," she whispered.

"We will care for him here. Beyond that . . . we are all agreed that you are no longer welcome here. You and Sandrel. Whatever else you may be, you are lord and lady of an outpost, and you brought a mob down on us, a mob that put our trees to the axe and burned our forest."

The fire. "Can I help put it out before I go?"

"No need. The trees retreated to form a firebreak and the rain will do the rest, now that the humans have stopped spreading the flames. You need to go before the rain washes away your daughter's scent."

"I understand." Faris rose to her feet, already feeling steadier. "I appreciate all the help your people have given us, even though, as you say, we brought trouble to you. When I get my daughter back, when I take back our outpost, perhaps we can forge a more . . . mutually satisfactory arrangement?" Her people were likely even now tearing baby saplings from the ground in the name of keeping the forest at bay. Faris shuddered. "What you've built here"—she gestured to the hollow tree around them—"should be inspiration for us."

Biyana nodded but looked unconvinced. Only action would change her mind. But first, they needed to take back Gantry Forest Outpost, take back Ela.

They packed clothes, and Peter strapped them to Faris's wolf's back. It wouldn't do to show up . . . wherever Ela was . . . naked, and they couldn't risk travelling as humans on the road. The pack bumped against Faris's shoulders as they trotted past the firebreak to the edge of the trees. Faris lurked and paced under the cover of the trees while Peter snuck into the deserted camp to where Ela had been taken and picked up her scent.

She'd been dragged into a cart, but Peter was familiar enough with her scent markers to follow it, regardless; he had to be. Faris hadn't had time to press him on whether he and Ela had spoken about becoming mates or not, but she certainly would. It was part of her role, both as mother and alpha, to make sure Ela was entering into a partnership for the right reasons. *A partnership with a fox.* Her father's voice popped into her head, his dark eyes boring into her. He was the alpha of their pack, so far away across the sea, a pack that she hadn't heard from since she'd been tossed on a ship and bid good riddance decades ago. If mating a human was the ultimate punishment, it was nothing to being mated to a lower creature like a fox.

No, Peter wasn't a lower creature. He and Ela had saved her life. And even if that hadn't been the case, Ela had looked at him with such devotion, and he'd had such faith in her abilities, even though she'd come to shifting so late in life.

The fox himself trotted back to her through the blackened grass, yipped once, and trotted away westward—toward Gantry Outpost. They stuck to the edge of the forest, Peter occasionally scampering off to ensure they were still following the scent, until it became clear that Gantry Outpost was exactly where they were going.

Faris's heart sank. They'd planned to shift, dress, and blend in wherever they ended up, get the lay of the land and get Ela out, but breaking her daughter out of Gantry Outpost, her own people . . .

Faris jerked her head a little deeper into the woods as the sounds of axe striking wood floated to them on the noon breeze. They shifted and dressed in silence. It wouldn't do for some rogue woodcutter to come upon them naked in the woods.

Faris smoothed her tunic. "You'll have to find Ela alone. I can't go to the outpost."

Peter recoiled. "I can't do it alone, alpha."

"I'm not your alpha. Don't betray Biyana like that."

Peter shrugged. "Wolves have such hierarchies. You are Michaela's alpha, and I'm . . ."

Had he been about to claim her as his mate? This wasn't the time. "I will be recognized the second I set foot in the outpost."

"Surely that's an advantage. They'll tell you where Ela is."

"Sandrel isn't here. He's the lord. Look, humans don't trust shifters. I worked hard to hide my true self from them. If I come back, after what Lord Heinrich has no doubt told them, dressed like this . . ." She gestured to her homespun men's clothes.

"Then what?"

What indeed? What would Julia do when she spotted her lady traipsing out of the forest? What fate would MacIntosh choose for her? Did they know that Ela was being held by Heinrich?

"I think you're underestimating your people," said Peter. "They won't be swayed by some dandy lord from the north. Nor by some shifter appearing from the woods." He gestured to his own similar garb.

Peter was right. Sending him in alone would get him killed, like as not. MacIntosh had a good head on his shoulders. He at least would hear her out.

"It's decided, then."

As she marched out of the woods, Peter grabbed their discarded pack and hurried to catch up with her.

11

The sun warmed Faris's face as she stepped from the shelter of the trees. Cultivated fields swept up the hill toward the outpost, a road winding through them to where they stood. A woodcutter sawed a fallen tree into lengths, bending into the rasp of the blade cutting through wood. The axe strikes hadn't abated, still punctuating the birdsong further along the treeline. A row of women with their skirts tucked into their waistbands bent over, pulling tiny saplings and piling them in a cart for kindling. One of them straightened and drew a sleeve across her glistening forehead. *Julia.*

She waved and sauntered over, slowing as she came close enough to identify Faris and her companion. She shaded her eyes with her hand.

"Who's this, my lady?" Her gaze skittered over Faris from her tousled hair down her marked neck, over her homespun clothes, to the boots that were a size too big.

"Peter," said Faris. "I'm looking for Ela. I know she's here."

Julia's eyes narrowed, but she gestured up toward the outpost. "Whole column of soldiers arrived in the night. Didn't see who they were exactly. MacIntosh has been holed up with them all morning. You think Ela was with them?"

"Thank you, Julia."

She frowned, but Faris and Peter continued up toward the outpost without answering her question.

Faris put a hand on Peter's arm. "Don't look back. She's already wondering about you."

"Wondering? Seems as though she's trying to see through me into my very soul."

Faris had been a fool to listen to Peter. As long as Sandrel had been by her side, no one had dared treat her as anything other than the lady of the outpost, but now that he was gone, they were of course treating her like the shifter she was. She held her head high and kept on up the road.

A farmer raised a hand from his plow, and Faris waved back. He didn't stop to talk to them, though. As they got closer to the outpost, they passed cottages and a scattering of houses. A dog tied in the yard of a cottage barked and growled as they passed, and a woman with a kerchief on her head popped out the door. She sized them up, glared, and retreated, slamming the door and setting the dog off again.

"Are they always like this, or is it me?"

"Humans don't much like shifters. I would have thought the incendiary mob on the doorstep of the forest got that through to you."

"But you know these people. You're their lady."

"Apparently, I don't know them as well as I thought." Faris scented the air. The smells of the outpost that she'd grown so accustomed to ignoring assaulted her: refuse, cooking food, smoke, and so many humans. Even if Ela was here, her scent would be lost in the cacophony. Not to mention that shifting in the middle of the outpost would be inadvisable. "There's nothing for it. We'll have to go in."

Peter followed her so closely up the steps to the kitchen door that her heel almost gouged his knees. If only the shifters had had proper clothes with proper undergarments, maybe she wouldn't feel quite so outmatched. The homespun clothing was serviceable enough, but playing the part of the lady was not coming to her naturally as she clomped up the wooden steps, hiking up her loose breeches.

The kitchen staff stopped to stare. A red-faced woman elbowed her companion, who stopped peeling potatoes to eye them as they crossed the kitchen to the stone stairs beyond.

"Hey!"

Faris turned. Sepp sauntered around the kitchen to crowd Faris. She stood her ground and looked up at him.

He shook his head slowly. "You shouldn't have come back again."

They didn't stand a chance of escaping—not without harming Faris's own people. Sepp marched them to the cellar doors. Thankfully, the rats sensed that they were predators and scurried away when Faris and Peter were shoved in and the door bolted behind them.

Faris had been silly to expect that anyone would speak up on her behalf. She'd been absolutely right: her people weren't loyal to her, not without Sandrel to legitimize her role. Now that Heinrich had taken over the outpost, she was just a shifter to them. Peter slumped against a crate of imported furnishings, hands dangling between his knees. The cellar had no windows, just rows of barrels, casks, crates, and bottles, but the two of them could see in the darkness. Faris shivered. The chill cut right through the single layer of homespun.

She paced from a hogshead of pickled eggs to a rack of brandy bottles, dust obscuring the labels. Sandrel refused to uncork any, except on special occasions. After their wedding, when he'd first brought her back here, he'd cracked one to celebrate the life they were going to build together. And, of course, when Ela was born, once they were sure both she and Faris would survive.

"How long until one of your people frees us?" Peter sounded tired but not worried.

Faris turned slowly to face him. Did he really still have such faith in the people here—surely no longer *her* people—to support her? How could he, who had known her family for a mere few days, be so certain that they wouldn't be killed outright? Or kept and toyed with for sport? It was not beyond Heinrich's capabilities.

"That crate you're using as a backrest was supposed to be Michaela's dowry. Part of it, anyway. Did she tell you she was supposed to marry Lord Heinrich? Perhaps she still will. His lordship depends on it, after all."

"And you think Michaela would marry him?"

"Will she have a choice? Without Sandrel . . ." He'd been the one to chase Heinrich off in the first place. Maybe it would have been better if he'd listened to her, made concessions, accepted Heinrich's terms. They could have arranged to keep Ela and her children safe. But Sandrel would never accept such disrespectful terms for his only daughter. Which was why Heinrich forced the issue, and they were now trapped in the cellar while Sandrel lay incapacitated deep in the forest.

"So we kill him." Peter said it so matter-of-factly.

"That would mean retaliation from Castle Redcliff, something our outpost would certainly not survive. Earl Anders appointed Lord Heinrich and would not take kindly to someone else removing him." On the other hand, Earl Anders appointing a northern lordling to the most strategically important keep in his earldom may not have been his choice alone. Perhaps he would privately be thankful to whoever removed Heinrich from the picture—though it would be in private only. He would be obligated to make an example either way; they would find no quarter there.

"If they get married . . ."

"Ela is tied to him for life." Then again, if Faris had already made an enemy of the earl just by virtue of being a shifter, what would it matter if she killed Heinrich and was executed in turn? Ela would remain Sandrel's daughter and could at the very least be spirited away to the forest. Surely Peter would do as much to allow Ela to live a peaceful life?

"In the forest, we've taken in shifters from as far away as Brayside. Some who had never before shifted."

"What about you?" said Faris. She was no longer welcome in the forest. If Peter was trying to convince her to bring Ela and escape with them, Biyana would never allow it. She'd made that perfectly clear.

"I learned to help them."

"Like you helped Ela." Had he engaged in so very personal a strategy to help the other shifters who came to them, their nature totally unknown to them?

"No," said Peter. "I've never helped anyone the way I helped her. No one has ever responded to me that way." He shook his head in wonder. "A wolf showed me her belly."

"I'm glad you appreciate the significance. I'm not sure that Ela does. She's had dalliances in the past, but the way her wolf responded to you . . ."

"I have the power to hurt her."

More like the power to destroy her. Faris just nodded.

Muffled voices came through the door, and the bolt slid slowly across. Peter leaped into a crouch. Faris squared her shoulders. The door creaked open.

MacIntosh stood framed in the doorway, a torch held high.

"So it's true then, is it? You've returned with a shifter, neck bite and all." He shook his head. "I never thought I'd see the day."

He gestured his two companions forward, and Faris and Peter submitted to having their hands bound behind them. "When Lord Heinrich told us what happened . . ." He shook his head again. "But, seems he was right, even after we all welcomed you and took you in."

He led them through the outpost, up to the hall where Lord Heinrich sat alone on the dais. Julia flanked him, her arms crossed over her chest, her axe now back in its habitual place at her side. MacIntosh joined them once he had led the shifters into the hall and rapped his quarterstaff on the floor.

It seemed every member of the outpost had gathered in the hall, leaving off their work for the moment, flour or dirt still dusting their hands, to see the spectacle of this shifter trial of Heinrich's. His men's armour and weapons glinted in the light pouring through the windows behind the dais. Her people, Sandrel's really, had calluses from weaving and whittling instead of archery and sparring.

"I'm glad you've seen fit to join me," said Lord Heinrich.

It would be so easy to shift and rip his throat out right now. They still needed to find Ela. Faris pushed her wolf down.

"It's good to see you are enjoying the hospitality of my halls." Faris looked from Julia to MacIntosh, but they both returned her stare stonily. She'd get no help from them.

"Quite. I fully intend to execute both of you. However, I require something of you first. Change my betrothed back into a person."

Ela? He had her here, still in wolf form? Peter tensed next to her. Ela had had trouble shifting back to human form, and a threat like Heinrich would only exacerbate the issue.

"We've tried a few methods," said Heinrich conversationally. "But she hasn't responded to the stick or the flame like the dog she is."

Faris closed her eyes out of habit, the wolf lunging and snapping inside her undeniably showing through her flashing gaze. Peter needed

Ela's whereabouts before Faris could rip this lord's throat from his neck and taste his heart's blood in her clamping jaws.

She pried her eyes open; Julia and MacIntosh both had the grace to look unsettled. It seemed they hadn't been privy to the torture. Julia's hand dropped to the head of her axe. Would they stand by and watch her be executed, the lady they had purported to serve for two decades?

The priority was determining where Ela was being kept. Peter, as a fox, would make sure she was freed. He could slip away from the hall the second he knew where to find Ela, something a wolf as large as Faris could never hope to do.

"Let me see her," said Faris to Heinrich. She tried—and failed—to keep the steely hatred from her voice.

He shook his head and clasped his hands behind his back. "So that you can mutate into a horrible beast along with her and murder us all? I don't think so."

"There is no hope for her to shift without someone she trusts present. Surely you understand that she must be brought to us. Look at us, bound and guarded before you. What danger do we pose?" Playing on his hubris couldn't hurt. He had no way of knowing that their bindings would be immaterial should they decide to shift.

"I believe she's safer in the tower than here in the open," said Sepp.

The look Heinrich gave him was murderous, but it was too late.

Faris and Peter shifted almost in tandem. Peter launched himself sideways and shifted in the air, landing on his fox paws and slipping between suddenly stampeding feet and streaking out the door. Faris leaned forward and shifted, then launched herself onto the table that stretched along the dais. She had Heinrich on the ground, arms pinned beneath him, before their guards could so much as move.

A blow to her shoulder barely budged Faris; she was so close to tasting the blood of her enemy, teeth pricking his flesh.

"That's for murdering our lord," said MacIntosh with another blow, this time to her ribs. "Taking a shifter mate after we all accepted you."

What was he saying? Faris cocked her head to look at her old friend, tears streaking his face. Murdered? New mate? They thought Peter was her mate? They thought the claiming bite was his. Heinrich had told them she'd killed Sandrel and taken a new mate. No wonder they hated her! Surely they would believe her over him if she told them the truth. Of course, to tell them anything at all, she would have to shift—and lose her advantage.

She couldn't let them keep believing this *lord's* lies. Faris shifted, her human form not nearly heavy enough to keep Heinrich pinned. He threw her off and pulled his dirk. Faris scrambled back, but a hand wrapped her throat, and she was slammed against the wall. Sepp practically lifted her off her feet. She thrashed and tried to get words out through her closed throat: *Lord Sandrel is alive, the claiming bite is his.*

Heinrich picked himself off the floor and straightened his clothes. The stone wall bit into Faris's naked back, and she saw stars as the guard shook her again, rattling her teeth. Heinrich brought his face inches from hers.

"How do I make her human?"

Faris wheezed out a breath, and Heinrich nodded to Sepp, who released her neck. She fell to her knees—bruises she would feel tomorrow if she survived this. Heinrich crouched next to her and laid the point of his dirk against her throat. She could shift again, still kill him, even kill all his men. But that was not why she'd changed back to her human form.

She got slowly to her feet and looked past Sepp to address MacIntosh, who retreated a pace, and Julia, who stared defiantly back at her.

She brushed her fingers over the bite on her neck, clearly visible now that she was divested. "Lord Sandrel gifted me with this claiming bite the night before Heinrich's man tried to gut him and Heinrich himself kidnapped our daughter. My shifter blood and the fox, Peter, saved your lord's life."

Understanding dawned on MacIntosh's face. Julia took a moment longer, her eyes still narrowed. Faris searched the hall. Her people had scattered when she shifted, leaving five of Heinrich's men, Sepp, and himself, dirk still in hand. Even if Faris shifted again, she couldn't hope to take so many—not without getting her people killed. She took in MacIntosh's quarterstaff, Julia's wood axe hanging at her belt, and took her leap of faith.

Faris shifted, filled her chest, and threw back her head in a howl. The sound practically shook the walls: a log fell in the fireplace, sending up a shower of sparks; the stained glass behind her rattled, and Heinrich took two steps back, fear showing in his eyes for the first time.

A cry of *To Lady Faris!* swelled from the rest of the castle, and Heinrich's guards turned to meet this new threat. The people of the outpost came pelting into the hall wielding hammers, frypans, and bare fists. Heinrich's men were wildly outnumbered.

Faris jumped back as Sepp lunged for her again. MacIntosh raised his quarterstaff and, with a solid blow, laid Sepp out prone. Julia hefted the woodsman's axe from her belt and used the head to knock Heinrich's dirk from his hand, sending it skittering across the floor out of reach. Heinrich's gaze flicked over the hall for an escape like a cornered rabbit. He clutched his hand and backed away on stilted legs as Faris advanced on him, hackles raised, a growl rumbling in her chest.

Heinrich had to know that his men were defeated. Those that had not surrendered were senseless on the floor, and her people blocked

Heinrich's retreat. Faris could hear his heart pounding and licked her lips. Enough toying with the lordling. His blood would feed something starved inside her. She padded closer, claws clicking on the stone.

"Mom, no!"

Faris whipped around. Ela pushed past a farmer wielding a scythe with hay still clinging to the blade. A half-healed burn marked her face, but she was alive, alive and well and human. Peter followed close behind her, clearly having scrounged some clothes from the guards below the tower.

Ela didn't hesitate to lay a hand on Faris's nose. The scent of her daughter's skin soothed her wolf in a way not even her enemy's blood would have been able to manage. Her wolf huffed out a breath and then retreated, allowing Faris to shift. Her human form landed painfully on one knee at Ela's feet, hands braced on the cool stone, her chest heaving. She hadn't shifted so frequently since she was a child. A tunic was drawn over her head, and Faris fought down a moment of panic while she freed her arms through the armscyes.

She'd gathered her pack with a howl, and they had answered. Her own pack. Peter and Ela drew Faris to her feet, and it was only when Ela brushed a tear off her mother's face that Faris realized she wept. Her hands shook as she took Ela's in her own and finally tore her gaze from the smooth flagstones.

Ela beamed at her through her own tears.

"An alpha needs a pack," said Peter softly.

MacIntosh stood stoutly at Ela's side and nodded sharply, a movement taken up by the red-faced woman next to him and echoed all around the hall.

"You say the word, and we'll gut Lord Heinrich or toss him in the forest and leave him for dead," said Julia.

Faris swallowed and cleared her throat. "That won't be necessary. I'm sure he understands now that his neighbours are not to be trodden on." She squeezed Ela's hands and dropped them so she could turn to face Heinrich, her people at her back. She lifted her chin. To his credit, he didn't cower overmuch.

His gaze flicked to the door once before he nodded. "Absolutely, Lady Faris. I understand completely."

She turned her back on him and stalked to the stairway, nodding to her people as she passed, each one of them bowing to her in turn. Her own pack. And she was their alpha.

12

Faris straightened her collar to show off her claiming bite. Ela and Peter's wedding, already beginning in the hall below, was their best chance to prove to Biyana that they were serious about working with the forest instead of against it. All the more important now since they couldn't count on any of their neighbours for the supplies they would need to maintain their efforts to beat it back.

But even Julia had agreed, if begrudgingly, to hear the shifters out when Peter had enlisted their advice on living in harmony with the forest.

"You're sure she's not doing it to spite that worm Heinrich?" said Lord Sandrel from behind her.

"Not at all, my love," said Faris. "Let me." She took her time affixing his chain and belt for him. Sandrel was still stiff from his wound, but it had healed without infection, and he'd been moved—with instructions never to return—from the forest settlement two days ago. "There, perfectly lordly. The way they look at each other . . . giving Earl Anders an excuse to out Heinrich from his lordship is a side-benefit."

Sandrel settled his belt around his hips, shaking his head. "We'll have to keep an eye on the earl. That he would use my daughter's hand as a condition of Heinrich's lordship without consulting us . . ."

"I suppose he thought it an honour for us and a test for Heinrich."

"Arranging Ela's marriage before they'd even met?" Sandrel ran a hand through his hair.

Faris smiled. "You're forgetting that we didn't so much as meet before we were married."

"Those circumstances were different—and much more motivated by sweeping embarrassing children under the rug."

The second son who refused to come home from the uncivilized south and the female wolf shifter who turned out to be an alpha. A match made in heaven. Faris had never dreamt that she'd have her own pack, not even back when she'd been living among shifters. But now that she had her own people, it felt right, especially to her wolf, who perked up whenever she barked an order to a guard, cared for a child, or helped a pack mate with their laundry. Not only that, but this had been her pack for years, something that had happened so gradually she hadn't noticed. She'd been so focused on smothering the growls and bloodlust that she'd inadvertently smothered the pack loyalty and alpha ability to inspire her pack right along with it.

But not anymore.

Sandrel wrapped his arms around her. "And you're sure you won't change your mind and pin Peter to the floor?"

Faris laughed. "I'll leave pinning Peter to Ela. I'd much rather pin you." She kissed him carefully, mindful of his recent injury, but he deepened it and pulled her to his body.

"You can try anytime, alpha."

***

Thanks so much for reading *Second Acts of Weary Warrior Women*! If you liked it, please leave a review on your platform of choice. Even a line or two is very helpful for other readers!

If you want to be the first to hear about new releases, consider joining my newsletter at join.elizabethshearly.ca.

DEAR LOVELY READER

When I had the idea for a vampire story where any vampire could be compelled to summon their sire, I didn't realize that it would blossom into an entire collection. As it turns out, the concept of a "second act" really resonated with me, allowing me to create all these women. Each one has trapped herself in a life that is unfulfilling, due to circumstance, fear, and avoidance. Each one breaks out of that life and smashes through the fear, ending up in a vibrant and cozy place that she would never have been able to reach otherwise.

It's not hard to draw a parallel to my life, considering my foray into a writing career was just beginning when I planned out this project. Moving from a safe job that pays the bills into a career in the arts where you're lucky if you break even is a risk, like the risks all these women take. Theirs pay off in the end, and the privilege of being able to share all these stories with you makes mine pay off as well.

The King's Pixie Seer was the last story in this collection to be written. It's about the struggle to bring one's whole self to a relationship, and the fear that weaknesses will be used against you. Too often, we shut our vulnerability away to protect ourselves, but in so doing we lose something of ourselves as well.

To Break A Dragon Bond ended up being a platonic romance between a woman and her dragon. Their friendship is shattered by their trauma, their communication breaks down, and it seems like their relationship can never be fixed. Raisa is driven to the very edge of her sanity until she realizes that Kalanthi isn't trying to torture her; Kalanthi loves her. It's their trauma that needs to be processed, not their relationship that needs to be destroyed. (If you were hoping for Raisa and Thane to bang it out before Raisa's impending execution, I'm planning an alternate scene where that happens. I thought it was a bit too dark for the way the story turned out, since it was much more about Raisa and Kalanthi in the end.)

The Swordswoman and the Vampire was the flash of inspiration that got this entire collection going. What if it was the human who wanted the vampire bite and the vampire who refused? What if there was a vampire who wanted his human to feel safe and in control? It's no revelation to depict a masc partner as a vampire and a femme as a helpless bite victim; it's not even all that uncommon to have them end up meeting as equal partners as they get to know each other. But Ama takes her addiction to the adrenalin rush of being bitten and transforms it into an empowering experience, where she is in control, with her frail(ish) human body unchanged. And of course, for Lazarus's part, he struggles with his sire the way many of my generation struggle with the previous generation, trying to do better for our children than our parents did for us.

A Pentagram of Candles and Spectres was a struggle for me to write. I think it shines through in the story that the circumstances the characters are working through are just a bit too real, just a little too close to the current real-life struggles of children to maintain their rights in schools, the struggles of care-takers and teachers who have to watch as activists' words are twisted and used against what they believe. (If you're disappointed that Pauline and Landon never made sweet ghost love, I'm working on a bonus scene so their desires can finally come to fruition. The scene didn't end up working in the story, since the story ended up being more focussed on Pauline herself rather than her relationship with Landon.)

And, finally, *Her Castle, Her Howl, Her Pack* is a twist on the current trends in the shifter genre where the shifter is most often the masc partner, the animal nature a parallel for masculine aggression, protectiveness, and violence. But what if a woman is protective? So many of us have a side that we are afraid to show, afraid of how others will perceive us if we do. But Faris shows that side; she embraces it, and when she does, those around her embrace it as well, beyond anything she could have imagined. Often, we won't stand up for ourselves but we refuse to allow our daughters to endure what we dismiss on our own behalf. Inevitably, in fighting for them, we end up finding the courage to fight for ourselves as well.

If *Second Acts of Weary Warrior Women* means something to you, as it does to me, that's all I can hope for as a writer. I'm so glad we could share these pages together. <3

Looking forward to our next adventure,

E. F. Shearly

Elizabeth F. Shearly

ENDLESS SEA OF STARS

The ground shakes under Jeanie's feet, and she staggers across the pristine corridor. Her blowtorch digs into her hip when she collides with the wall. The blaring alarm pounds through her head. We get it, the moon is imploding! She's still far away from the ship that's her only escape from the disintegrating base. Too far away.

Years ago, Jeanie and Liam thought the isolated moon base would be a middle ground between her spacefaring lifestyle and his need for the stability of a space station. It didn't take long to realize that the life they chose was making both of them miserable.

But now it's literally falling apart around them, with no escape in sight. No escape but one slim chance they have no choice but to take. It may not be comfortable or pretty, but it just might keep them alive long enough to save their marriage.

ALSO BY ELIZABETH F. SHEARLY

Endless Sea Of Stars
Dread Spring
Keep the Good Parts

Second Acts of Weary Warrior Women

The Swordswoman and the Vampire
To Break A Dragon Bond
A Pentagram Of Candles and Spectres
Her Castle, Her Howl, Her Pack
The King's Pixie Seer

ABOUT THE AUTHOR

Elizabeth F. Shearly writes science fiction and fantasy tales, from flash fiction to novels and everything in between. She holds a B.Sc. in physics, and you'll find plenty of science in her science fiction, though the fiction always takes precedence. No matter what she writes about—spaceships or magic, walking cities or medieval castles—romance always finds a way to blossom, whether as the main plot or as a background story.

When she's not watching characters play-act in her head, you can find her relaxing on the couch with her two cats, playing a video game or knitting a sweater.

instagram.com/stitchnscribble/

bookbub.com/authors/elizabeth-f-shearly

facebook.com/ElizabethFShearly/

goodreads.com/elizabethfshearly